"I'd like to make you my wife."

His hand was bare, she realized dimly, and warm where hers was cold. He must have removed his glove at some point and his skin against hers set fireworks wheeling through her insides, each one trailing countless sparks. On the day he had lifted her onto his horse, she'd felt the power in his grip, but now it was gentle, allowing her to pull away if she chose. But as she looked up at him and saw the honesty in his eyes, she knew that she would not.

"But...but *why*? Why would you ask *me*?"

"That's a fair question. I think I'd say the same if someone I'd only met twice before offered me their hand."

He still held hers and Emily felt herself begin to burn, aware his palm was big enough to eclipse her fingers within it.

"Do you want to go a hundred miles away to be a governess?"

His unexpected bluntness startled her into honesty. "No, sir."

"Would you rather stay in Warwickshire and perhaps continue the hunt for your father?"

"Why...yes."

"If you decide to marry me, I could help you with both of those things." Andrew's voice was level, neither wheedling nor pushy and speaking with the quiet frankness of a man telling the truth.

Author Note

The first inkling of *A Marriage to Shock Society* came while I was rereading my favorite Jane Austen novel, *Emma*.

I always felt Miss Woodhouse's friend Harriet was a far more interesting character than the heroine. Where Emma was brought up in luxury, illegitimate Harriet Smith was raised as a "parlor boarder" at a school for young ladies, not learning the identity of her father until much later in the novel. By some lucky chance, she was taken under Emma's wing and so was exposed to Society, which given her station, she couldn't have accessed otherwise. But it left me wondering what would have happened to "natural daughters" who lacked such sympathetic (and well-bred) friends.

Emily Townsend is one such unclaimed daughter. Her background is similar to Harriet's, spending her childhood at school with no knowledge of her parentage, although sadly she lacks Miss Smith's influential mentor. Unwanted and unloved, it seems her destiny is to be sent far away from the town she grew up in, to take a job where nobody knows her shameful origins...

Until she meets Andrew.

Although now the Earl of Breamore, Andrew Gouldsmith understands what it's like to live on the fringes, and he doesn't want a wife from among the *ton*. Emily piques his curiosity from their very first meeting, as a young woman very different from those he knows, although the mystery of her parentage poses problems he hadn't expected. He fears for his new countess's happiness if she insists on trying to find her father—but much like Emma Woodhouse, Emily will not be deterred once her mind is made up!

A MARRIAGE TO SHOCK SOCIETY

JOANNA JOHNSON

HISTORICAL

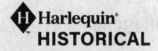
Harlequin®
HISTORICAL

ISBN-13: 978-1-335-59627-7

A Marriage to Shock Society

Copyright © 2024 by Joanna Johnson

Recycling programs for this product may not exist in your area.

 Harlequin Enterprises ULC
22 Adelaide St. West, 41st Floor
Toronto, Ontario M5H 4E3, Canada
www.Harlequin.com

Printed in U.S.A.

Joanna Johnson lives in a little village with her husband and too many books. After completing an English degree at university, she went on to work in publishing, although she'd always wish she was working on her own books rather than other people's. This dream came true in 2018 when she signed her first contract with Harlequin, and she hasn't looked back, spending her time getting lost in mainly Regency history and wishing it was acceptable to write a manuscript using a quill.

Books by Joanna Johnson

Harlequin Historical

Scandalously Wed to the Captain
His Runaway Lady
A Mistletoe Vow to Lord Lovell
The Return of Her Long-Lost Husband
The Officer's Convenient Proposal
"A Kiss at the Winter Ball"
in *Regency Christmas Parties*
Her Grace's Daring Proposal
Their Inconvenient Yuletide Wedding

Visit the Author Profile page
at Harlequin.com.

For Sissy

Chapter One

Staring up at the intimidating frontage of Huntingham Hall, Emily Townsend knew there was no turning back.

The five-mile walk from the neighbouring town of Brigwell had taken longer than she'd anticipated and she feared she looked dishevelled, pushing aside a limp strand of hair and wishing the back of her neck wasn't quite so damp from the summer sun. She had to be at her very best when she finally worked up the courage to knock at the door and, taking a deep breath, she peered up once again at the biggest house she had ever seen.

It was hewn from the same pretty Warwickshire stone as the school she had lived in since birth, but any scant similarity between the two buildings began and ended there. Miss Laycock's establishment comprised little more than a largish cottage, the second floor reserved for the parlour boarders that included Emily. Despite the lofty claims of advertisements placed in the Brigwell

Gazette it was neither particularly exclusive nor pres-
tigious. It had never truly felt like *home*, even though
she had never known any other, and the smallest flutter
of excitement stirred now despite her jangling nerves.

If she was right…

The flutter grew stronger and Emily tried her best to
check it. If she let herself get her hopes up too high it
would be even more painful if they were then dashed,
especially with so much at stake. It had been made abun-
dantly—and abruptly—clear that there was no longer a
place for her at the Laycock School for Young Ladies and
she'd been left with no choice but to act, now throwing
all her faith in what she'd seen on a smudged piece of
paper more than twelve years before.

The hand she raised to the ornate bellpull shook un-
controllably, and she swallowed rising apprehension as
she listened to the chime. In a matter of moments the
door would open and she'd step inside, mere minutes
away from a scene she'd imagined countless times, and
then—

And then—what?

He'd be delighted to see her, this stranger whom she'd
given no warning she was coming…wouldn't he? If he
wasn't, she might die of shame right there in Huntingham Hall's no doubt magnificent parlour, but she had
no choice. There were no other options left to her, and
as the door opened Emily forced a smile, clasping her
hands together to hide how they trembled.

'Good morning. I would like to see Lord Breamore.
Is he at home?'

She spoke with as much confidence as she could muster, glad of the hours she'd spent rehearsing before her

bedroom mirror when the newly emerged butler bowed instead of immediately turning her away.

'Yes, ma'am. Please come inside.'

The man withdrew and with one final glance over her shoulder Emily followed. She'd succeeded in getting past the front door and that in itself felt like a victory, although any triumph was rapidly replaced by awe as she stepped over the threshold.

The entrance hall alone was bigger than Miss Laycock's entire drawing room. High ceilinged, gleaming with marble and lit by sunshine cascading in through tall windows, it was more a palace than a house and she'd never felt so out of place in her life as she removed her faded bonnet and handed it to a waiting maid. Even the servants were better dressed than she was and hurriedly Emily tried to hide a visibly mended hole in the palm of one glove. If the other parlour boarders could see her now they'd be amazed at her nerve in daring to set foot in an Earl's home, somewhere a person of her position had no right to *think* about let alone visit, and she prayed for the frightening gallop of her pulse to slow as the butler turned back.

'I shall inform His Lordship of your presence. What name may I give?'

'Miss Townsend. Miss Emily Townsend.'

She watched keenly for his reaction, but it seemed her name meant nothing to him.

'Thank you, ma'am. His Lordship will be down directly.'

Emily attempted another smile, although her limbs felt like water as the maid began to lead her away. Her nape was still too hot and her heart still flung itself against her ribs and, when she was shown into what seemed to her the grandest parlour on earth, she all but fell onto a sofa rather than sat.

The maid withdrew, leaving Emily alone and at the mercy of her thoughts.

'His Lordship will be down directly.'

Another surge of excitement rose and again she attempted to master it. She'd dreamed of this day since she was nine years old, when she had forced open the forbidden drawer of the late Mrs Laycock's desk to hunt the secrets she knew lay within, and what she'd found had turned her world on its head. Many questions had been answered by that piece of paper, none of which her guardians had shown any intention of addressing themselves then or since, but the biggest still remained and Emily's heart leaped into her mouth as she heard footsteps approaching and knew the final piece of the puzzle was about to fall into place.

She sprang to her feet, hardly breathing as the door swung open. A man stood on the threshold, his face momentarily hidden by shadow, but then he stepped fully into the room and Emily felt as though she had been kicked in the stomach.

'Good morning. Miss Townsend, is it? I am Lord Breamore. I believe you wanted to see me?'

The Earl smiled, the unfeigned warmth of it reaching his dark eyes. He was tall enough that she had to lift her chin slightly to look into his face—a pleasant one, as she might have been more aware if a crushing weight hadn't just come slamming down across her chest.

But he's far too young. Surely this can't be right?

It was like being doused by a shower of cold water.

Every trace of excitement vanished instantly, all tentative hope draining away as she gazed up at the man who wasn't who she wanted him to be, and the first words she spoke to him came far more bluntly than she'd intended.

'You are Lord Breamore? The *only* Lord Breamore?'

His almost black eyebrows raised a fraction at her forthrightness, but so did one corner of his mouth, a half-smile that even Emily couldn't miss.

'I'm afraid so. There's generally only one of us at a time.'

He seemed to consider for a moment. 'Perhaps you were expecting my uncle, Ephraim Gouldsmith? The previous Earl?'

Emily swallowed, the sudden dryness of her throat almost choking her. 'Perhaps.'

'In that case I'm afraid I have bad news. He died two months ago.'

The unexpected Earl gestured for her to sit and Emily found herself folding back down onto the sofa she had sprung from so eagerly. Dismay and confusion crowded her, although from somewhere she managed to dredge up the only socially acceptable response.

'I'm sorry, sir. My deepest condolences.'

The Earl inclined his head. He seemed unmoved by the recent bereavement and Emily wondered fleetingly at his coolness before reality returned to eclipse all else.

I'm too late. If Ephraim Gouldsmith was indeed my father I'll never know him now...and we'll never have the happier future together I hoped for.

The weight in her chest shifted to make room for a shard of ice. For *years* the only thing that had made her sad existence in any way tolerable was the dream of one day meeting the father nobody wanted to tell her anything about. No one at the school, where she'd been deposited as a newborn, had ever truly cared for her. Mrs Laycock had occasionally bestowed a tight smile or stiffly encouraging word, but after she died and her daughter took control even that meagre approval came to an end. *Miss* Laycock was even more austere than her mother, never hesitating to use the cane in her attempts to shape Emily into a respectable young woman, although it seemed illegitimacy was a stain no amount of rapped knuckles could erase. The only future deemed appropriate for such an unfortunate creature was as a governess for a family prepared to overlook her dubious origins in exchange for a pittance, a grim prospect she'd been informed was now imminent. A position had been found for her with a family almost a hundred miles away from Brigwell, practically on the other side of the country and far from everyone and everything she'd ever known, and to evade that fate she'd finally played the single winning card she thought fate had dealt her.

But I left it too late.

Vaguely she heard the Earl ring a bell by the fireplace and then seat himself in a chair to one side of her sofa, the tread of his boots muffled by expensive rugs. Each one must have cost as much as her board and schooling did for a year, and she stared blindly down at the woven designs, despair washing over her like a chilly breeze.

Was this really the outcome of all that time spent looking forward to this day? The paper in Mrs Laycock's desk had stated her anonymous mother was deceased, dying in childbed and leaving Emily behind, but to discover she had a father still living had given her nine-year-old

self the strength to go on. A maddeningly placed smudge
had obscured his surname, leaving only his title exposed
alongside a smeared impression of a coat of arms courtesy of his ink-spattered signet ring, but that had been
enough. There was only one Lord living near Brigwell
and that was Breamore, and without ever having laid eyes
on him Emily knew it *had* to be his signature scrawled
on the dotted line. Who else could not only afford to pay
for her lodging and education in advance but would take
the trouble to do so, spending what must have added up
to a small fortune by the time she'd come of age?

Such generosity had been enough to convince her that
he cared, and as the years had passed that certainty had
taken root in her lonely, affection-starved heart, which
cherished the notion of her distant papa until she'd built
him up into an almost mythical figure for a girl who
had nothing else to cling to. In her desperation to belong somewhere she had seized on what she ached to be
true, a fiercely held conviction she'd reminded herself of
every time her cold life at the school grew too much to
bear—that fathers existed to love their daughters, even
if they couldn't always keep them, and that one day hers
would come to take her away from the bleak situation
he must have had good reason for making her endure.
He had invested money and effort in placing her with
the Laycocks, surely proof he wanted to know where to
find her when the time was right, and only the looming
prospect of forced servitude had made her abandon her
patient waiting and seek him out for herself.

There was a loaded pause. Clearly her unwitting host
expected some kind of explanation as to why he had a si-

lent, obviously unhappy woman in his parlour, but when it became plain one was not forthcoming, he leaned forward.

'We've established I'm not the one you want, but can I assist you anyway? Perhaps if you told me why you'd come to see my uncle?'

Emily glanced up. He was watching her with interest, and for the first time she noticed the liveliness of his eyes, dark but simultaneously alight with intelligence and good humour. He was attractive, she realised now she looked at him properly. Twin grooves beside his mouth suggested he smiled often and the line of his jaw could have been shaped by a sculptor's knife. His nose was slightly crooked, broken and mended long ago, but the small flaw lent character to what could otherwise have been a far blander kind of handsomeness. In all he was a man it was no hardship to look at, which only managed to make her current position feel even worse.

The only possible justification she'd had for calling at Huntingham Hall had been the belief her father lived there and now her audacity had no basis at all. She ought to leave at once, running away before the new Earl realised what kind of woman he had allowed into his home, but to her horror she wasn't sure she could. Despair had sapped her strength and made it all but impossible to stand, pinning her to the sofa while Lord Breamore politely waited for an answer she was powerless to find.

What was she supposed to tell him? That she had come to ask if his newly buried uncle was her absent papa, the only person who could save her from being sent miles from home to slave for pennies it was assumed an illegitimate girl ought to be grateful to receive? It wouldn't paint either of them in a particularly flattering light—his uncle as an errant father and herself as the secret, unwanted product of an indiscretion—and she fumbled for an answer that wasn't an outright lie.

'I understood he was a friend of my mother's.'

That might have been true, she reasoned uncomfortably as she watched Lord Breamore's brows knit together.

There must have been *some* kind of relationship between her poor nameless mama and the previous Earl, even if only the most transient. A child could be made in a matter of moments, one of the older school boarders had told her once, and although at the time Emily hadn't been *entirely* sure what the other girl had meant, she now had enough of an idea for her current blush to deepen another three shades.

'You say your *mother* was a friend of his? That's… interesting.'

The corners of his mouth turned down. There was a small cleft in his chin and he rubbed it thoughtfully, his uncertainty making Emily hold her breath. 'I wouldn't have thought he ever had a single friend in his life, let alone a woman.'

He hesitated, clearly choosing his next words carefully. 'He wasn't known for his regard for ladies. I take it you never met him?'

The question struck at the very centre of Emily's unhappiness. 'No, sir. I never had that pleasure.'

'Well. It might be best to consider that a blessing.'

The Earl's mouth twisted and Emily felt herself frown. What could he mean by that? There was now no chance of her meeting Ephraim Breamore and his nephew was her only link to him, the sole person who could tell her anything about the man she'd never had the opportunity to know.

'Wasn't he a pleasant man?'

To her surprise Lord Breamore gave a short laugh. It rang hollow in the room, and at her obvious confusion he held up an apologetic hand.

'Forgive me. It's only that there are many words that could have described my uncle, and *pleasant* wouldn't be one of them.'

He nodded towards a painting hanging against one richly papered wall. 'See for yourself. Even in his portrait he glares, and that's nothing to how he would scowl when he was alive.'

Emily turned at once. She had no idea what the former Lord Breamore had looked like and she braced herself to come face to face with him, even if that face was rendered in oils rather than flesh and blood. Perhaps their noses had been the same shape, or they'd shared the same unusual reddish-gold hair? It was a chance to see whether her imaginings of him had any root in fact, and she almost forgot she was being watched as she craned her neck to take a better look.

She'd expected to find at least some resemblance between herself and the man in the ornate frame…but there was none.

It was as if the artist had been tasked with creating a subject the opposite of her in every conceivable way. The painted face was square where hers was rounded, his skin olive-toned in place of her pink and white, and the thick hair waved in a much less distinctive mid-brown. His eyes were dark too, in stark contrast to her own blue, and the expression in them was exactly as his nephew had described. Ephraim Gouldsmith glowered down at her, dislike etched into every painted line, and for the first time she felt a glimmer of doubt.

Was I wrong?

There was absolutely no likeness whatsoever, not even the most tenuous. Between uncle and nephew there was an undeniable similarity, their colouring and jawlines clearly passed down through the generations, but for herself there might have been no family link at all. If it hadn't been pointed out to her which painting was Ephraim she never would have guessed he was the man she suspected of being her father, and the longer she gazed up at him the stronger her sudden doubts became.

But if not him...?

Out of the corner of her eye she saw her host like-wise studying the portrait. There was little affection in his expression and, when he spoke, she heard a note of distaste loud and clear.

'I don't believe he ever thought well of anyone. If your mother was the exception, she must have been a singular woman indeed—he thought ladies a waste of time only fools pursued, which was why he never troubled him-self to marry. His money was the only company I ever knew him to enjoy.'

He gave his uncle another lingering look before turning away, and Emily followed his lead. Meeting Ephraim's painted eye made her feel cold. His gaze was too hostile, as if angry with her for daring to enter his home, and the lack of anything approaching a paternal resemblance...

Was a man who apparently disliked women so much

likely to have fathered an unwanted child? To hear Lord Breamore speak of him, the former Earl had been more concerned with his fortune than pleasure-seeking. Between his disinterest in the fairer sex and his looks so opposite her own, the evidence against him was mounting, and Emily's confusion grew likewise.

First I thought he must be my father, then I discover he's died, and now I'm not sure he was my father at all. For years I was so certain, but now...

There was too much to process while sitting in such a luxurious parlour, a place she was growing ever more uncomfortable to have invaded with every second that passed. She needed to go away to think and it was an immeasurable relief to find some of the strength had returned to her legs as she prepared to stand.

'Thank you for your time, my lord. I've taken up far too much of it. I'll bid you good day now.'

She saw him lean forward as if about to speak but the opening of the parlour door beat him to it. A servant with a tea tray appeared and set it down on a nearby table, answering the Earl's murmured thanks with a neat bob before silently leaving the room.

He smiled as the door closed again. His face had taken on a tightness when viewing the portrait but that seemed to have passed, the upward tick of his lips effortlessly catching Emily's eye, and she had no time to wonder at herself for noticing such a thing, at such a time, before he reached out.

'If you've decided to leave, at least have some tea first. Without wishing to sound rude, you look as though you need it.'

* * *

In what might be considered an uncharacteristic move for an Earl, Andrew picked up the teapot himself, simultaneously stealing a glance at the mysterious Miss Townsend's downturned face. She was pale again now, the pretty flush replaced by a curiously unhappy pallor, and he couldn't help but note the way her fingers shook when she unconsciously pushed back her hair. It was a striking colour, somewhere between russet and blonde, and he wondered again why such an attractive young woman had come to Huntingham Hall.

He poured out a cup and pushed it towards her. She did indeed look in need of a drink, although perhaps of something stronger than tea. When he'd first entered the room she'd looked as though she was about to fall over, her blue eyes wide with shock that had rapidly turned to obvious dismay, and he was no closer to understanding why. The only thing that was plain was that she had come expecting to see Uncle Ephraim, and the news of his passing had affected her far more than the old devil deserved.

'Oh… Thank you, sir. You're very kind.'

He saw how she hesitated before reaching for her tea. Her thoughts were evidently elsewhere and he took the opportunity to let his own unfold as she stirred a fragment of sugar into her cup.

Had she and Uncle Ephraim been having some kind of liaison? Was that it? The idea made him want to grimace, the thought of such a soft-spoken young woman in that gnarled grasp not an agreeable one, but then he dismissed it out of hand. She had never met the previous

Earl, and besides, what he'd told her was the truth. His uncle had never looked at women with desire, only ever disdain, and the likelihood of him being interested in her even if they'd crossed paths was surely less than zero.

She claims her mother had been a friend of his but that has to be a lie. All Uncle cared for was money, and it's very clear this Miss Townsend has none.

Her clothes were clean but mended, and the soles of her shoes were worn thin, he saw with the empathy of one who had once been in a similar position. His uncle had only ever been able to tolerate those with wealth, as though poverty was contagious...as Andrew knew all too well.

As if sensing he was trying to puzzle her out, Emily looked up, colouring slightly when she met his eye. She shifted uneasily on the sofa and Andrew was glad she hadn't caught him in his survey of her dress, aware she must already be feeling ill at ease in his grand home.

Just as I did as a boy, whenever Uncle deigned to summon me here. It always felt more like entering a viper's nest than a house, hoping he wouldn't notice how my cuffs were frayed and my shirts always slightly outgrown.

It was a memory he didn't particularly want to examine at that moment, and instead he sipped his tea while pretending not to observe his guest. Every now and again she took a surreptitious glance around the room, apparently marvelling at the costly furniture and rich velvet curtains at each window, and eventually he couldn't restrain his curiosity any longer.

'You said my uncle knew your mother, but not why *you* came here. Are you quite sure there's nothing I can do?'

He'd expected her to jump for another unconvincing

lie but instead she merely shook her slightly bowed head, gazing steadily down into her cup.

'No, thank you. It doesn't matter now. I think I made a mistake.'

Her voice was carefully neutral, but the tiniest quiver of a muscle near her mouth gave her away. For some reason she was both upset and trying to conceal it. Despite his piqued interest, Andrew's conscience pricked him to change the subject.

'I hope you didn't come too far. It's warm today and I assume from your dress that you walked here.'

'Yes, sir. From Brigwell.'

His eyebrows rose. Brigwell had to be at least five miles away, across a patchwork of fields and lanes too rough to be called roads. To reach it was more of a trek than a stroll, and one that only an individual with a real purpose would set out on...which brought him once again to the lingering question of *why* Miss Townsend had thought it worth the bother.

'That's some distance away. I feel a gentleman would send you home in his carriage.'

For the first time since he'd entered the parlour Emily granted him a smile, small but immediately drawing his attention to the shape of her lips.

'No gentleman should ever trouble himself on my account, my lord. I enjoy walking. A couple of miles is no hardship for me.'

She sought refuge behind her teacup again, her blue eyes hidden by the sweep of her lashes, and it struck Andrew that whatever she might be thinking was as mysterious as her appearance at his home.

What he *did* know was that he liked her answer. The

days where *he* had to walk everywhere were gone now, of course, vanished the moment Uncle Ephraim had taken his last breath, and part of him missed the freedom of setting out across a field and feeling the sun shining down on his upturned face. Venturing among the forests and fields had been one of the few pleasures in his old life. His new duties now took up much of his time, the title he'd so recently inherited a heavy responsibility alongside the many privileges—and adjustments—it brought.

Not that I'd wind back the clock, however. Not after what Mother and I endured to bring us to this moment.

More for something to occupy his hands rather than out of any real desire for one, Andrew poured himself another cup and drank it in three gulps, wishing it was port or wine or anything better equipped at helping him outrun unwanted memories.

Andrew's father had been Ephraim's intended heir, and when a fever carried him away the Gouldsmith inheritance had transferred to his then barely five-year-old son. Most people would have assumed Lord Breamore would make some arrangements to care for his poor sister-in-law and her now fatherless child, stepping in to support and comfort them in their grief, but that had not been the case. Uncle Ephraim never lifted a finger to help in the dark days following Father's death and, even now, over twenty years later, Andrew could still picture his mother's tear-stained face as they'd been forced to pack their things and leave the home they could no longer afford. Mother's widow's jointure was small, and in the absence of any other family to turn to she'd had to make it stretch, dismissing servants and selling trinkets until only the bare bones of her once luxurious existence remained. Andrew might have been in line for an earldom, but anyone looking at him in those lean years would have struggled to believe it, and any pride he might have felt at the prospect had faded while he was still a child.

The old Earl's only interest had come later, when advancing age had made him demand occasional visits from his reluctant heir, although such calls gave neither party much satisfaction. Ephraim had been displeased with his nephew's lack of regard for wealth and status, and Andrew frustrated by his uncle's obsession with both, and it was always a relief to leave for his home in Derbyshire again, even if the roof sometimes leaked and the doors squeaked on their hinges with every strong wind.

A movement from Emily's sofa stirred him. She had set down her cup and looked as though she was about to stand, and Andrew firmly pulled himself back into the present.

'You're preparing to take your leave. Joking aside, you'll allow me to call for my uncle's—for *my* carriage?'

Rising, Miss Townsend shook out her skirts. She hadn't touched any of the dainty biscuits arranged on the tea tray so there could be no crumbs to dislodge, giving the distinct impression she was instead trying to avoid looking at him. 'No thank you, my lord. I'm very happy to walk, although even if it was a distance of twenty miles I couldn't accept such a generous offer. It wouldn't be right.'

'Wouldn't it? Why not?'

The careless question slipped out before Andrew thought the better of it. At once he realised his mistake, watching the colour in Emily's cheeks deepen into a crimson flush.

Of course she wouldn't accept his offer of a carriage. A woman like Miss Townsend would be painfully aware of the difference in their stations and never want to give the impression she'd forgotten her place, even if he was still struggling to come to terms with his own.

To Emily's eyes he was privileged and wealthy and existing in a world far removed from hers, even if he knew there was more to his position than the obvious. Doubtless he had more in common with his slightly shabby uninvited guest than with the refined young ladies that showed him such interest when he set foot in a ballroom, although to tell her so would be absurd. She was a stranger; given their opposing social circles it was very unlikely he'd ever see her again, and it would be foolish to behave as though nothing had changed, when in fact his life would never now be the same again.

His mother had tried to prepare him. Since he was a boy she'd told him of the grand inheritance he stood to gain and the title that would be bestowed on him, doing her best to ready him for a world his father's death had excluded them from so mercilessly, but still Andrew felt like a fraud. Lady Gouldsmith had done as much as she could to mould him into an Earl-to-be, teaching him to dance and play cards and grasp the varying subtleties of upper-class etiquette, and yet the lower sphere their poverty had forced them to enter had influenced him more than anything else.

His playmates as a child weren't the offspring of knights and baronets as they would have been if his father was still alive. They were apprentice clerks and rectors' sons, respectable enough but with no prestige, and it was alongside these pleasant but ordinary young men that he'd become a man himself. He'd even sought employment as a tutor once he was old enough, something the *ton* would have considered an unthinkable humiliation, but he'd taken satisfaction in knowing the money he presented to his mother each week was honestly earned. For years he'd lived as a simple gentleman, never rich but at least comfortable in the modest existence he had carved out for himself, and when the black-edged letter had come that announced Ephraim's death he had felt as though the rug had been pulled sharply from beneath him.

'Very well. If you've made up your mind.'

A flicker of relief crossed Miss Townsend's face. It seemed she was eager to make her escape, and he had no wish to detain her, the feeling of having just put his foot in it not one he wanted prolonged.

He bowed. 'It was a pleasure to meet you, Miss Townsend. I'm only sorry I couldn't be of more help.'

Another of those eye-catching smiles was his reward for such gallantry, though it struck him that perhaps this time it was a little forced. 'Please think nothing of it, my lord. I ought never to have imposed in the first place. I apologise sincerely for troubling you.'

Solemnly she dropped into a low curtsey, her knees almost touching the carpet, and began to withdraw. She walked with admirable poise and Andrew realised he wanted to carry on watching her as she turned back, dipping him one final curtsey before she left—to return to wherever she had come from, disappearing, without him knowing why she had come at all.

Chapter Two

Emily kept her attention firmly on her plate as she forced down her breakfast of thin porridge. If she hunched in her seat, and made herself small and quiet, perhaps Miss Laycock wouldn't notice her, sparing her conversation she was in no mood to entertain.

Or perhaps not.

'Are you ill?'

A sharp voice issued from the head of the table and, looking up, she found herself fixed by an equally sharp pair of eyes.

'No, Miss Laycock. I'm quite well.'

The school mistress didn't seem convinced. The stern eyes narrowed and Emily braced herself as they swept over her. It was true she probably did look ill, a night spent trying to untangle what had transpired at Huntingham Hall not allowing much sleep, although she would rather have bitten her own tongue than confess what was troubling her. If Miss Laycock learned one of her charges had dared stray near a *ton* house she would have boxed the girl's ears for having ideas above her station, and even at the grand age of twenty-one Emily suspected she wasn't immune to receiving the back of a righteous hand.

'You haven't said a word since you sat down. Are you bilious?'

'No, ma'am. As I said, I am perfectly well.'

Out of the very corner of her eye she caught two of the other parlour boarders exchange nervous glances. Miss Laycock was not a woman to rile, and Emily felt a flutter of apprehension as she was skewered with another pointed look.

'I'm glad to hear you aren't sickening for anything. The timing would be unfortunate, given I received another letter from Mrs Swanscombe this morning.'

A folded sheet of paper lay beside Miss Laycock's plate and she tapped it with a deliberate finger. 'She requires you to attend her no later than the fifteenth of this month. It seems each of the three previous governesses left after a short time and without much notice, and she is keen for the children's education to begin again as soon as possible.'

The flutter in Emily's insides spread its wings more forcefully. 'The fifteenth? But that's hardly more than a week away!'

'Correct. Now that your appointment is settled, neither Mrs Swanscombe nor I saw any reason to delay.'

Miss Laycock casually dabbed her napkin to her mouth as if she hadn't just changed the course of Emily's life in a few scant sentences and Emily herself could only stare with mute horror as the other girls diligently studied their laps.

Barely a week before she had to leave behind everything she knew and take up a position she hadn't wanted in the first place? The thought filled her with dread, coming to rest like an anchor in her chest, already heavy with the confusion and disappointment of the day before. Her visit to Huntingham Hall had been supposed to save her from being sent away, not make the prospect seem even more unescapable, although of course her reason for venturing there hadn't been solely to thwart Miss Laycock's plans.

If Lord Breamore *had* been her father, she would finally have found the family she'd always longed for. After a lifetime without affection she wanted nothing more than to be loved, to be held in a safe pair of arms and know she was valued and cared about, and for all her dreams to have fallen flat was almost more than she could endure. The old Earl was dead, and even if he had been her father—which she now doubted—she'd never have the chance to know him, everything she'd hoped for slipping through her fingers like bitter sand. Her life stretched ahead empty of all hope, the shining figure of her papa she had conjured to ward off her loneliness turned to a shadow, and the loss of that comforting warmth made her feel hollow right down to her toes.

A lump had risen in her throat and she tried to clear it with a sip of lukewarm tea, aware Miss Laycock was watching her. Those gimlet eyes were all-seeing, however, and she knew she was in danger when the school mistress pursed her lips.

'You might show a little more gratitude. It isn't everyone who would take on a governess with your background.'

Her tone was severe, setting the younger girls sitting around the table huddling lower into their chairs. From force of habit Emily jumped to make amends.

'I am grateful, ma'am. It's just… It's almost a hundred miles away. I shall know no one, and you said the house is somewhat remote…?'

'It's true there are no immediate neighbours nor a directly adjoining town, but what does that matter? Mrs Swanscombe has six children, all of whom she describes as "spirited". You'll be too busy to think of recreation.'

Miss Laycock spoke with the authority of one used to being obeyed, and Emily clamped her teeth together, wishing she knew how to argue back.

The prospect of her employment sounded worse with every added detail. She was to be marooned in a house in the middle of nowhere with nobody to talk to, attempting to wrangle six ill-disciplined children who had managed to chase off at least three other governesses, and all for a wage of next to nothing. It would be a living nightmare and one it seemed more and more imperative she avoid, especially now her first idea for doing so lay in tatters. If she'd found her father he would have taken her in, of course, but now she was entirely without help she would just have to find a way out of her situation alone.

'It isn't that I don't appreciate your efforts on my behalf, ma'am, but surely there must be an alternative? I realise money doesn't grow on trees and fully intend to pay my own way. If I could just find a position closer to Brigwell, nearer home—'

'You do not have a home.' Miss Laycock's reply was like

a whipcrack. 'You were brought here because there was nowhere else for you to go and my mother was paid to take you. Since you are now of age, the money for your board has ceased and I do not operate a charity. Mrs Swanscombe has offered you paid employment and frankly you should be glad of it, considering nobody in this town is likely to want someone of your origins beneath their roof.'

A tense silence fell over the room.

The desire to know more about the *origins* spoken of so cruelly stirred, but for perhaps the thousandth time Emily dismissed it, her stomach clenching into a tight ball. She'd asked so many times she'd lost count, begging to be told about her parents and the reason they had surrendered her, but neither Mrs Laycock nor her daughter had ever been moved to answer. Either from spite or a misguided sense of duty, every question had always been met with blank refusal, and there seemed little hope of that changing now, not when it was clearer than ever that Miss Laycock couldn't wait to be rid of her.

To her dismay she felt a tell-tale stinging behind her eyes. The absolute last thing she wanted was for anyone seated around the dining table to see her cry, and she rose swiftly from her chair.

'Please excuse me. I find I have little appetite this morning.'

One or two of the other girls peered over their shoulders at her as she slipped away, but Miss Laycock was the only one to call after her, the hard voice cutting in its indifference.

'Sulking won't achieve anything, Miss Townsend. You'd be much better employed in going to your room and starting to pack.'

* * *

Emily didn't go up to her room. Instead, she moved blindly for the side door into the garden, biting the inside of her cheek to stop her tears from beginning to fall.

A gate was set into the hedge that bordered the garden and she pushed through it, too intent on escaping to think where she was going. To the right a lane led to Brigwell's main street, while the left opened into the countryside beyond and instinctively she turned for the latter. In the fields she could be alone, although Miss Laycock's words rang in her ears every step of the way.

'You have no home.'

'There was nowhere else for you to go.'

'Someone of your origins...'

She plunged onwards for what could have been minutes or hours, paying scant attention to which direction she was heading in. Her insides had drawn into an unhappy knot and she blinked hard, her stubbornly restrained tears scattering shards of light before her eyes. They made her vision blur, the grass and hedges all around her reduced to indistinct green smudges, and by the time she realised a thick tree root lay sprawling across her path it was too late to prevent it from snatching at her foot.

The ground came up to meet her with a thud, knocking the wind from her as she landed in a heap of skirts and outstretched arms. Sharp stones grazed her palms, but it was a stab of pain in one ankle that was the final straw, the tears she'd been holding back at last springing free.

'Damn it. Damn it, damn it, *damn it*!'

She finished on a dry sob, shakily pushing herself up

to sit back against the trunk of the tree. The root had torn her stocking and she looked down at it despairingly, seeing it was ruined beyond mending. It had been darned three times already, and the knowledge that she couldn't afford a new pair clawed at her already tight throat. She had nothing and no one and now she even had to leave Brigwell behind, and in spite of her determination not to, Emily dropped her face into her hands and cried.

The tears poured down her cheeks, hot against her skin. The pain in her ankle echoed that in her heart and for some minutes she was helpless, only able to lean against the jagged bark as the weight of her sorrow held her down. Now the tears had started she feared they might never stop, but eventually she found the strength to lift her head and roughly wipe her eyes.

'There's no use crying about it. I might be impoverished, unwanted and quite possibly orphaned, but I can still attempt to keep at least some small measure of pride.'

She took a deep breath, holding it until her lungs ached before exhaling slowly. Allowing Miss Laycock to see the effect of her callous words was out of the question. It would give her satisfaction Emily had no intention of granting. She closed her eyes briefly as she wondered whether she could get back in time to avoid being missed. If she was gone for too long her absence would be noticed, and she braced herself to stand, gritting her teeth when a fresh crackle of pain arched up from her ankle.

'Come on. Get up.'

With a grimace she managed to lever herself off the ground, still leaning against the tree for support. An attempt to put her foot down was met with another sharp stab and she choked out a gasp, her fingers digging into the bark. It seemed that if she loosened her grip she might fall and it occurred to her that, short of crawling back on her hands and knees, she had little hope of returning the way she had come.

She glanced around. Perhaps there was a branch she could use as a walking stick? With growing concern she looked about her, seeing nothing of any use—although a large shape coming into view around the corner of the lane made her suddenly forget everything else.

A man was riding towards her on a great grey horse, the tails of his green coat flying out behind him. Even from a distance she could tell he was well-dressed, and as he came closer she felt her stomach plummet down to her scuffed boots.

She lurched backwards, pressing herself harder against the tree. He hadn't yet seen her. If she moved quickly she might just be able to hop out of sight, probably making her ankle hurt even more but the pure mortification of the alternative not worth considering. With any luck he would ride right past her, disappearing over the fields in the opposite direction, and if she waited a few minutes he'd be long gone before she tried to hobble back to the school.

Edging into the shadows as hurriedly as she could she heard the beat of hooves come closer. They grew louder and louder, horseshoes ringing out against the dry mud—and then to her alarm they slowed to a stop, halting dangerously close to where she stood with the bark digging into her spine.

'Ma'am? Are you there?'

If she'd had any doubts as to who the rider was before,

there could be none now. His voice was one she'd heard very recently, deep and cultured and not easily forgotten, and as she forced herself to peep out she wished the ground would open beneath her feet.

'I thought I recognised the colour of your hair. Good morning, Miss Townsend.'

The Earl was far too polite to ask *why* she was endeavouring to hide behind a tree, but Emily could tell he was thinking it as she peered upwards, feeling all her blood vacate the rest of her body to come rushing into her cheeks.

It would have to be Lord Breamore who saw her in such a state, she thought dismally as he gazed down at her, the sunlight scattering bronze threads among his dark hair. *Of course* it would be the most elegant man of her acquaintance who would witness her tear-mottled countenance and puffy eyes. After her entirely inappropriate visit to his house she would have been quite happy never to see him again, still mortified to have strayed into a place where she didn't belong, and the fact he was even more handsome than she remembered didn't help matters one straw.

'Good morning, my lord.' She attempted a curtsey, her face glowing hotter when all she could manage was an ungainly squirm. 'I would not have expected to see you here.'

High up in the saddle the Earl smiled, a slight quirk of his lips that did something uncomfortable to her already twisted insides. 'It's thanks to you that I am. Your visit yesterday reminded me how pretty the countryside around Brigwell is, and I made up my mind to come here on my morning ride.'

He waved one gloved hand at the sunlit lane bordered with swaying trees, although when he looked back at her he was frowning.

'Forgive me, Miss Townsend, but is something wrong?'

'Wrong, sir? No. Why should you think that?'

She'd never been a good liar, and Emily knew he had come to that conclusion himself when he immediately brushed her denial aside.

'Because the evidence is here in front of me. I don't pretend to be an expert, but I believe even I can tell when a woman has been crying.'

The Earl fixed her with a direct gaze. Clearly he was too much of a gentleman to remain unmoved by a lady's distress, although the lady in question wished he'd ride off again instead of prolonging her discomfort.

'You're kind to ask, my lord, but it's nothing I would have you trouble yourself about.'

'With respect, that wasn't what I asked.'

In one smooth motion he unhooked his foot from one stirrup and slid to the ground, landing in front of her before she had time to blink. The slight heel of his riding boot made him even taller, and for the first time Emily noticed his height was well matched by the width of his shoulders, broad enough to invite a second and perhaps even a third glance. He didn't come any closer, although he didn't need to for her to be able to look into his eyes. They were warm and brown, filled with concern so genuine it took her by surprise, so unused to anybody showing her sympathy that for a moment she forgot they were from two different worlds.

'I'd received some bad news—twice, in fact, in little

more than a day. Crying won't help anything, I know, but I confess I found myself momentarily overwhelmed by things I cannot change.'

Even as the final word escaped she regretted having spoken it. Why had she given him even the vaguest idea of what had upset her? He was an Earl and she was nobody, and she shouldn't have bothered him with her troubles even though he had asked...

Lord Breamore studied her face, his gaze lingering on the red marks framing her eyes. 'I'm sorry to hear it. I can see whatever it was must have been unwelcome indeed.'

He paused, one hand resting on his horse's neck. The mare snorted softly and he absently rubbed her nose, not seeming to care that it might leave a smudge on his pristine kid gloves.

'I wonder, Miss Townsend... Would I be correct in thinking at least part of your unhappiness relates to your visit to Huntingham yesterday?'

Emily stiffened, feeling the ridges of the bark behind her pressing through her gown as he went on.

'Learning of my uncle's death certainly seemed to affect you more than I might have imagined, considering you'd never met. Is it fair to assume that was part of your unwanted news?'

He watched her closely, giving her nowhere to hide. There was still concern in his eyes, but a spark of curiosity had joined it. Emily found herself wanting to back away, into the shadows of the trees or anywhere else he couldn't fix her with the look that made it so tempting to tell him the truth.

'I—'

The words caught in her throat, halfway between escaping and being swallowed again. Admitting that the death of Ephraim Gouldsmith had indeed dealt her a bitter blow would make his nephew wonder why she cared so much, and she shrank from the prospect of explaining herself. The Earl might—*would*—think the worse of her to learn she wasn't even sure of the identity of her own father, and for some reason the idea of his disapproval helped her make up her mind.

With as much conviction as she could summon, Emily forced a smile, hoping it would be enough to cover a breakneck change of subject.

'I must return home, sir. I didn't tell anyone I'd gone out walking and they must be wondering where I am.'

Giving him no chance to reply she gave another awkward attempt at a curtsey and abruptly turned away, managing only one ungainly step before her ankle ruined her escape.

'Ouch!'

She sucked in a harsh breath as pain lanced up from her boot. It felt sharper than it had even a few minutes ago, and she knew she was trapped as the Earl came towards her, cutting off any hope of flight.

'Are you hurt?'

'Just my ankle. I caught it on a root and gave it a wrench. It isn't anything serious.'

There was a different kind of concern in his face now, although every bit as appealing as the variety that had gone before it. 'Perhaps not, but evidently too painful to walk on.' He shook his head decisively. 'I can't leave you here like this. If you'll allow me, I'll take you home myself.'

Emily started. He couldn't take her back to the school—he just *couldn't*. Miss Laycock would be furious she had inconvenienced someone of such high rank and would probably banish her to Mrs Swanscombe's even earlier than planned. It was an unthinkable imposition for one of her standing, and she was trying to find the words to refuse when another of those eye-catching smiles stopped her in her tracks.

'I know what you're thinking, but don't worry. I'm not offering you a carriage this time—just Constance.' He nodded to the mare beside him and Emily saw how even the horse's bridle gleamed in the sun, the leather soft and more expensive than all her clothing put together.

'It isn't so much the carriage, my lord, as being in your company. If someone saw…'

'What would they say? That you should have turned down my offer in favour of staying here, clinging to a tree?' He laughed, the deep note one she realised she could have gladly listened to all day. 'There can be no impropriety for you in accepting my help. If anyone has a problem with either of our actions they can take it up with me.'

He smiled again and Emily knew it was hopeless. Surely resisting that handsome face was impossible and, when combined with the most kindness she'd been shown in a long time, she had more chance of jumping over the moon than refusing him. She ought to say no but it just wouldn't come, and when the Earl held out his arm she took it.

'Here. Lean on me.'

Her breath caught as he carefully helped her out from the shadows, his forearm solid beneath her fingers. Each hopping step jarred her ankle, but somehow the pain faded when he drew her to him, her head scarcely reaching his shoulder and the rich green wool of his coat almost brushing her ear. It was the closest she'd ever been to a man, she realised with a jolt. Most girls had attended at least one dance by the time they reached her age, but Miss Laycock would never countenance such frivolity, and so, instead of dancing, it was to raise her onto his horse that a gentleman first placed a hand on her lower back.

'You'll permit me?'

She nodded wordlessly, not trusting herself to speak. Lifting her seemed the easiest thing in the world: he swept her up as though she weighed nothing, that first touch by a strong pair of hands unforgettable. With expert gentleness he placed her into the saddle and she clung to the pommel, with what felt like an entire swarm of butterflies taking wing in her stomach as he climbed up behind her.

'Settled?'

Another nod was all she could muster. The hard breadth of his chest lay flush against her back, warm despite the layers of clothing between them, and Emily feared she might combust when a firm arm wound around her to anchor her in place.

'Good. Let's get you home. By the by—where is that, exactly?'

There was hardly anything to her, Andrew realised as he tightened his arm around Emily's waist and tapped his horse into a brisk trot. She was all angles and unpadded bone beneath another drab gown, but her hair smelled of wild flowers and sunshine and he had to curb the impulse to breathe it in as it stirred just beneath his nose, the breeze making her red-gold waves move as though they were alive. Her head was uncovered and she wore no gloves, something unheard of for any respectable young lady venturing outside, but he was too distracted by other things to spend much time wondering why.

The headache that had been his constant companion since he woke had eased a little since riding out from Huntingham Hall, some of the cobwebs blown away by the summer air. It had been a mistake to drink so much the night before and he was paying for it now, but Lady Calthorpe's ball had been so crashingly dull he'd had to make his own entertainment. It had been filled with people just like Uncle Ephraim—rich, self-important and humourless, on the whole—and he couldn't say he'd particularly enjoyed dancing with the unending succession of young ladies who had been dangled before him like beautifully dressed carrots on sticks. A new, youthful Earl was a fine thing for every mama with an unmarried daughter, and he'd been harried since the moment he'd stepped into the ballroom, forced to twirl one debutante after another with nothing much to say to any of them. As the highest-ranking man in the room it would be assumed he had much in common with these well-bred ladies, but that assumption was misguided as ever, and as Emily shifted in the saddle Andrew felt his interest in her return full force.

'How's your ankle? I hope the movement isn't hurting you?'

'Hardly at all, sir. I'm just thankful for your assistance.'

Her voice was little more than a murmur above the thudding of hooves and he had to lean down to catch it, sitting sharply back again when his cheek accidentally brushed her ear. With each of the horse's long strides she swayed against him, her slim waist undulating under his palm, and it was becoming difficult to deny he found himself infinitely more attracted to her than any of the women he'd danced with the night before.

But why, though?

He tensed as his horse stumbled slightly, the movement throwing Emily even harder against him as though to test his restraint.

Is it because there might be some scant similarity between us, given the years I spent with barely a penny to my name, or because she seems so determined to remain a mystery?

That was a distinct possibility. She still hadn't told him what had upset her so clearly, what she'd been doing out in the fields or even where she lived. His earlier enquiry as to the latter had produced the distinctly unhelpful reply of 'Brigwell, sir,' with nothing more to go on than that, and he had to wonder if she was doing it on purpose.

She could just be odd, I suppose. Why else would she have been attempting to hide behind a tree when I stumbled across her?

Perhaps she'd felt so uncomfortable after their first unexpected meeting that she hadn't wished to see him again, resorting to diving into bushes to avoid him? For his part, it was true that one motivation for stopping to help her was concern, but he couldn't deny another reason followed closely behind. Ever since she'd left his parlour he hadn't been able to stop trying to guess why she'd been there in the first place, and it seemed almost serendipitous he now had a chance to find out.

They reached the end of the lane and, in the absence of any direction from his passenger, Andrew spurred the horse straight on. The overgrown trees swept down too low for him to ride along the footpath Emily must have taken from town, and he found he was glad of the landowner's negligence—the obstruction meant taking the long way round. Although if he wanted to satisfy his curiosity, he realised time was running out.

Careful not to let his face graze hers again, he leaned down.

'What if I told you that my assistance came at a price?'

He felt her stiffen. Already seeming to consist solely of ribs and sharp edges, she became even more tense, her spine hardening as if encased in armour.

'I would have to ask you to set me down here and now, my lord. I regret I have nothing with which to pay you.'

'Not money, Miss Townsend.'

Aware of his poor phrasing, Andrew hurried to correct it. 'My price would be the true answer to a question.'

The smallest whisper of tension left Emily's iron backbone, but not much, and there was an uncomfortable pause before her reply was almost lost in the wind.

'I suppose I'd say yes, sir. You've been far kinder than I'd have expected. It would be ungracious of me to refuse.'

She waited, her sunlit hair sliding over her shoulders. It had come looser and looser from its knot as they'd ridden along, sprinkling pins into the dry mud behind them, and now it hung freely around her like a silken cloak. Its natural perfume was more enticing than ever and it tempted Andrew to abandon his questioning, instead feeling the urge to bury his face in its waves...

'Why did you really go to see my uncle?'

He covered his lapse of good sense with a blurted query. If the mere scent of her hair was enough to distract him it didn't bode well for when she got down from his horse and he saw her face again, disarmingly pretty even when streaked with dried tears. A shabby gown did nothing to set her at a disadvantage. If anything, it made her shine all the more brightly, like a precious jewel half hidden in rubble and waiting to be found, although the image faded when he heard her sigh.

The deep breath seemed to come all the way up from the very soles of her mended boots. 'I suppose it makes little difference now. I'll be gone from Brigwell in a few days and then my foolishness won't matter.'

She rearranged herself slightly, tucking her elbows closer against her sides. A glance over the top of her head showed her hands had tightened on the pommel, and Andrew felt the rigidity in her back return with a vengeance.

'I'm not altogether sure where to start.'

He kept silent as she gathered her thoughts, her slender fingers never loosening their vice-like grasp of the saddle.

'I've been a parlour boarder at Miss Laycock's School for Young Ladies since the day after I was born. Neither Mrs Laycock nor her daughter, when she became mistress, would ever tell me anything about my parents or why I was placed there, other than to make it clear there was nowhere else for me to go.'

Emily turned her head slightly to the side and he saw the curve of her cheek glowed a brilliant crimson. Reading between the lines she had just admitted to being born on the wrong side of the blanket, and he heard the raw edge of shame in her voice, already difficult to catch above the wind in his ears but now even lower still.

'When I was nine I found the papers regarding my admission. I discovered my mother had died in childbed and my father was *Lord* someone, although I was unable to learn either of their names. My board and education were paid for in advance, obviously by my father, and I was always convinced he would return to claim me.'

There was a moment of silence, broken only by the horse's heavy breaths and the swishing of wind-stirred trees. Emily's iron spine had bent a little. She hunched now as if she had a pain in her belly, her shoulders rounded where previously she'd held herself so firmly upright.

'After my twenty-first birthday it seems the money for my keep ran out, and a few days ago Miss Laycock informed me she'd found me a position as a governess a hundred miles away, far from what I consider my home. She wouldn't countenance any refusal and so I sought to find my father, thinking to throw myself on his mercy until I found a position more to my liking, but it did not… turn out as I had hoped.'

'That's why you tried to see my uncle? Because you imagined *he* might be the man?'

It was a good thing Emily couldn't see his face, Andrew thought as he watched her give a single, tentative nod. It was all he could do to keep his hands steady on the reins, shock spreading through him like wildfire.

She thought Uncle Ephraim…?

The very idea was impossible. Of all the men in the

world, the late Lord Breamore had been the very least likely to create a child, his disdain for women and people in general rendering that an inarguable fact. Ephraim Gouldsmith had never looked kindly on a lady in his life, and certainly never with enough lust to seduce one, his cold heart moved only by money and the unceasing desire for more. Miss Townsend couldn't have been more wrong in her assumption, and Andrew had to marvel at the extent of her error—but that didn't make her current dismay any less real. For whatever reason she'd convinced herself Ephraim was her father, and her reaction to learning of his passing now made perfect sense, the inaccuracy of her belief taking nothing away from the pain she must have felt to discover he was gone.

'I see.'

Taking great care to keep his voice level, Andrew cast about for the right words, wishing the education his mother had scraped to afford had taught him how to manage unhappy young women as well as Latin. 'And I, like a fool, dropped the knowledge of his death on you with no warning. I'm truly sorry for that.'

Emily's answering shrug set a surge of pity rising inside him. 'You needn't apologise, my lord. How could you have known?'

She huddled into herself, perhaps regretting laying herself so bare, and Andrew cursed himself for forcing her to it. His curiosity had made her admit things she probably wanted to keep locked away, private loss and unhappiness he was ashamed to have caused her to relive.

He would have to break the truth about Uncle Ephraim to her gently. She couldn't be allowed to carry the old wretch in her heart when he didn't deserve to be there, the thought of the old Earl's reaction to her if he'd still been alive making Andrew's jaw harden. The late Lord Breamore would have rained humiliation down on her for daring to have ideas so above her station and Andrew tried not to imagine it, the picture of Emily's tear-stained face when he'd found her that morning flashing before his eyes.

'He wasn't a man much interested in women, Miss Townsend. I see no resemblance to him in your face or temperament... You also said the money stopped when you were twenty-one?'

'Yes, sir. My birthday was just last week.'

'In that case I'm afraid he really can't have been your father. My uncle lived in Italy for a few years around the time of your birth. He wouldn't have been in England to meet your mother or to secure your place at school.'

Bracing himself for despair, arguments or perhaps even more tears, it was a relief when instead Emily simply shook her head.

'In truth, sir, I had already begun to doubt it myself. As you say, there is no resemblance between us, and when you spoke of his distaste for women it seemed unlikely that he might have...'

There was no need for her to finish. Both parties knew what went into the making of an illegitimate child, and the sliver of Emily's profile he could glimpse behind her hair was still flushed a deep, unhappy pink.

'Of course, any financial assistance would have been very much appreciated but it was the man himself I truly wanted to find. I suppose I'll have to reconcile myself to it and accept my new position with Mrs Swanscombe—

there are worse fates than living among strangers, even if it wouldn't be of my choosing.'

'You'll leave town? Is there no other way?'

'I think not. I must make money to support myself and Miss Laycock has made it very clear to me there are few in Brigwell who would countenance a woman of my standing having care of their children.'

Her bare hands looked as though they were carved from ivory as they held onto the saddle, so stiff and white they might have belonged to a statue. One glance at them told Andrew her face must be much the same, tight and pale aside from the flare of shame in each cheek, and as they drew closer to town he realised he hadn't the faintest idea of how to reply.

The stigma of her illegitimacy would indeed be a problem. He'd seen similar in his village in Derbyshire, with a young woman widely rumoured to have been fathered by a passing tradesman. It was supposed that as her mother had been loose so must the daughter be, and the local men had barely given the poor girl a moment's peace until at last she'd eloped with the baker's son to the horror of his parents. A woman's reputation could be her glory or her downfall, and the unfairness of it didn't affect the truth, someone like Emily placed at a disadvantage while still in her swaddling clothes.

He opened his mouth—and closed it again just as quickly. An offer to help her had pushed forwards and very nearly made its way out, although at the last moment he managed to snatch it back.

Be sensible. Think before you speak.

How could he be of help to her? He had no children of his own in need of a governess, and giving her money would be a mistake. It would suggest she'd done something to earn it and he knew exactly what that *something* would be, an act that would fan the unkind whispers already swirling about her until they burst into flames.

'Can you not ask this Miss Laycock for more information? Surely she would have records, documents...?'

He caught the smallest breath of a laugh. 'I've tried, sir, many, many times. Either she doesn't know or has made up her mind to tell me nothing—there's no hope of learning anything there.'

'I see.' He thought for a moment. 'And the paper you found? It gave no hint as to his identity, other than his title?'

'No. His name was covered by an ink blot, leaving only the *Lord* exposed. There *was* a smudged crest alongside his signature, as though his signet ring had brushed the ink and left a stamp of sorts, but it was so smeared I could hardly tell what it was supposed to be without the original to compare it to.'

She lapsed into silence and Andrew didn't attempt to draw her out again. There seemed little else for her to add, or at least little she *wanted* to, and neither spoke again until eventually she tentatively cleared her throat.

'You can set me down here, please, my lord. I'm sure I can walk the rest of the way myself.'

Caught up in his thoughts he'd barely noticed they were on the edge of town and he reined his horse in abruptly, bringing her to a stop at the end of the lane that led to the market square. There was nobody around, but it seemed Emily wanted to take no chances, slipping out from beneath his arm and sliding to the ground without waiting for him to hand her down.

He heard her draw in a pained hiss as she straightened up, but at his move to dismount she held up a hand.

'There's no need, sir. As I said, I can walk from here quite easily.'

'Really? With that ankle?'

'Hobble, then.' She smiled up at him, a false smile, but one that emphasised her pretty cheekbones nonetheless. 'But it's best I'm not seen with you. You understand.'

She stepped back, slightly lopsidedly but still managing some of the poise he'd so admired as she left his parlour. Clearly the education her mysterious father had paid for had focused heavily on deportment, although when she raised her chin to look at him she didn't quite meet his eye.

'Thank you for your help, sir. I don't doubt it was a small thing for you, but for me it was a moment of kindness when all seemed bleak indeed.'

The spot of colour in each cheek blazed brighter and Andrew suspected her unsteady curtsey was a ruse to hide her countenance—a reprieve for which he found he was grateful.

His earlier suspicion had been proved right. Looking into her face again did nothing to lessen the fledgling attraction to her that had begun at first glance, and when coupled with her gratitude he found he had nothing to say, his chest oddly tight as he gazed down at her bowed head.

For such a small act to mean so much to her she must have led a cold and empty life. He'd had his own struggles, but at least he'd always known he was loved, his mother taking great pains to teach him money was not the most important thing to strive for. A secure home and the chance to understand herself were all Emily wanted, things even the lowest farmhand took for granted but she had been denied, and there was a strange heaviness around Andrew's heart as he tipped his hat to her and turned to ride back the way he had come.

Chapter Three

A light was still burning in the Dower House's window when Andrew returned from Captain Maybury's dinner party, the single lamp casting an eerie glow over the drive. It was past midnight, but his mother clearly had not yet retired to bed, and he gritted his teeth on a yawn as he took a detour from Huntingham's front steps to knock at her door.

It was no surprise that she answered it herself. Old habits died hard, and although she could now have afforded an army of servants she preferred only two maids to live in, young girls who would have been sent to their beds some hours before, while their mistress sat up to keep watch.

'You're back earlier than last week. Was the music not to your liking this time?'

She let him into the shadowy hall, the candle she held throwing strange shapes against the wall. With a white shawl over her nightdress and her greying hair in a plait there was a touch of Shakespearean ghost about her, and Andrew felt as though he was following a spectre as she led him down the corridor and into her parlour.

'The music was fine. I just wanted to leave.'

He dropped into a chair beside the fire, stretching his legs out towards the blaze. 'I wish you wouldn't wait up for me. It's not necessary now we live in a respectable neighbourhood again. What do you think might happen to me when I'm taken everywhere by carriage?'

'I don't know. I suppose it'll just take a while for both of us to adapt to the change.'

Lady Gouldsmith settled into the chair opposite, drawing her shawl around her shoulders in another relic from the years they'd spent living in draughty houses. 'How was it?'

'The same as always.'

'Oh. As enjoyable as that?' His mother gave a wry smile. 'Was Mrs Windham there again?'

'Yes.'

'And Mrs Forsythe?'

'Yes.'

'And their daughters, of course?'

'Of course.'

Another yawn was building and this time he let it out with an audible crack of his jaw. It had been another long and tedious evening and he wanted to go to bed, weary from the effort of juggling two ambitious mamas both vying for the same thing—himself.

'I wish you'd come to these dinners too, Mother. You're always invited. It would help divert some of the attention from me.'

'I'm afraid the presence of an old widow couldn't do that. Until you've taken a wife you'll be the most interesting man in the county, and there's nothing I or anyone else can do about it.'

The fire had died down and Lady Gouldsmith leaned over to take up the poker, deliberately looking away from her son as she prodded the flames. It was glaringly obvious what she was about to ask, and Andrew wondered how she'd phrase it this time, the same question as always but delivered in a hundred different ways.

'So…still nobody has caught your eye?'

He'd meant to laugh at her predictability but tonight it caught in his throat. For the first time since they'd arrived back in Warwickshire he might have answered *yes*—although the woman on his mind for the past two days had not been among those seated around Captain Maybury's grand dining table.

Miss Emily Townsend would never receive an invitation to such a gathering, Andrew thought, as he watched his mother cast a length of kindling into the fire. Captain Maybury and his fine friends would never have heard of her, far too refined to know anything of unfashionable Brigwell or its residents, and even if they had she would *not* have made the guest list. In her faded gown she wasn't anywhere near smart enough and her plain speech would amuse them, and the fact she didn't even know who her father was placed her miles beyond the pale.

And yet to me none of that seems to matter. If anything, it makes me like her all the more.

He let his head rest against the back of his chair, gazing up at the firelight moving over the ceiling. The image of copper-gold hair and flushed cheeks had lingered ever since he had left Emily at the side of the road. It flickered before him now, a pair of bright blue eyes joining the attack. They had been made raw by crying and the sympathy he'd felt then came again as—not for the first time—he allowed their meeting to replay itself through his tired mind.

It wasn't just money she'd wanted from her father, he was certain. It had been to know the man who bore half the credit of making her, someone that, despite the passing of more than twenty years, he still felt his own loss of every single day. The initial wound had closed over but a scar remained, and he knew how easy it would be to tear it open again, grief fading into the background but never fully going away. Miss Townsend had known her own unhappiness and that made them the same, in a way, and he suspected that they could have grown to understand each other if only they'd had the chance to try.

But we won't have one.

Andrew frowned up at the ceiling, surprised by the sudden intensity of his disappointment.

She's leaving Brigwell in a few days and then I shan't see her again.

He sat forward, hoping his mother had missed the pinch of his brows. 'My circle boasts many young ladies now, all of them amiable, but there's nothing on which to build a connection. Our lives have been too different to find much common ground.'

Lady Gouldsmith nodded as she propped the poker back in its place beside the hearth. 'A solid foundation is important for a successful marriage. I would not have you wed where you couldn't agree, even if the lady was the richest woman in all of England.'

'Money doesn't come into it. I've enough now to last several lifetimes—I can't see that I need any more, even if to say that would make my uncle turn in his grave.'

At the mention of Ephraim a shadow crossed his mother's face. The previous Lord Breamore had strongly disapproved of his younger brother's choice of bride, determined that any marriage should have been to the advantage of the family coffers. Mother's only fortune had been her face and good nature, however, and Ephraim had never forgiven her for it, his decision not to help her after Father's death rooted in resentment he'd carried until his very last day.

'How that man and your father were brothers I shall never understand. I'm glad a woman's money matters little to you. Your father was the same, and although we paid the price for it later I wouldn't have had him any other way.'

'Nor I.' Andrew slowly shook his head, thoughts of Emily still lingering. 'It was difficult at times but I'm grateful for what that taught me. I don't need carriages and expensive clothes to be content, and I'd like the same to be true of my wife.'

'That would be a fine thing. As your mother I only ever want you to be happy…although, of course, as the latest Lord Breamore, it's also necessary for you to produce an heir.'

Lady Gouldsmith slid her son a hesitant glance from beneath the lace edge of her cap, the dark eyes they shared glinting with reflected firelight. 'Your father and I weren't granted time enough to provide you with siblings. Unlike your late uncle you have no nephew to save you from matrimony, and it would be a shame indeed if your father's name were to die out.'

She spoke lightly but Andrew could hear her sincerity. Uncle Ephraim had done little to garner admiration, but Father had been a good man. He deserved for his legacy to live on, and besides, it would be a wonderful thing to have a family again. The five short years he'd had with both his parents had been the happiest of Andrew's life, and he found he wanted to recreate it himself, the building of a better future perhaps the best cure for a sad past.

The romance of his parents' relationship was something he would have liked to experience, although now a love match was out of the question. As mere Andrew Gouldsmith he'd had the luxury of time, able to wait for as long as it took to find a woman who could capture his heart, but for the Earl of Breamore duty must come first. He owed it to his father's memory to wed quickly, setting his own desires aside for the sake of the man whose life had been cut so tragically short. All that remained was for him to attempt to find a wife, among those with whom he was supposed to feel more commonality than his early years meant he ever could.

'I've no intention of letting it. I'll marry as soon as I've found a woman with whom I feel at least some accord.'

He pressed his fingers against his eyes, feeling some slight relief from an ache growing behind them. He'd drunk too much again. It was beginning to be a pattern, and not one he wanted to continue, his dislike of the Society events he was obliged to attend making him seek solace in the bottom of his glass. If he wasn't careful he might end up doing something unwise next time and then he'd be known as the scandalous Earl rather than the desirable one, although the idea of escaping the determined mamas that hunted him was almost enough to make him consider downing an entire bottle.

'I'm going to bed. You'll go to yours now too, I hope?'

'Yes. I'll be able to settle now I know you've returned.'

His mother rose and Andrew followed her back to the front porch, pausing briefly to stoop and kiss her cheek before stepping out into the night. The door closed behind him and he heard the scrape of a key in a lock, and then the single light in the Dower House window was extinguished, leaving him alone in the dark.

For a moment he didn't move. The moon hung above him in a silvery arc and the stars winked back as he gazed up at them, enjoying the cool air on his skin. Captain Maybury's dining room had been loud and stifling and he relished the silence that surrounded him now, only the faraway cry of a fox interrupting the peace of the night. In the darkness he wasn't an Earl or a gentleman or anything else someone might label him. He was just Andrew, standing still looking up at the stars, and he found himself wondering if Emily was doing the same.

Of course she's not. She's far too sensible to be loitering outside at this time, catching her death of cold.

He'd definitely drunk too much if that was what he was thinking, he rebuked himself as he turned towards the Hall. Miss Emily Townsend would be tucked up in bed by now, her beautiful hair probably bound up in a braid and her eyelashes sweeping down onto smooth cheeks, and for a split second the mental picture made it difficult to concentrate on climbing the front steps.

She might be softer, somehow, in a nightgown, less

stiff than when she'd sat in front of him on the horse and he'd locked an arm around her waist. That hadn't made the experience of holding her against him any less enjoyable, of course. She was still warm and the secret sweep of her waist was still unmistakably womanly, and when the curve of her backside had fitted so neatly into the space between his thighs—

He grabbed the front door handle and pushed it open. It wasn't a gentlemanly thought and he tried firmly to leave it outside, attempting to turn his mind in a more respectful direction as he nudged the door shut behind him…

And then, quite without meaning to, he stumbled onto an intriguing idea.

The sound of a pianoforte being tortured floated up from the floor below as Emily folded her spare nightgown into a neat square, her bedroom window open to the fresh morning air. The rest of her belongings were already packed into the small trunk that lay open on her bed, and she placed the nightgown on top, her meagre possessions barely filling it halfway. All that remained was to fetch her books and winter cloak and that would be everything, a whole life able to fit in a case with room enough to spare, and as she straightened up she wished she could stow her unhappiness inside it too.

There was a brief pause in the strangled Mozart. Probably Miss Laycock had just brought her fan down sharply over the knuckles of whichever unfortunate girl was currently struggling her way through and, despite her despondency, Emily felt a flicker of sympathy. Music lessons with Miss Laycock were often fraught affairs and her own knuckles had paid the price more than once, although at this moment she would have gladly suffered the same thing again if it meant she didn't have to leave. In two days she would board a post carriage, and then another and another, riding a whole chain of the uncomfortable, rattling things until she'd left Brigwell far behind. And once at Mrs Swanscombe's house she'd face loneliness worse than any she'd known before.

The despair that was never far away placed its hand on her shoulder and she was powerless to shrug it off. The only positive she could think of was that her ankle felt better that morning, the stabbing pain now reduced to a slight ache, although even that scant silver lining ebbed when she recalled who had helped her at its peak.

With a sigh she sat down on the edge of her bed. Had she been right to tell Lord Breamore the truth? After his kindness to her she could hardly have refused, and surely his opinion of her hardly mattered. Even if she'd stayed on in Brigwell, an Earl wouldn't care about the life story of someone like herself. He'd been curious, no doubt, rather than truly interested, and would forget all about her now they were destined never to meet again. If he thought badly of her after hearing about her shame then it should make no difference…

So why, then, did she seem to care so much?

One corner of the trunk was digging into her back and she pushed it away, passing a hand over her face when she heard something inside it fall over.

She had other far more pressing concerns than what a near stranger thought of her. Her entire life was about to change and it was a waste of time to daydream about a man so hopelessly out of her reach, with his kind, dark eyes and hands strong enough to lift her into a saddle without breaking a sweat. Men like that weren't meant for women like her, and she'd be a fool to imagine he'd given her a second thought once she'd slipped down from his horse, their worlds so far apart there was no hope of bridging the gap.

A brisk knock brought Emily's head jerking up. She hadn't realised she'd placed it in her hands, and she stood up hurriedly as a face appeared around her bedroom door.

'There you are. You've a visitor waiting in the back parlour.'

The other young woman seemed almost as surprised by this development as Emily herself. In all her twenty-one years at the school nobody had ever come to call on her, and she frowned as if she'd just been told a particularly difficult riddle.

'What? Who is it?'

'A *man*. Andrew somebody. I didn't catch his last name.' The messenger paused, took half a step into the room and lowered her voice. 'If you come down quickly Miss Laycock might not see. I don't think she heard the bell above the din of Jane's playing and you could speak to him without her knowing.'

She raised her eyebrows meaningfully, although Emily continued to stare at her without any understanding whatsoever.

The only Andrew she knew was the local butcher's son. They'd exchanged perhaps ten words in as many years and even then only about a side of beef. Why he would come to see her was a mystery, but definitely one she preferred to solve without Miss Laycock breathing down her neck. Male visitors were strictly forbidden and her caller would be dismissed as soon as he was discovered, the doctor the only man ever allowed to darken the Laycock door.

'I'll come down now. You said he's in the back parlour?'

At an affirming nod Emily left the room, slipping silently out onto the landing. The sound of murdered Mozart showed no sign of stopping and she was glad of its cover as she crept down the stairs, careful to avoid the creaking tread at the bottom. The back parlour was situated behind the kitchen, in a leftover from the times a housekeeper had ruled the domain instead of Miss Laycock, and Emily felt her heart begin to beat faster as she stole down the corridor and tentatively—still unsure of what she might find—pushed open the door.

It was fortunate she wasn't holding anything. If she had been there was no way she wouldn't have dropped it when the man standing by the empty fireplace turned around, his face familiar but most certainly not the one she'd expected.

'Lord Breamore!'

His answering smile set her already skipping heart bounding even faster. 'Good morning, Miss Townsend. I hope you'll forgive me for calling unannounced.'

He bowed, as casually as if finding an Earl in the second-best parlour was an everyday occurrence. 'I thought it would be better not to use my title. For myself I couldn't care less whether the whole school knows who I am, but I guessed you'd prefer discretion.'

Lord Breamore—*Andrew*—smiled again but Emily didn't return it. The question of what he was doing there

was so overwhelming it drowned out everything else—
aside, perhaps, from the wish she'd thought to tidy herself
up before leaving her room, acutely aware of a tea stain
on the front of her apron. By contrast the Earl looked
as immaculate as ever, his boots gleaming and hair perfectly arranged, the healed break in his nose the only
flaw in his features and yet somehow managing to en-
hance them rather than the reverse...

A particularly discordant note from the distant pianoforte brought her back to her senses. Miss Laycock
would be furious if she realised rules were being broken. Emily stepped into the room, hastily shutting the
door behind her.

'It's an honour to have you here, my lord, but I'm
afraid I'm not allowed male visitors. The headmistress
will be finishing her lesson soon and if she catches me
with you she'll be severely displeased. Was there something you needed from me?'

What could have brought him there was impossible
to guess. In his beautifully tailored coat and silk cravat
he seemed as out of place as a thoroughbred in a field of
ponies. She wasn't sure where to look, suddenly shyer in
his presence than she'd ever been before.

*That's because you know how strong his hands are
now*, a little voice in the back of her mind piped up help-
fully. *And how it feels to have his arm around you. It
was firm and unyielding, and more muscular than you
might have expected a gentleman's to be—*

Fortunately, Andrew didn't appear to have noticed
how heat had rushed into her cheeks. He was still beside
the unlit fire, the arm she was so enamoured of resting

on the mantle, and to her surprise he now seemed somewhat ill at ease himself.

'If time's short I won't waste it. I came with a propo-
sition—or, more precisely, a propo*sal*.'

'Of what kind?'

He glanced at her, a swift flit of his dark eyes that sent
a thrill skittering down her spine. 'Perhaps you'd like to
sit before I continue?'

'I'd rather stay here by the door, sir. If I hear Miss
Laycock coming I can intercept her while you slip out
through the kitchen. I know from experience that her
lessons can end abruptly.'

Andrew inclined his head, a slight crease appearing
between his straight brows. His air was definitely bordering on the uncertain now. He gave the impression of
one teetering on the brink of something, one finger unconsciously tapping the top of the mantlepiece.

'Very well. It's a proposal of the usual kind a man
might make a woman.' The Earl paused for a moment,
his finger abruptly ceasing its restless twitch. 'Marriage.'

Emily blinked.

*How funny. I could have sworn he just said 'mar-
riage'.*

'I'm sorry, my lord. I must have misheard you.'

'No. I think you heard me perfectly.'

She felt her face slacken into blank incomprehension.
Her ears had caught the words, yes, but she couldn't
grasp what they meant, and she stared at him, wondering what other definition of marriage he could possibly
be referring to. It couldn't be the one *she* knew, with the
church and the rings and the 'til death us do part, and her
confusion only grew when he came closer, and slowly,

as if being careful not to frighten her into running away, reached out to take her hand.

'I'm in earnest. If you'll have me, I'd like to make you my wife.'

His hand was bare, she realised dimly, and warm where hers was cold. He must have removed his glove at some point and his skin against hers set fireworks wheeling through her insides, each one trailing countless sparks. On the day he had lifted her onto his horse she'd felt the power in his grip, although now it was gentle, allowing her to pull away if she chose, but as she looked up at him and saw the honesty in his eyes she knew that she would not.

'But…*why*?'

It was the only response she could think of, and one Andrew seemed to have been expecting, a ghost of the smile he'd flashed when she'd entered the room reappearing to draw her attention sharply to his mouth.

'That's a fair question. I think I'd say the same if someone I'd only met twice before offered me their hand.'

He still held hers and Emily felt herself begin to burn, aware his palm was big enough to eclipse her fingers within it.

'Do you want to be sent a hundred miles away?'

His unexpected bluntness startled her into honesty. 'No, sir.'

'Would you rather stay in Warwickshire and perhaps continue the hunt for your father?'

'Why…yes.'

'If you decided to marry me, I could help you with both of those things.' Andrew's voice was level, neither wheedling nor pushy and speaking with the quiet frankness of a man telling the truth. 'You said your father was a Lord. As my Countess and the mistress of Huntingham Hall you'd have access to every high-ranking man in Warwickshire and could easily carry on your search. For my part I am in need of a wife and, having met many, *many* of the young ladies in this county, I've come to the conclusion that my best match would be you.'

He nodded as if to emphasise his point and Emily watched him, hoping her face wasn't that of the simpleton she currently felt. He was offering her everything she wanted in the whole world and yet she couldn't make herself understand, her mind working at a far slower pace than her racing heart.

'I don't… How could I possibly be a good match for you? For an Earl?'

'As I said, I've met many young ladies since I came to take my inheritance. In general they've been pleasant, accomplished and credits to their families, but that is not what I want.'

A shade flitted over his handsome face, half a second and then it was gone, a nameless emotion Emily saw with shock-glazed eyes. 'You see an Earl when you look at me, but I didn't grow up with wealth. My mother and I knew what it was to count every penny and, as such, I feel little kinship with those who might be thought of as my peers. I don't place great value on having a new carriage every year and I'd like my wife to be the same— someone who has lived in the real world and understands it, and is grateful for things money can't buy.'

He looked down at her, serious now, with no trace of a smile, and Emily felt something twist.

Surely the whole thing was folly, still so unlikely she

half suspected she was dreaming. She couldn't marry an Earl no matter what he said—it just wasn't *done*, the chasm between them too wide and too dark for anyone of her station to cross. For all his sweet words and the undeniable attraction that had her in its thrall, he was still above her, from a sphere entirely separate from her own, and the sudden desire to abandon all good sense and go along with his madness was only just held in check by the equally strong knowledge that he would regret his choice as soon as it was made.

'I can't.'

Her throat was dry. 'I thank you for your offer, my lord, but I can't accept. It would shame you to marry me. I couldn't allow your reputation to suffer for my sake.'

Andrew shook his head, his brows knitting together again in a frown so determined she wanted to trace it with her fingertips.

'I don't see why it would. Nobody outside of Brigwell knows you, and certainly none of my new circle. You'd have the chance to reinvent yourself, should you choose. Whatever version of Emily Townsend you wished to be would be up to you.'

Very gently he increased the pressure on her hand, drawing her towards him, and Emily found she couldn't stop herself from allowing it.

For all her conscious mind's warnings, her baser instincts cut through the fog of her sluggish mind, instructing her to obey the quietly insistent pull of Andrew's fingers. It was magnetic, unfightable, and when she stepped near enough for him to take her other hand she thought her leaping heart might burst out through her ribs.

'Do you really think I could stand beside you and feel

shame?' he murmured, his gaze holding hers and refusing to let go. 'Knowing your circumstances makes me respect you more, not less. If I can look past your station, past the things about yourself you cannot change, do you think you could do the same for me?'

His face was very near to hers. Probably she should pull away, some tediously puritanical part of her thought, pretending offence that he presumed to get so close, but such a thing was impossible. If he leaned down just a fraction more he could kiss her, something no man had ever done before, and only the most untimely of interruptions stopped Emily from losing her head entirely and rising up to kiss *him* instead.

Far too late she realised the pianoforte had stopped its tuneless tinkling. The door behind her had opened and she hadn't even noticed, too spellbound to focus on anything but Andrew's scandalously enticing mouth, but Miss Laycock's cry sent her flying back from him as though she'd been scalded.

'What is this? Who is this man?'

Even the Earl seemed slightly taken aback as the headmistress stormed into the room, although Emily had to marvel at how quickly he recovered.

'Good morning, Miss Laycock. My name is Andrew Gouldsmith.' He gave a sweeping bow, the very image of well-bred charm. 'Please forgive my calling. There was something I needed to speak to Miss Townsend about that was too important to be delayed.'

At the mention of his name Emily felt her stomach drop, already writhing like a bag of snakes. If Miss Laycock realised she had somehow crossed paths with an Earl there would be hell to pay, but the schoolteacher merely primmed up her mouth, evidently failing to connect the name with the title it disguised.

'It didn't look much like speaking to me.'

Turning her back on him she reached to take hold of Emily's arm. 'Come away at once. This is a disgrace. You'll return to your room and stay there until the carriage comes for you, and I don't want to see your face downstairs again before you leave.'

Angry fingers brushed her sleeve but Emily pulled away, for the first time in years failing to jump to do as she was told. Miss Laycock stood on one side of the door and Andrew on the other, and Emily took a step towards him, the same magnetic pull that had drawn her into his grasp guiding her again to move closer to his side.

She risked a glance up at him. He was watching intently as she made her choice, his eyes never leaving her face, and the unspoken encouragement she saw there made everything fall into place.

She'd never expected to marry. The lonely life of a governess was all she'd ever envisioned for herself, on the off-chance Lord *Somebody* never came to claim her, and it had seemed foolish to aspire to more when Miss Laycock had always made it seem so inevitable…but with Andrew things could be different. For the first time in her existence she could have a real home and help to find her father, at last able to know his love as she'd yearned to since she was a neglected child, and with growing wonder at her uncharacteristic defiance, Emily lifted her chin.

'Please give my apologies to Mrs Swanscombe, but I won't be taking the position of governess. I hope she won't be too inconvenienced.'

'What? Whyever not?'

Miss Laycock's eyes flashed. Beside her Emily felt Andrew move and then the snakes in her stomach turned to butterflies as his finger traced the lightest of reassuring touches across her wrist.

'What do you think you'll do instead? If you think for one moment you can stay here, you can't. I've told you before I don't offer charity.'

The headmistress glared but somehow her displeasure had lost its power to make Emily shiver. There was nothing to fear from that wrath any longer, she realised, not now Andrew stood so close beside her, that smallest of touches enough to make her want so much more—and she could have it, if only she was brave enough to say the words out loud.

'I don't want charity, ma'am. I'm still leaving, but of my own choice. I hope you'll be happy to hear I'm going to be wed.'

Chapter Four

Staring up at the unfamiliar ceiling of an unfamiliar bedroom, Emily wondered if she'd taken leave of her senses.

A maid had come to help her dress—*another* unfamiliar development—but she hadn't yet gathered the courage to go downstairs. Once she set foot outside her new bedroom she would have truly begun her first day as a resident of Huntingham Hall's Dower House, and the bizarreness of the fact seemed to have rendered her unable to stand up. She wasn't sure exactly how long she'd spent lying fully clothed on top of the most comfortable bed she'd ever experienced, but it was probably too long, the clock on her bedside table ticking the minutes away accusingly, and it took all her self-control not to bury her head beneath her pillow and stay there.

Instead, however, she forced herself to sit up. Lord Breamore's mother would be at the breakfast table and it would be unforgivably rude to keep her waiting, especially as she'd been gracious enough to take a stranger into her home. Her face had been a picture of shock when her son had brought Emily to her door the previous evening, but to Lady Gouldsmith's credit she had collected herself quickly, any surprise hidden behind hospitality that Emily couldn't quite tell was genuine or forced.

'Either way, you can't stay up here all morning,' she mumbled now towards the ceiling's elaborate cornicing. 'Like it or not, it's time to go down.'

A mirror hung above her washstand and, finally dragging herself to her feet, she glanced at it, immediately wishing she hadn't when her eye fell upon the sleeve of her gown. She'd neatly repaired a small rip in it but the mend was still visible, and she grimaced to wonder whether her hostess would notice. Lady Gouldsmith would be dressed impeccably, no doubt, drawing more attention to the difference between them that the Earl seemed so determined to overlook, and once again Emily questioned whether she had made a catastrophic mistake.

He said he didn't grow up with wealth, but surely what one considers wealthy is subjective? An Earl might consider himself impoverished if he only had three footmen instead of ten, without ever knowing what it's really like to live on slender means.

The one thing he had decided they had in common wasn't really true at all, she thought as she tried to tuck a stray thread out of sight inside her cuff; and surely as Lord Breamore got to know her he'd come to that conclusion himself. Every moment she spent with him would be an opportunity for him to realise his mistake, which was unfortunate, considering that to spend more time with him was exactly what she wanted.

I'll have to be more careful.

Getting carried away would be unwise, she tried to tell herself as she headed for the stairs. The Earl had thrown her a lifeline and she was grateful for it, but she shouldn't let that gratitude—or the attraction to her bewildering new fiancé, which showed no signs of diminishing—cloud her judgement. Lord Breamore had made his offer to her based on an assumption and she had accepted out of necessity and temptation, and that was not a firm enough foundation for anything more. Until both of them had a better understanding of who they were marrying it would be sensible to exercise restraint, although as Emily reached the bottom of the stairs she couldn't stop her heart from making a sudden, excited leap.

Voices were issuing from the dining room, one of them so deep and delightful she recognised it at once. Clearly the Earl had come to take breakfast with them and Emily stopped in her tracks, caught between running back the way she'd come and pushing on into the room. The door was slightly ajar, the low conversation taking place beyond it *just* audible, and without intending to she found herself listening as she groped for the courage to go in.

Lord Breamore's voice came alongside the clink of metal against China. 'How is Emily this morning?'

'I couldn't tell you. She hasn't yet been down.'

'Perhaps she didn't sleep well.'

'Perhaps. Such a drastic change of surroundings would make it difficult for anyone to get much rest.'

There was a pause in which Emily barely breathed,

still unable to move either forwards or back. She'd hardly spoken to Lady Gouldsmith since arriving at the Dower House, pleading exhaustion as an excuse to retire early the night before, and with such scant acquaintance it was hard to tell whether the other woman's remark held any kind of reproach.

It seemed the Earl was wondering the same thing. 'You disapprove?'

'Of course not. She seems a sweet girl, if entirely out of her depth—which is why I'd urge caution.'

A sensation not unlike a trickle of icy water crept down Emily's back. She *was* out of her depth, and the situation *was* strange enough to require caution, and to hear it said out loud made her feel as though the Earl's mother had found a window into her mind.

'You know the *ton* only care for their own,' Lady Gouldsmith continued, entirely unaware Emily now hung on her every word. 'Your uncle was furious when your father married me, a gentleman's daughter with a modest dowry, and Miss Townsend's background is far more uncertain than that. If you bring her into this world I hope you're prepared to protect her from what might follow, especially given the disadvantage from which she begins.'

For a moment there was quiet.

'If anyone asks about her past, we'll tell the truth.' Lord Breamore's deep voice was level. 'That she lost her parents as a child and was brought up by respectable people. There's no need to go into more detail to satisfy idle curiosity.'

'You might find that easier said than done.'

A gentle splash suggested Lady Gouldsmith was pouring herself a cup of tea as well as dispensing wisdom. 'Just be sure to take good care of her. It would be sad indeed if she found herself having escaped one unfortunate future only to stumble into another.'

Emily drew back from the doorway, not wanting to hear any more. Her heart was beating hard enough that she could feel it in her ears, and a knot sat in her stomach like a fist, clenched so tight the idea of eating breakfast held no appeal at all.

Clearly the Earl had already shared the private details of her background with his mother. He would have had to eventually, of course, but somehow knowing the elegant woman on the other side of the door was aware of her shameful origins made the fist grip harder still. Lady Gouldsmith evidently had her reservations about the match and, although she'd spoken kindly, she hadn't *quite* given it her blessing, managing to shoot an arrow directly into the centre of all Emily's uncertainties.

Before she could consider the matter further, however, a movement behind her caught her attention. A maid was crossing the hall and quickly Emily stepped back towards the door. The servants were probably already whispering about her, and being seen eavesdropping wouldn't help make a good impression, something that currently seemed very important as she squared her shoulders and—reluctantly—tapped on the door.

The voices on the other side ceased immediately. There was a short pause and then a chair scraped against a wooden floor as someone got to their feet, boots coming nearer as the unseen person came to answer her tentative knock—

The door swung open and for the briefest of beats the Earl's smile chased away all her fears.

'Ah. Good morning.'

He gave a slight bow, his crisp white shirt dazzling in the sunlight streaming through a window at his back. She couldn't see past him, his tall frame filling the doorway, although even if they'd been the same height his face made it impossible to look anywhere else.

'You don't have to wait to be allowed in. Until the wedding, we'd like you to consider this your home.'

At Miss Laycock's establishment the girls had been required to knock before entering any room, probably to stop them from becoming too comfortable, but Emily didn't tell him that. His welcoming smile had fleetingly loosened the vice in her innards, but it tightened again at the thought of the school, the place she *should* have woken that morning if the world hadn't been turned upside down.

'I'm sorry, my lord. Force of habit.'

'Andrew. I'm not "my lord" or "sir" any longer. I'd like you to call me by my name, if that's acceptable to you?'

He looked down at her in polite inquiry. He was very close and she could see where he had recently shaved, the skin of his jaw slightly pink from the razor's edge. The cleft in his chin she'd noticed the first day they met was more obvious when he was freshly shaven, and she realised she'd been looking at it for a fraction too long when the lip above it began to curve.

Hurriedly she nodded. 'Of course.'

'I'm glad to hear it. Will you sit down?'

Andrew stood aside and she scuttled past, careful not to brush against him. A place had been set for her at the table and, with a curtsey to Lady Gouldsmith, she sat down, intensely aware that Andrew's chair was right next to her own.

His mother smiled, genuinely, as far as Emily could tell. She'd been just as kind the night before and it seemed she was keen to put her guest at ease, even if she harboured doubts not intended to be overheard.

'Good morning, Miss Townsend. Or, following Andrew's example, perhaps you'd prefer I call you Emily?'

First names were less formal and therefore marginally less frightening, and Emily nodded at once.

'Yes, Lady Gouldsmith. Please do.'

'Oh, but we must be fair. There's no need to use my title around the breakfast table, surely. We'll be Emily and Eleanor here—although once you're wed, of course, you might find you *like* being called Lady Breamore.'

She smiled again and Emily tried to return it, although her face suddenly felt as though it were carved from marble.

Lady Breamore.

Even Andrew taking his seat beside her, accidentally brushing her arm as he sat, couldn't entirely distract her. Somehow in all the confusion of the past few days she hadn't fully grasped exactly what becoming his wife would mean, and for a moment she felt almost dizzy, the change from an illegitimate girl to a Countess far too huge to take in one leap.

'I can guess what you're thinking.'

Eleanor was watching her, one eyebrow raised knowingly. 'I wasn't born Lady anything either. I gained my title on marriage, just as you will, and I remember how strange it felt the first time someone said it. You'll get used to it, though, and more quickly than you'd imagine.'

With an encouraging nod she reached for a tray of cold ham, leaving Emily to stare down at her own empty plate. There were plenty of things with which to fill it but she couldn't bring herself to take any, anxiety making her feel unable to eat so much as a crumb.

'Can I pass you something?'

Andrew's voice was very close to her ear. There was something unexpectedly reassuring in it—more the depth than the innocuous question, and she busied herself in spreading her napkin over her lap as she tried to rein in her nerves enough to answer.

As Lady Breamore she would have a much better chance at finding her father, she reminded herself firmly. Wasn't that why she'd taken this path in the first place, to meet the one person she had long since convinced herself loved her as she had always wanted to be loved? Andrew was a risk, an attractive one she doubted could ever turn into something more, but her father was a far more certain prospect. Even if her husband ended up regretting her, she was sure her papa never would, and now that she had taken the first steps on this unexpected journey she had to stay the course.

She glanced to the side, feeling her nape prickle when she met Andrew's eye. He was waiting for her to say something and she quickly scanned the table, seizing on the first thing she saw despite not being hungry in the least.

'Yes, please, my lo—Andrew. Perhaps a piece of toast?'

She hardly took more than a mouthful, Andrew saw as he sat back in his chair and drained the dregs of his coffee. Few remnants remained of his own breakfast but

Emily's plate still held almost all of her toast, crumbled to appear smaller, although the definitive way she set down her knife suggested she'd finished. Either she always ate like a bird or something had stolen her appetite, and he realised—with slight discomfort—he didn't know her well enough to tell which was the truth.

And yet we're to be married.

It was still a good idea despite some small uncertainties, he told himself. The reasons he'd given her for their match were sound even if he felt some natural hesitation now that there was no turning back. Emily wanted a home and the chance to find her father, and he wanted a sensible wife who understood money wasn't a God-given right, and they had both made the right choice given the limited other options available to them.

Hadn't they?

Unwilling to dwell on the question, it was a relief when his mother posed one of her own.

'Do you have any plans for today?'

'I thought I might show Emily the grounds.' He turned to her with as careless a smile as he could manage. 'If you wanted to see them, that is?'

'Yes. I'd like that.'

She nodded, her piled-up hair swaying slightly as she moved. It was dressed more neatly than he'd seen it before, a few curls artfully arranged around her face to show her features to their best advantage, and he made a mental note to reward whichever maid was responsible. The style emphasised the almond slant of her eyes—the same soft blue as a hydrangea in full bloom, he'd already decided—and when she fixed them on him he felt his prior reservations waver.

Their rapid engagement would be even more difficult for her to adapt to than for himself. Leaving his modest life in Derbyshire and taking his place among the *ton* was an uncomfortable adjustment for him, but he had at least known it would happen eventually, aware of his position as Ephraim's heir since he was a child. For Emily there had been no such time to prepare. Blindsided by his proposal, she had agreed to become his wife without any real understanding of what she was agreeing *to*, acting out of necessity above anything else, and it was now his job to make sure she didn't come to regret it. Wedding a stranger was a gamble for both of them but she had more at stake, her decision to marry him catapulting her into a world she'd never set foot in before. He ought to spend less time contemplating his feelings and more time trying to help her with a transition that must have been like something from a dream.

'Good. If you'll excuse me for a short while, I have a letter to finish. Shall I call for you again in an hour?'

Another nod was his cue to rise from the table. Pushing back his chair he prepared to stand—but a warm touch on the back of his hand made him stop dead.

'I'm sorry. I was trying to move out of the way.'

Emily shuffled in her seat, the leg of her chair somehow caught on his. In attempting to detach herself, however, she instead leaned closer still, her arm brushing his hand again and her flushed face suddenly so near he had to act quickly to curb the first thought that came to mind.

He was still too late.

In the school's back parlour he would have kissed her and the picture came to him now, flaring vividly in spite of his attempt to hold it back. With her chin tilted and eyes wide Emily had been the most tempting thing he'd ever seen—and what was more he could have sworn she'd *wanted* him to bend his head and claim her, her lips slightly parted and breath coming shallow and fast. She might only have accepted his proposal as an alternative to exile, but in that moment at least she had felt something stir, he was certain of it, and if he'd managed it once there was hope he could do it again. A marriage of convenience didn't necessarily have to mean a marriage devoid of desire—although that wasn't something to consider in detail while his mother sat opposite, watching with amusement barely concealed behind her teacup.

At last, after what felt like far too much of a struggle, Andrew unhooked his accursed chair and stood up. Emily was far too busy rearranging her cutlery to return his bow but his mother smiled up at him...perhaps slightly too knowingly, he thought uneasily, not entirely comfortable with the expression in her dark eyes as she watched him leave the room.

Emily was already waiting for him when he had finished his letter an hour later, the hairstyle he so admired now hidden beneath a shabby bonnet as she hovered in the Dower House's porch. If she was to be a Countess she would have to be dressed like one eventually, although that was a concern for another time. Today he would begin by easing her into what was to be her new home, starting with the prettily unthreatening grounds, and Andrew made sure not to let his eyes wander to her more frayed edges as she descended the front steps.

'Ready to survey your new domain? Or the outside of it, at least?'

'Yes. I'm looking forward to it.'

She followed him to the gate that separated his mother's more modest garden from Huntingham Hall's sprawling back lawns. They reached out seemingly endlessly, punctuated with manicured hedges and paths bordering flowerbeds filled with colour, the grass sloping gently downwards until it met a line of trees at the very edge of the park beyond. To one side an artificial lake reflected the clouds gathering overhead, the sunshine that had been present at breakfast now fast disappearing, although even the increasingly brooding light couldn't dim the beauty before them as Andrew paused to allow Emily to savour her first glimpse of what she would soon call her own.

'What do you think?'

Her petal-blue eyes were round. 'This…all of this… is yours?'

'That's right. The parkland behind those trees makes up the rest of the estate.'

'The rest of the estate? There's more?'

'Yes. Just a few hundred acres.'

She'd risen on tiptoe, peering around her from the paved patio that afforded an elevated view down to the water, and for a moment he feared she might lose her balance.

'A few hundred? A few *hundred acres*?'

'It used to be much more before my great-grandfather inherited. Apparently his tastes ran to expensive women, wine and horses and he had to sell off some farms to cover his debts.'

Emily's lips parted in wordless disbelief. Her amazement couldn't have been more different from the feigned nonchalance of the young ladies of the *ton*, and he found he much preferred her willingness to show what she was really thinking. It was an impressive sight and he was glad she didn't try to pretend it wasn't, still just as struck by it himself even after visiting year after year.

Her enthusiasm made his own rise to meet it.

'Come with me. I'll show you my favourite place when I was made to come here as a boy.'

He led her down a set of stone steps towards a path between two hedges, winding away from the shadow of the Hall. It reared up behind them like a mountain carved from pale yellow stone, its windows dulled beneath the clouds but still as magnificently many-eyed as a peacock's tail. Emily peeped back at it as they walked, as if she was worried it might rise from its foundations and come after her, and he was glad to have something up his sleeve as a distraction.

'In here.'

They turned into a kind of courtyard, the walls made from well-tended hedges that stretched above even Andrew's head. In the very middle of the gravelled space was a raised pond with a statue standing guard over it, some kind of Grecian figure he had no clue how to name, and he let Emily go ahead of him to look down into the water.

She leaned over the elaborately carved edge, at first not seeming to see anything, but then she gave a gasp.

'What—?'

'Uncle Ephraim's prized collection. Goldfish, imported all the way from Portugal.'

Emily glanced at him over her shoulder, eyebrows raised beneath the worn brim of her bonnet.

'Goldfish?'

At his nod she twisted to sit on the edge of the pool, one hand trailing at the surface of the water. Several bright, metallic shapes followed the dabbling movement and he saw her face light up when a greedy little mouth fastened on one fingertip, her delight so unselfconscious he couldn't look away.

'I've never seen anything like them. Then again, I suppose I shouldn't be surprised even your uncle's *fish* were gold.' She paused. 'I'm sorry. That was impolite.'

'But not uncalled for.' Andrew shrugged, unwilling to allow Ephraim to spoil the moment. 'He was extremely proud of them. Anything with even the slightest suggestion of value interested him very much indeed.'

He moved to stand beside her, watching as the gleaming fish cut effortlessly through the water. If he looked closely he could make out Emily's face reflected back at him, distorted by ripples, but the sudden soberness of her expression clear all the same.

'I feel I should apologise.' She traced a finger through a knot of pondweed, apparently either unmoved by its unpleasant texture or too set on her own thoughts to notice. 'For suggesting he was my father, I mean. I shouldn't have made assumptions about someone I never knew, and in doing so implying his conduct was not always… gentlemanly.'

Andrew shook his head. 'There's no call to apologise. If anything, to be considered was a compliment he didn't deserve.'

Emily didn't look up, her face still turned to the water. The rippling mirror showed she was frowning, and he sought to change the subject before the late Lord Breamore could spread even more unhappiness from beyond the grave.

'It should be me saying sorry. I haven't yet asked after your injury. With everything that's happened since it occurred, I realise I neglected to enquire.'

Still perched on the edge of the pond Emily flexed her foot, Andrew not quite managing to stop himself from taking an admiring glance at the flash of slender ankle. 'It's much better. Only a slight ache now rather than real pain.'

'I'm glad. I can't imagine you'd want to limp down the aisle.'

'Down the aisle.' She repeated the words slowly, more to herself than to him. 'How soon will that be?'

'It depends. To read the banns takes three weeks, but with a common licence we could wed within days.'

He tried to sound casual but knew he'd failed when her gaze flickered over him, towards and away again, as quickly as blinking. It was a conversation they had to have at some point, but he hadn't expected it quite so soon and he had no idea how to go about it. Planning a wedding was not something he'd imagined he'd be doing even a few days before.

'What would be your preference? As the bride-to-be?'

'I hardly know. If we waited for the banns that would at least give you more time.'

'More time for what?'

There was a pause, and then a deliberately downward tilt of her head hid her face from him, even her reflection now concealed by the peak of that blasted bonnet. 'To change your mind, should you wish.'

'Change my mind?' Andrew frowned. 'I have no intention of it. Unless…?'

A unpleasant sensation crept over him. Was she speaking of her own thoughts rather than trying to guess his, wanting to break their engagement almost as soon as it was made?

He leaned down, trying to see beneath the straw brim. She kept her eyes fixed firmly on the goldfish, however, refusing to allow him to read anything in them, and he was just about to press harder for an answer when he felt the first raindrop land squarely on the top of his head.

'Oh!'

Evidently Emily had just suffered the same experience. She jumped up as the pond's surface broke out into countless dimples, the fish turning to golden blurs as the rain began in earnest. The downpour was as heavy as it was sudden, and within seconds Andrew felt dampness beginning to spread over his back, his light summer coat ill-equipped for the barrage crashing down on their heads.

Emily squinted up at him. 'Should we run back to the Dower House?'

Her worn old bonnet was little match for the deluge. Already the curls around her face had darkened to bronze rather than gold, and she held her hands above her head in an ineffectual umbrella, the rain spattering onto her gown to mould the thin muslin to her shoulders.

'No need. There's a folly just through here we can shelter in until this passes.'

He turned for the far corner of the courtyard where another path led beneath a stone arch, Emily scurrying behind him. Beyond it a mock-Gothic ruin stood among a small knot of trees, its walls intentionally crumbling but the roof intact, and he waved her inside just as the first rumble of thunder sounded somewhere far away.

Leaning against one wall he watched her trying to catch her breath. Her chest rose and fell rapidly and he had to make himself look away, her damp bodice clinging to her like a second skin. For all her angularity there was still a distinctly feminine curve to the swell of her bosom, and he turned his attention firmly to the ceiling, all too aware that a large part of him was reluctant to make the change.

For a short time neither spoke, only the drumming of rain on the roof breaking the silence between them.

Perhaps she was thinking about what she'd hinted at beside the pond, Andrew mused, studying a spider spinning its way down from a beam. He certainly was. His stomach felt as though someone had kicked it, an unsettling mixture of disappointment and unease. It had definitely seemed as though she was having second thoughts and he wondered at how instantly he had wanted to reassure her, his first reaction being the desire to talk her round...

'This is a beautiful little place. Did your uncle build it?'

He looked down. Emily was examining the arched windows, following the winding progress of a rose climbing through one empty frame. She seemed entranced, and not even the laughable idea of Ephraim being responsible for something so fanciful as a folly was enough to distract Andrew from her expression, no longer hidden by the bonnet she had removed while he was diligently looking elsewhere.

'No. My grandfather commissioned it for my grand-mother as a wedding present many years ago. My uncle had no patience for anything even slightly romantic or whimsical—it's a miracle he never had it knocked down.'

'I'm very glad he didn't.'

She lifted her head to peer up at the ceiling, the movement revealing the pale line of her throat. It shone pearl-like in the grey light and Andrew found himself gripped by the desire to touch it, perhaps running one finger from her ear all the way down to the dip between her collar bones.

'If you like it that much, consider it yours.'

The air hung heavily, warm and richly scented with wet soil. All around them the sound of rain on the roof came in a constant pitter-patter like the rapid beating of a heart, mirroring Andrew's own as he turned to face her full on.

'So, Emily. Do you?'

'Do I what?'

'Intend to change your mind. As you suggested *I* might.'

He saw her throat move as she swallowed. A stray ribbon of damp hair hung at her ear and, without stopping to think, he reached out to brush it aside, his chest tightening when he heard her take a shaky breath.

Her eyelashes swept down but the rosy flush of her cheeks gave her away. They glowed almost as pink as her lips, her mouth drawing Andrew's gaze like a moth to a flame, and despite the overwhelming temptation to drop his head and kiss her he forced himself to hold back. If she was having doubts as to their marriage, then trying to kiss her would be the very worst thing he could do…

but that didn't make it any easier to fight the urge, every fibre of his being now trained on that downturned face.

At last, she put him out of his misery.

'No.'

Her voice was low and not entirely steady. 'I think I made the right choice. My only fear is you might come to think otherwise.'

'That's a worry you need not entertain.'

It was a struggle not to allow the relief that threaded through him to show on his face. She wasn't thinking of fleeing, then—only feeling the kind of natural uncertainty he himself had experienced that morning, although the depth of his relief gave him pause. Already it seemed he was set on the marriage going ahead, far more strongly than he'd realised, and he wasn't entirely sure how to feel at the knowledge his mind was apparently so firmly made up.

The rain continued to patter gently on the roof, the occasional droplet slipping through a gap to splash onto the floor. With Emily so close by the desire to kiss her lingered, and with great difficulty he stepped away, peering out of the window at the full-bellied clouds. It didn't seem as though the sun would be reappearing any time soon and they would have to make a run for it eventually, she back to the Dower House and he to the Hall, although soon there would be no need for them to part at two separate front doors.

The thought spurred him into action.

'Will you come to the Hall tomorrow afternoon?' He looked back at her, attempting not to notice how her damp gown still clung so tightly. 'I think it might help ease your mind if you were more familiar with it before moving in. My greatest wish is that in time it will start to feel like home—both to you and myself.'

'I'd like that.' Slowly, and far more endearingly than Andrew knew she intended, Emily smiled—still slightly uncertain but determined to be brave. 'I very much hope you're right.'

Chapter Five

The moment she saw him at breakfast the next morning Emily knew something was wrong.

Andrew's fingers seemed to have a life of their own, tapping distractedly on the tabletop, his teacup and against the saltshaker, and no sooner had she sat down than Lady Gouldsmith confirmed Emily's suspicions.

'You're fiddling. What's the matter?'

He looked up from his misuse of an innocent butter knife. For half a second he glanced at Emily, piquing her apprehension, but then he addressed his mother. 'Do you recall the date?'

'The fourteenth, I think. Why?'

'Ah. It seems that you, much like myself, forgot what that means.'

His hair was more disordered than usual, perhaps indicative of having an agitated hand pushed through it, and Emily only had a moment to note how such dishevelment suited him before he went on.

'Monroe just reminded me I'm supposed to host a card party this evening. Only a small one, something I agreed to weeks ago and subsequently disregarded given far more important things, but I can't back out of it now.'

He turned to her, the butterknife still balanced between two fingers. 'I'm sorry. I can imagine this is the last thing you want so soon, but I'm afraid my guests already know you're here.'

Emily felt herself pale. 'You wish me to attend a *ton* party? *Tonight?*'

Out of the corner of her widened eye she saw Lady Gouldsmith purse her lips. 'I forgot how quickly news travels when you have a lot of servants. It was only ever a matter of time before rumours began, and unfortunately an Earl's engagement is like manna for gossips.'

'But I can't.' Horrified, Emily looked to Andrew as if he might save her instead of being the one throwing her to the wolves. 'All those high-ranking people... I wouldn't know where to begin.'

'I'm truly sorry. If there was any way of avoiding this situation I would take it. We could say you were indisposed, but—'

'But that wouldn't lessen their curiosity one jot.' Eleanor finished her son's sentence with grim understanding. 'If you wanted to minimise the scrutiny around your engagement, as for certain delicate personal reasons I believe you would prefer, then we must try to avoid making you a point of interest. There are few things more intriguing than someone else's secrets, and if it seems as though Andrew is keeping you hidden away people will wonder why.'

Emily stared down at the tablecloth, trying to master her panic. In only a few hours she would have to walk into a room filled with the best and brightest of Warwickshire Society and pretend she belonged? Two days ago the only member of the *ton* she'd so much as said 'good morning' to had been Andrew, and now she was expected to be centre of attention for a whole crowd of them. The idea of having so many well-bred eyes on her made her want to shrivel in her chair.

'I thought I'd have more time to learn how to be a real lady before I had to be one in public. Such people will see immediately that I'm not one of their kind.'

The moment she set foot in the Hall her origins were sure to show themselves in a multitude of ways she didn't even know existed, probably from the way she spoke right down to the way she held a spoon. Tongues would wag and speculation begin in earnest, and all too soon Andrew would realise he'd made a mistake in bringing her there, the idea of causing him embarrassment making her insides feel like tangled rope.

Another realisation added the final touch to her unhappiness.

'All that aside, I have nothing fit to wear.'

Shame stole over her to admit it out loud, but it was the truth. Her limited wardrobe was comprised of dresses that had been made over so many times they were more patches than gown. Beside Andrew and Eleanor she would look like a scullery maid, and she felt her face grow hot to realise they must be thinking the same thing.

'Don't worry about that.'

Lady Gouldsmith came to the rescue, cutting through Emily's inner turmoil with genteel ease. 'I have dresses I'm certain will fit you. With a few tweaks I'm sure you'll outshine us all.'

There was a clatter as Andrew finally laid down the knife.

'Would you excuse me? There are things I need to see to before tonight. With your permission, we'll postpone your tour of Huntingham until another day.'

He stood up without looking at her, vaguely bowing to the room at large before striding to the door and disappearing. Emily watched after him with the knotted rope of her innards pulling tighter still.

She heard Lady Gouldsmith sigh. 'Off he goes. As I knew he would.'

'He did leave rather quickly.' Trying to sound calmer than she felt, Emily made herself take a slice of toast, although she knew there was scant hope of choking it down. 'I hope he wasn't angry that I had reservations about the party?'

'No, no. He would never be upset with you for that.' Eleanor shook her head, her face sombre as she reached for the teapot. 'You're not the only person wishing they didn't have to go this evening. Andrew dreads these occasions too and won't be easy until it's over and done with.'

'Is that so?'

Emily's surprise was met with a wry half-smile. 'Oh, yes. I think he feels almost as out of place among these people as you do. He might be an Earl now, but for years he considered himself quite the nobody.'

Carefully stirring a piece of sugar into her cup Eleanor gave another sigh, barely audible above the gentle clinking of her spoon.

'Sometimes, you know, I'm not sure which state he preferred.'

Night had fallen before Emily saw her fiancé again, by which time a transformation had taken place.

Andrew's eyes flickered wider as she ascended Huntingham Hall's front steps and came towards him, walking beside Lady Gouldsmith as stiffly upright as a jointed doll. Her borrowed dress was the most beautiful—and expensive—thing she'd worn in her life, and the fear of tearing it made her already heightened anxiety shoot skyward. Only the frank admiration in Andrew's flame-lit face stopped her from fleeing back to the safety of the Dower House.

'You look—'

He broke off as if finding the right word was momentarily beyond him. His eyes never left her, however, sweeping from the top of her befeathered head to the gauzy hem of her gown, and only his mother discreetly clearing her throat prompted him to try again.

'Forgive me. I know it's rude to stare, but I'd defy anyone to resist if they were to see you now.'

He bowed and Emily only just remembered to curtsey in reply. In the light of the torches on either side of the Hall's front door Andrew's features had taken on a new sharpness, the lines of his cheekbones and jaw thrown into relief by the shadows of the flames, and she marvelled that it was even possible for him to become more handsome than before. For herself she knew she had the borrowed gown to thank for any improvement in her ap-

pearance, giving it full credit for Andrew's flattering reaction, but it would be churlish to scorn a compliment
just because it wasn't strictly deserved.

It was as if he'd read her mind.

'It isn't the dress every man in the room will be admiring tonight, if that's what you imagine. You lend your
charms to the gown—not the other way around.'

Andrew's smile was almost as dangerously delightful as his words. The two together nearly succeeded in
making her already weak knees give way entirely, and
it was only the timely intervention of Lady Gouldsmith
that prevented an accident on Huntingham's front steps.

'Goodness. I had no idea I'd raised such a smooth-
talking gentleman.' She arched an amused eyebrow at her
son before squaring her shoulders like a soldier marching
to war. 'I'll go in and mingle, shall I? I suppose at least
one of us should pretend to be pleased to see your guests.'

She sailed inside, her voice rising to greet someone,
leaving Emily and Andrew alone in the warm night air.

Unsure what else to do with herself, Emily smoothed
down her skirts. They glistened in the torchlight, falling from just below her bosom in a cascade of pistachio
silk that contrasted strikingly with the copper-gold of her
hair. Every time she moved her head she could feel the
strange weight of the ostrich feathers on top of her curls,
a feat of engineering it had taken two maids to achieve,
and she wondered how Society ladies could bear having so many pins sticking into their scalp. She might
look more like one of them now but she *felt* as much a
stranger in a foreign land as ever before, although some
of her misgivings retreated into the background when
Andrew held out his arm.

'I'm sorry for being so inattentive to you all day. I promise that from this moment on I won't leave your side.'

That was an agreeable prospect indeed, and she tried not to seem too eager as she slipped her fingers into the crook of his elbow and allowed him to draw her towards the door. It was a secret pleasure to be so near him again. His shoulder gently brushed the curls at one ear, setting the nerves there tingling, and the breadth of his forearm under her fingertips reminded her of the strength in his hands. Even the smell of him tempted her to take a deeper breath, soap and a woody undertone she didn't recognise, but was so unmistakably *him* that she found herself wanting to bottle it, although a swift glance at his face brought her growing fancies up short.

A casual observer might have missed the set of his mouth or faint hardness around his eyes, but to Emily both were plain as day. They hinted at unease, manfully concealed but impossible to hide completely, and as they stepped over the threshold and into the entrance hall her mind reeled back to recall what his mother had said only that morning.

He doesn't want to do this either.

Clearly he didn't feel quite at home among the *ton*, just as Eleanor had told her. She'd been sceptical when he had declared they had that much in common, but to look at him now she could see he'd been in earnest, catching a glimpse of the real man behind the glossy façade of an Earl. Something had happened to make him feel that way, and she wanted to know what it was, his life before he'd come to Warwickshire something she suddenly burned to understand. Whatever had occurred had forged a link between them that surely wouldn't have existed otherwise—but now was not the time to ask. The parlour door was before them, opening to show a roomful of faces turning in their direction, and all other thoughts were chased away when Andrew bent to murmur into her ear.

'This wasn't how I wanted your introduction to Huntingham Hall to be, but there might be a silver lining. You'll meet some of the highest-ranking men for miles around here tonight—one of which could be your father.'

The smile she'd managed to force froze painfully in place. Somehow that idea hadn't occurred to her, although at present she had no chance to consider it. The moment she entered the room it seemed as though everyone in it swung round to stare, strangers breaking off their conversations to peer at her, and the fact there were probably only twenty people in the parlour didn't stop it from feeling like a crowd of hundreds.

'Don't be afraid. As I said—I won't leave your side.'

Her fingers still lay in his elbow and her heart leapt as she felt him give them a reassuring squeeze. Evidently he was determined to set his own feelings aside to focus on hers, and Emily found her throat had grown tight, unable to speak as the first of his acquaintances came forward.

In all the years she'd lived at Miss Laycock's mercy nobody had ever put her wellbeing above their own. She had never expected it, unsure how to grasp the notion, but that one gentle squeeze said more than any words. Andrew knew she was uncertain and afraid and was inviting her to rely on him, a prospect so perilously wonderful she didn't dare accept.

You're not married yet.

He'd said he wouldn't change his mind, that day in Huntingham's gardens when they'd sheltered from the rain—but how could he be so sure? There had to still be a risk, even if only a small one, that he could rethink their engagement before they were wed. A young lady of his own rank would be far better placed to help him fully find his feet among the *ton*, someone who could support him rather than the other way around, and until she had a ring firmly on her finger it wasn't safe to allow her hopes to carry her too far.

'Sir Montfort. May I introduce my fiancée, Miss Townsend?'

A man had materialised through her distracted haze and she made herself focus on him as he sank into a flourishing bow.

'A pleasure, madam.'

He straightened up, his silk cravat gleaming in the light of a chandelier swaying above them. 'We were surprised to hear of your sudden engagement, Breamore, but now I think everyone will understand why you had no desire to delay.'

The elderly knight nodded gallantly at Emily and she smiled weakly in reply. If the other man had known the truth, she was certain he wouldn't have spoken so approvingly, although it seemed he was by no means the only one intending to pay her the courtesy of an introduction. Over Sir Montfort's stooping shoulder she saw another man hovering, flanked by three women and a stylish couple who looked her up and down with undisguised interest, and she was very glad Andrew's arm showed no sign of loosening its grip on her hand.

'The Earl for less than two months and already you've bested your old bachelor of an uncle. Very well done.'

Sir Montfort clapped Andrew on the shoulder and withdrew, his place taken immediately by a mother and daughter, who dropped into curtseys so deep Emily wondered how they kept their balance.

'Good evening, my lord. Thank you for inviting us to Huntingham.'

'You are always most welcome, Mrs Windham, and of course Miss Windham.'

Mrs Windham smiled tightly. Both she and her daughter were frighteningly fashionable. Their gowns must have cost a fortune, and despite the relatively informal occasion they glittered with jewels, earrings and necklaces that caught the light, making them twinkle like fallen stars. There was such glamour in their finery that Emily had to remind herself not to examine them too closely, so splendidly turned out that they reminded her of a pair of exotic birds she'd once seen in a travelling show.

As if sensing Emily's awe Miss Windham glanced across at her. She was extremely attractive, with golden hair and the effortless elegance of a woman who knew she was admired wherever she went, and Emily shrank slightly from her cool green gaze. Beside such a creature she felt more out of place than ever, like a child dressing up in her mother's clothes. Surely Miss Windham was the kind of young lady Andrew ought to have proposed to, a far better match for an Earl than she herself could ever be—although it seemed he still disagreed.

'Please allow me to introduce you. This is Miss Townsend.'

To her amazement, she thought she caught a trace of pride in his voice as he subtly brought her forward, refusing to allow her to half hide behind him. 'You may have heard we are recently engaged.'

'Indeed we did.'

Mrs Windham sounded far less pleased about the situation than Andrew. She allowed Emily a smile, a chilly stretch of her mouth that didn't reach her eyes. 'We heard a rumour, although as the news only reached us through a third party we weren't entirely sure it was true.'

If there had been pride in Andrew's voice, Mrs Windham's held ice. Evidently she was most put out to see undisputable evidence that her daughter would not be the next Lady Breamore, and it was left up to Miss Windham to smooth over her mother's obvious disapproval.

'Clearly it is, Mama. Congratulations my lord, Miss Townsend.'

With a neat curtsey Miss Windham took her mother's arm and drew her away, their skirts whispering behind them as they retreated, and Emily watched them go, the unease already sitting in her stomach beginning to flutter harder.

'I think perhaps Mrs Windham will not be a friend to me.'

'I think perhaps you might be right. But never mind.' Andrew shrugged, pausing to nod politely to a guest passing towards the card tables. 'She was once intent on marrying Uncle Ephraim, many years ago, so I'm not sure her opinion is worth much.'

The parlour door opened and closed repeatedly. More people arrived, the room growing hotter and louder as the evening progressed, and acquaintance after acquaintance came forward to meet their soon-to-be hostess. Every time Andrew waved towards her, with satisfaction that she could hardly dare to believe was genuine, introducing her to what felt like a never-ending stream of ladies and gentlemen, whose names she forgot almost as soon as they were revealed. It was like being in another world, the effort of playing the part so exhausting that her head began to ache, and only the knowledge that Andrew was pushing through his own discomfort to help with hers gave her the courage to carry on.

He was true to his word. He didn't leave her alone for so much as a moment, remaining a constant and reassuring presence at her side. Even when talking to someone else she could sense his awareness of her, never allowing himself to be distracted by anyone in the room, which was more than Emily could say for herself.

Andrew took up the vast majority of her focus—but not quite all of it.

She'd determined within the very first half-hour that there were four men in attendance who were the right age to be her father. Two of them she discounted at once, one whose hair was much too dark and the other with a complexion the handsome olive of the Mediterranean, although neither of the remaining two filled her with much confidence. One gentleman was fair, although the shape of his face was nothing like her own, and the last contender seemed too shy to have spoken to a woman in his life, let alone father an illegitimate child. On the whole she doubted any of the men beneath Huntingham's roof were who she was looking for, and her disappointment was bitter, not even a glass of sweet punch able to wash it away.

'Will you join us for a game of whist, Miss Townsend?'

A voice at her shoulder made her turn. A young man stood behind her, some baronet's son whose name she had been too nervous to absorb when told, and her worry piqued sharply at what should have been an innocuous request.

Heaven help me. What do I do now?

Was this how she was to be caught out? By a friendly game of whist, of all things? It was the kind of thing well-bred young ladies were born knowing how to play, probably, but she had no idea of the rules. Miss Laycock had frowned upon card games of any kind, believing them to be a gateway to gambling and sin, and for a moment Emily wondered if it was too late to turn and run. Any second now he'd realise she hadn't a clue, would think how odd it was for an Earl's fiancée to have such a gap in her accomplishments, and would begin to wonder why...

'Ah. I was actually just about to ask Miss Townsend if she would play for us,' Andrew cut in smoothly. 'There's a pianoforte just through there. You'd be out of sight, I'm afraid, but we'd still be able to hear you.'

He gestured towards a half-open door on the other side of the room, flicking her the briefest of glances that left her in no doubt that he understood her predicament, and she seized the lifeline at once.

'I'd be glad to. If you'd excuse me, sir?'

The nameless baronet's son bowed but she didn't stay to see it. The choice between being looked at by the *ton* or merely listened to was an easy one. She crossed the room as quickly as elegance allowed, for the first time in her life grateful for Miss Laycock's insistence that all her girls were forced into music lessons whether they liked it or not.

Slipping into the adjoining room she felt herself relax slightly. The curious eyes that had tracked her all evening couldn't see through walls, and as she seated herself at the pianoforte—an extremely expensive looking instrument and definitely the handsomest she'd ever seen— some weight lifted from her chest.

It was unfortunate that none of the men present were likely to be her papa, but that didn't mean her search was a lost cause. To stumble across him during her very first foray into Society would have been unlikely, surely, and today's failure didn't necessarily mean more would follow. She would just have to keep her nerve, keep forcing herself not to hide from the prospect of being seen by the very people she was afraid might see *through* her, and eventually she would find the missing piece she knew could make her whole.

She placed her fingers over the ivory keys, appreciating their cool smoothness before she took a breath and began to play.

The hum of conversation from the next room grew quieter. For a moment the only sound was melodic tinkling before the talking and laughter resumed, lower now to allow her audience to listen as they bent over their cards. Somehow knowing a roomful of landed gentry could hear her was less frightening than being required to play whist, and Emily let herself be borne away by the music, not realising someone had entered the room behind her until they came to sit beside her on the pianoforte's upholstered stool.

Startled, she looked up from her busy hands, although she knew instinctively who she would see.

'Don't stop playing. I just thought you might need someone to turn the page for you.'

Emily nodded, not quite trusting herself to speak. The stool wasn't large and there was no way for Andrew to stop his leg from touching hers, the long line of his thigh pressing against her skirts. To reach the music book he had to lean across her slightly, and she almost fumbled a wrong note when his cheek was suddenly before her, clean shaven that morning but now dusted with the lightest suggestion of stubble. The urge to see what it felt like rose so sharply she could barely hold it back.

It was essential she say something to break the tension building inside her, tension she knew must be one-sided. Andrew had come because he'd promised to stay by her side, not because he'd *wanted* to, and she grasped for the first thing that came to mind as she struggled to remember that dampening truth.

'I've been thinking. I'm not sure any of the gentlemen here tonight could be my father.'

She kept her voice down, her hands still moving with unthinking skill. For Andrew to hear her he had to lean closer, something that did nothing to help regain control of her wayward thoughts. 'None of them bear any resemblance to me in any form. I've looked and I really don't see any likeness at all.'

Out of the corner of her eye she saw him incline his head thoughtfully. 'I agree. I don't believe any one of our guests could claim the credit for your beauty.'

Emily's fingers slipped, a jarring note ringing out.

'I'm sorry.' Andrew sounded mildly amused, although

there was an undercurrent of something else. 'Was that too forward?'

'No. I didn't… I don't mind.'

She stared down at the keys as if her life depended on it, not looking up even to read the music.

He could have said whatever he liked. The truth was that his mouth was so close that even curse words would have sounded sweet issuing from it. But he had instead called her beautiful, and she was in danger of swooning off the stool.

Her body had unconsciously begun to curve towards him, wanting to shrink the already slim gap between them down to nothing at all. One of his hands lay on his lap, the other raised waiting to turn the page, and she bit her tongue against the desire to feel them on her. With his leg still pressed against hers, and the edge of his cheek so near, she felt as though she was burning, only the necessity of keeping her fingers on the keys helping her to fight the feelings coursing through her like a flood; although no amount of Bach could drown out the insistent thought that ran unchecked through her head.

I wish he'd kiss me. At this moment there's nothing I want more.

Don't kiss her. Do not kiss her.

Andrew tried to concentrate on following the music, anticipating when to turn the next page, but it was damned difficult when half of his brain was busy with far more interesting things.

Every time Emily moved her arm grazed his, a continuous light touch that was impossible to ignore. She was all but sitting in his lap, the pianoforte's stool smaller than he'd anticipated, and he wasn't sure how much longer he could contain the ache to slide an arm around her waist. She seemed focused on the ivory beneath her fingers, now apparently determined not to look at him, but even that didn't make much difference. Her profile was just as pretty as when she faced him full on, the soft curve of her lips mere inches away, calling out to be kissed, and he clenched his jaw as he prayed for the strength to resist.

He was supposed to be shielding her from whispers rather than exposing her to them, he reminded himself, trying to heed his own wisdom as Emily's elbow accidentally caressed the inside of his arm. They might be engaged, but it would still draw comment if anyone were to look into the room and find them intimately entwined, and besides—hadn't he decided to take things slowly?

She'd expressed doubts as to their match once already and he didn't mean for it to happen again. In both appearance and behaviour her presence at Huntingham that evening had convinced him he'd made the right decision in choosing her above any highborn lady, and he found he was more determined than ever to see their engagement through.

If he hadn't already known she was uncomfortable to be among the *ton* he wouldn't have guessed. Her nervousness on entering the parlour had seemed the kind any young lady might feel on meeting a roomful of strangers, mostly concealed behind good manners almost as polished as those honed at court. For all her faults it seemed Miss Laycock hadn't stinted on lessons in decorum, and he'd felt an absurd amount of pleasure to see Emily receive the admiration she deserved, none of his guests suspecting for a moment that she was anything other than one of their kind.

But she isn't.

He dared a sideways glance at her, noting the perfect petal-like smoothness of her cheek as she kept her eyes trained immovably on the keys.

She feels like me, an outsider acting a part. And unless I'm much mistaken I believe she's worked that out already.

Probably his mother had hinted at the truth, but it wouldn't have taken Emily long to figure it out for herself. He hadn't wanted to attend this party either, despite it being under his own roof, and he had the feeling he'd done a poor job of hiding it at the breakfast table that morning. He had meant for his presence to be a comfort for *her*, not the other way around, but something about her hand on his arm made it easier to slip into the impenetrably well-bred shell of an Earl. The usual sensation of being the odd one out was absent with Emily beside him, no longer feeling like the only one in the room who had experienced life's harsher shadow, and as she came to the end of the piece, the pianoforte lapsing into silence, he considered if he ought to tell her so.

I think not. Or at least not yet.

There was a smattering of applause from the next room. Emily flexed her fingers but didn't resume playing, and he sensed her hesitate.

'Should I go on?'

'Please do. You play extremely well.'

A trace of colour crept into the cheek closest to him, pink against the strawberry-blonde ringlets at her ear. 'I don't know about *extremely*, but I'll continue if you wish.'

She lifted her arm to shuffle a new sheet of music to the front, the feathers in her hair waving as she moved. The maids must have spritzed her curls with rose water, the subtle floral sweetness tempting him closer still, and he wondered briefly if he would have to resort to sitting on his hands.

The smell of her, the barely perceptible warmth of her leg against his… It was a delight and a torment to sit so near yet be unable to touch her, and when he heard a light cough from the doorway it was almost a relief to stand up and move away.

'Andrew? A few of your guests are wondering where you went.'

Lady Gouldsmith's countenance was impassive as she withdrew again, for which Andrew was grateful, although Emily's face when she finally looked at him properly was enough to throw the innocence of the situation into doubt.

Her cheeks were flushed, for all the world as though she'd been caught doing something she shouldn't, and the thought almost brought him to his knees.

Stop. Control yourself.

'Do you want me to stay?'

He half hoped she would say yes, although he supposed the shake of her head was far less dangerous. 'You need to attend to your guests. I think I'm safe enough in here.'

'Very good.'

She gave him the smallest of smiles as he stepped back, turning her attention almost immediately to the sheet of music in front of her. There was a short pause, a rustle as she adjusted her skirts, and then the sound of the pianoforte beginning again ushered Andrew from the room.

He barely saw her again for the rest of the evening. She continued to play until refreshments were served, although by that time it seemed she had relaxed slightly. She no longer looked quite so worried when spoken to, and when his guests began to leave she even managed a convincing smile, perhaps not completely genuine but close enough for a passing glance.

'You don't have to do that.'

Leaning against the fireplace, Andrew watched her rearranging the cushions on the now empty sofa, fastidious as any well-trained maid. His mother had retired to bed shortly before and they were alone, the parlour quiet aside from Emily's well-intentioned—but entirely needless—attempts to tidy up.

'I can't help myself. At the school there would have been hell to pay if we'd left a room like this.'

She smoothed down an embroidered throw on the back of a chair, her practical domesticity at odds with the ostrich feathers and silk dress. Evidently it would take more than one card party for her to make the transition from school boarder to future Countess, although in Andrew's opinion that wasn't necessarily a bad thing.

'Was this evening as you'd feared?'

'No.' Straightening a stray antimacassar, Emily shook her head. 'Most of your acquaintances were very pleasant. I'm not certain whether they'd be quite so welcoming if they knew my true background, but they were by no means as frightening as I imagined.'

'I'm glad. I wouldn't have you distressed in what will soon be your own home.'

A large, tasselled cushion had fallen onto the floor near the fire, and slowly she moved to pick it up, bringing her closer to where Andrew leaned against the mantle.

For a moment she fiddled with the fringing, running her fingers through it as if untangling invisible knots. 'Miss Windham in particular was charming. Very pretty, too. And extremely well-dressed.'

Andrew nodded absently. She was within arm's length now, he estimated, close enough for him to see how her sandy eyebrows had drawn together slightly, her face angled away but her cheekbones glowing in the dying candlelight.

'I suppose she is.'

'Are you still quite sure…' She stopped, even her fingers pausing in their phantom unpicking.

'Am I quite sure…?'

'That you wouldn't prefer someone like her? Miss Windham?'

Her eyes were averted but he could sense her full attention was fixed on him. 'I know you said you had no intention of changing your mind, but now that I've seen the kind of woman you might have chosen…it makes me wonder.'

From beneath her lowered eyelashes Andrew thought he caught a flash of blue dart in his direction, but he was too preoccupied to pay it much mind.

This again? Surely, after tonight...?

He stood up properly, no longer lounging against the fire. At the movement she turned towards him, now looking at him rather than that damned cushion, and he felt the same desire to move closer to her he'd been fighting all evening stir with renewed vigour.

He took half a step towards her—and she didn't back away.

Hadn't she guessed he had no interest in any woman but her? He'd been trying so hard to control himself, but he wasn't made of stone, and as he looked down into Emily's uncertain face, now perhaps only a hand's breadth from his, he realised he had reached the end of his endurance.

'Never mind. Forget I said anything. Goodnight.'

Hurriedly she turned to leave the room—but his hand on her wrist brought her spinning back again.

For a split second confusion flared in her eyes, but they closed the moment he pulled her towards him, the cushion falling forgotten onto the floor as he bent to bring her mouth to his.

Her lips were warm and yielding and he swallowed a groan to finally taste them, scarcely able to breathe as he heard her feather-soft sigh. Of their own accord his fingers moved from her wrist to the sweep of her waist and he felt her sway against him, his blood heating as she seized hold of his shirt to steady herself. Tentative at first, her lips moved more forcefully, opening to allow the very tip of his tongue to delve inside, and it was almost more than he could stand when she ventured to copy him, hesitance turning to boldness that set his skin ablaze.

Emily's hands were braver now, pulling him down, and he was happy to obey, his own palm pressed flat on the curve of her lower back and tilting her body to his. Probably she'd be able to feel how much he wanted her, inexperienced but certainly no fool, but he couldn't manage to feel ashamed that she might guess how for him their wedding night couldn't come soon enough.

The thought of it was the only thing that could have brought him to his senses. Before there was a wedding night there had to be a wedding, and against every desire he pulled back, breaking the kiss but unable to loosen his vice-like grip on her waist.

'Do you still think I have even half a thought to spare for Miss Windham? Or any of the others you might meet?'

Her eyes were glassy and her lips still parted as she looked up at him, flushed as a poppy in a field. It seemed she was either unable to speak or had forgotten how, as she merely shook her head in a dazed little quiver that made him want to pull her to him all over again.

'Will you stop questioning now whether I know my own mind?'

This time his question was met with a fervent nod.

'Good. Because next time I might have to kiss you properly to make my point.'

At last she managed to find her tongue, although her voice was little more than an unsteady murmur. 'That wasn't properly?'

'No.'

He gazed down at her, feeling the pounding of his heart all the way down to his boots. It raced as though he'd been running, and it was only the refusal to push her too far, too fast that stopped him from showing her exactly what he meant.

'Not even close.'

Chapter Six

Arriving at the Dower House the next morning, Andrew almost tripped over a large parcel sitting in the middle of the hall's floor. It was wrapped in brown paper with no label attached, but that didn't stop him from knowing at once what was inside.

The morning room door opened and his mother appeared, Emily a few paces behind. Lady Gouldsmith's interest seemed fixed on the mysterious package, but he saw Emily cast him a swift glance, her eyes lingering briefly on his mouth before she looked away again. The memory of their late-night entanglement must have been just as fresh in her mind as it was in his, he realised with a stir of interest somewhere too intimate to mention, and he was relieved to see he hadn't frightened her away with his reckless declaration that there was much more to come.

'We've been waiting for you.' His mother poked the

package with her foot, making the paper rustle. 'That was delivered at the crack of dawn this morning. What is it, and why is it in my hall? As I'm not expecting a delivery myself I believe it must be yours.'

'It's not exactly mine.' Andrew raised what he knew she'd think was an annoyingly enigmatic eyebrow. 'And if I'd told you to expect it, it would have ruined the surprise.'

He turned to Emily, for the first time noticing she wore another borrowed gown. The sage-green morning dress was pretty but didn't fit her as well as one made with her in mind, and the secret anticipation already forming climbed another notch.

'Do you recall I went away to finish a letter on the morning I showed you Huntingham's grounds? Just after breakfast?'

She nodded cautiously, a rosy trace appearing now he addressed her directly. 'Yes. Why?'

'I was writing to my man in London, asking him to send me this.' He jerked his head towards the parcel. 'It's for you.'

'For me? What is it?'

'If you open it, you'll find out.'

He smiled, trying to ignore a loose thread of uncertainty. Surely any woman would be pleased with what he'd arranged for her. But he couldn't know for definite until she unwrapped it, and there was a distinct air of hesitation in the way she came forward and knelt to untie the strings.

With its bindings undone the brown paper fell open. Andrew felt a twinge of relief. The wooden chest standing among its wrappings was just as handsome as

he'd hoped. Made from oak it was larger than he'd expected, with mother-of-pearl flowers on its lid that he
thought would delight its new owner, who at present
looked as though she didn't understand.

'For your wedding trousseau,' he clarified, seeing
the need for an explanation. 'I thought we could go to
Leamington today. The shops there are far better than
those in Brigwell and you can fill this chest with whatever you like.'

Kneeling on the floor beside the mess of crumpled
paper Emily's eyes widened. She didn't speak, however,
and he felt the thread of uncertainty unravel a little more.

'It's my understanding a bride usually has a chest of
clothes and other things to bring with her when she weds.
Forgive me for assuming, but I didn't think you already
had one. Would you be willing to let me correct that?'

She'd reached for the inlay of the lid, her fingertips
hovering over a pearlescent petal. It seemed she didn't
quite dare make contact, and she retracted her hand again
without touching, instead smoothing her skirts down
over her lap in the unconscious gesture Andrew knew
meant she wasn't sure what else to do.

There was a pause.

'I don't know what to say.'

'A simple yes would suffice.'

'But it's so generous.' Emily shook her head slowly,
the morning sunlight coming through the still-open front
door making her hair gleam with the movement. 'I never
would have presumed anything like this.'

'I know you wouldn't. That's in large part why I'd
like you to accept it.'

That bewildered shake of her head spoke of a need

for greater persuasion. Clearly there was a danger she might reject his offer out of some kind of unnecessary modesty, and with a meaningful glance over the top of her head he summoned reinforcements.

Lady Gouldsmith leapt in at once. 'You're in need of clothes befitting a woman of the station you'll soon occupy. As fond of you as I am, you can't wear mine for ever, and you'll certainly need something to wear for the wedding.'

It appeared his gift was easier to accept when put in more practical terms. At the prospect of no longer being a burden on her hostess's wardrobe, Andrew thought he sensed Emily reconsider—still doubtful, but at least not refusing it outright.

'Thank you.' She rose to her feet, dipping a small curtsey as she stood up, and then his heart lurched sideways to see a ghost of a smile. 'Your kindness means more to me than you know.'

That hardly perceptible upward curve was all the reward he could have wished for. He wasn't sure what it made him want to do more, stare at her lips or taste them again, but as he could currently do neither he settled for a polite nod of his own.

'Don't speak of it. I wouldn't be much of a man if I begrudged my future wife some gowns.'

Her spectral smile flickered a fraction wider. The idea of a new dress was agreeable, it seemed, and he was glad of it, her initial reluctance only reinforcing what he thought he already knew.

She didn't *require* fine things to be content. Emily would value her expensive clothes and never take them for granted, just as he himself was conscious of the need to be appreciative of what he had. The lean years of his youth had taught him that lesson, and it made him feel warm inside to think she shared his sentiments—perhaps the common ground between them even fertile enough to allow something more to grow in time.

Evidently, with her acceptance of his gift, her nerve had increased. She allowed herself to touch the pearl flowers now, following the iridescent line of a stalk with wonder he loved to see.

'I know that usually a young lady's family provides the trousseau.' Carefully Emily lifted the petal-shaped clasp that held the chest closed. 'I'm certain that when we find my father, he'll pay you back for providing what he couldn't at the time.'

She opened the lid to peer inside, Andrew suddenly thankful her attention was elsewhere so she might miss his involuntary frown.

What? Is that really what she thinks?

Did she truly believe her father was likely to take such an interest? Discomfort nudged in beneath what had previously been uninterrupted satisfaction. Surely she couldn't be that naïve. When he'd agreed to help her find her father he'd assumed it was for the sake of answers, not affection, and that she was prepared for the cool—at best—reception she would receive from a man who had never made any attempt to know her. Now it seemed Emily's hopes were much higher than he'd realised, and his concern grew as he caught his mother's eye, Lady Gouldsmith looking as worried as he was beginning to feel.

Perhaps I should try to talk her into lowering her expectations.

She would be hurt to discover her father's apathy if she was expecting anything more, and Andrew felt a sharp stab of something at the thought. An unhappy Emily was a sight he'd seen once before, when she'd attempted to hide her tear-stained face beneath the shadows of Brigwell's trees, and to imagine her in such a state again made him harden his jaw.

I'll have to say something. As much as I'm coming to care for her, it would be a miracle if her father felt the same.

The niggling unease at the back of his mind didn't subside for the duration of the carriage ride to Leamington, a distance of about ten miles, which that morning felt like much more.

It wasn't only the disquiet of his thoughts that were responsible for the dragging passage of time, however. Emily sat beside his mother on the seat opposite him, her face turned to the window so he could see the crescent of her profile like a pale waning moon, and he couldn't help but watch how the sunlight played over it as the carriage rattled down the dusty roads. The morning was warm and the subtle flush at the base of her throat was mesmerising, reminding him how her skin had burned beneath his hands the night before, and the desire to touch her again—but knowing he could not—made the journey seem very long indeed.

Simmer down. There are other things that require your attention.

Andrew tapped his fingers against his knee as he tried to order his thoughts. How could he broach a subject that she would no doubt find upsetting *without* upsetting her?

There was a simple answer—he couldn't.

However he tried to approach the topic of her father, Emily would end up distressed. She was already lacking in confidence—something for which he credited Miss Laycock—and to suggest her father might not be over-joyed to meet her would do nothing to help build her up. He had imagined she wanted to find this mysterious Lord to satisfy her curiosity and fill in the gaps in her history, not because she believed it would be possible to cultivate a relationship with him, and when he inevitably didn't want to know, her feeling of rejection would be complete.

The rapidity of Andrew's tapping increased, and not even a warning look from Lady Gouldsmith could stop it.

To bring his own father back he would have done anything, and he could well understand why Emily had deceived herself in pursuit of her own. She only wanted what so many never gave a second thought...but it wouldn't happen. The man who had signed her into the school's care hadn't wanted her when she was a newborn and he wouldn't want her now, and no amount of opti-mism on her part would change that inescapable fact.

'Is something the matter?'

Emily's question wasn't one he particularly wanted to answer. He could hardly look into her eyes and lie, that hydrangea-blue gaze holding him prisoner from the other side of the carriage, but at the same time he couldn't quite manage the truth.

Fortunately luck was on his side.

'Look. We've arrived.'

The carriage was beginning to slow as the traffic in-creased. Rows of tall white buildings had risen on either side of the road, houses and gleaming shop windows welcoming them as they passed, with well-dressed people thronging the pavements. In comparison with Brigwell, Leamington had all the polish and sophistication of London, and Andrew saw Emily had forgotten she was waiting for him to answer as she peered out of the window, her nose all but pressed against the glass as she drank it all in.

'Have you ever been to Leamington before?'

'No. Miss Laycock mistrusted towns larger than Brigwell.'

'I see.' Despite his unease he had to hide some amusement at the headmistress's interesting world view. 'Don't worry. We'll make sure nothing untoward happens to you.'

The carriage had come to a halt and he opened the door, not waiting for the footman to do something he was more than capable of doing for himself.

Still not half as Earlish an Earl as Uncle Ephraim was—but then, I hope I never am.

He handed his mother down the carriage steps and then Emily, her fingers resting lightly in his palm. It was the slightest contact, over and done in a matter of seconds with two pairs of gloves in between, but still he felt his pulse increase. The last time she'd willingly put herself in his hands had been moments before he'd kissed her, when she allowed him to map out the landscape of her body like an explorer in a new world, and from the tiny breath he heard her snatch as his hand grazed hers, he guessed she had made the same connection.

Surrounded now by crowds that made it difficult to move, Lady Gouldsmith took charge.

'We'll be knocked over if we keep standing here in

the middle of the street. Ought we begin with dresses? If you'd like, I can show you to the best modistes.'

'Yes, please.' To Andrew's regret Emily moved away from him to take his mother's outstretched arm. 'Left to my own devices I'm certain to get lost.'

Without further ado Lady Gouldsmith began to lead her away, cutting through the mass of fashionable shoppers with elegant ease. Andrew followed, his thoughts still bound up in the troubling matter of Emily's unlikely hopes—although that didn't stop him from noticing the subtle sway of her waist as she walked in front of him, something he found himself quite unable to ignore.

Allowing herself to be measured for what felt like the hundredth time, Emily tried not to focus on the ache in her legs. Almost a full day of trekking from dressmaker to milliner to dressmaker again had left her exhausted, but she still couldn't sit down, currently stripped to her shift and keeping obediently still as the latest modiste's assistant laid a measuring tape against her back. Her feet were sore and she was in desperate need of a cup of tea—and yet she couldn't remember ever having been so happy in all her life.

All afternoon Andrew had insisted on buying her anything she so much as glanced at, the number of gowns and bonnets and ribbons and *everything* mounting by the hour, but it wasn't the gifts themselves that had had lit such a spark inside her. His consideration was responsible for that, the offer of a trousseau rooted in kindness she valued more than any silk dancing shoes, and as the modiste regarded her with an expert eye she wondered how she had stumbled into such an impossible dream.

For years the only person she'd ever thought would care for her had been her mysterious father, but now... was there a chance Andrew might, too?

That he desired her she now had no doubt—not since he'd shown her so plainly only the night before, the memory making her heart flit faster beneath the scant cover of her shift. His grip on her had been strong but his mouth so gentle, drawing her into an embrace that had engulfed her in flames, and all day it had been difficult to meet his eye without blushing. To provoke a physical reaction in the man who would be her husband was one thing, however, while appealing to his heart was another; and perhaps it was too much to hope for that an Earl marrying for convenience might leave the way open to anything more.

'How are you getting on in there, Emily?'

Lady Gouldsmith's voice came from beyond the fitting room door. She was seated just outside, although Andrew—as a male and therefore an intruder in such a feminine space—was relegated to a quiet corner of the shop, tucked away where no customers might take fright at his presence. Apparently he had tea and a comfortable chair in which to drink it, and until his pocketbook was required it seemed he had little to do but relax.

'Well, I think?'

At her questioning look the modiste, the intimidatingly stylish Mrs Sedgewick, nodded authoritatively. 'Very well indeed. If I could just ask you to turn the other way?'

Obligingly Emily turned to face the wall behind her, well used by now to what was required. When she'd woken that morning she'd never visited a Society dressmaker in her life, and yet now she felt like an old hand, still scarcely able to credit she would soon be wearing gowns fit for a queen in place of her old mended muslins.

At last the endless measuring finished. The assistant rolled up her tape and Mrs Sedgewick returned to the helm.

'I'll show you some fabrics now. Once we've decided which colours suit you the best we can move on to embellishments.'

It seemed there was little scope for Emily to disagree. The assistant was despatched to fetch the samples, although it was only a few moments before she returned.

'I can't find them, Mrs Sedgewick.'

'What do you mean? You know where the swatches are kept.'

'Yes, ma'am, but they aren't there.'

The modiste sighed, catching Emily's eye in the mirror to offer an apologetic smile. 'Would you excuse me for a moment, Miss Townsend? I shall return directly.'

Shooing her assistant in front of her, Mrs Sedgewick left the fitting room, pulling the door firmly closed behind her. There were murmurs on the other side as she relayed the situation to Lady Gouldsmith, then the sound of footsteps retreating down the corridor that separated the fitting room from the rest of the shop.

Left alone, Emily stretched her aching back. It was a pity there was nowhere to sit down. The only things in the small room with her were an armoire and the elaborate mirror leaning against one wall. Idly she watched herself straighten her shift, the thin linen hardly preserving her modesty. Thanks to Andrew's generosity she had another ten on order, and she found herself wondering if he would ever want to see what he had paid for.

Stop it. You know that's not something you should think about.

Her subconscious spoke sense—but there was something in the idea of the Earl seeing her in only her under things that made being sensible seem very difficult indeed. It wasn't unreasonable to imagine a man might have certain expectations of his wife, and the hint he had dropped the previous evening, that the kiss she had found so thrilling hadn't even been at its full power, made her feel suddenly warm. Even a marriage of convenience could have passion, or so Andrew had implied, and she couldn't deny she was growing ever more curious to know for sure.

If he ever did see me like this...would he like what he saw?

The question posed itself without her permission, and she saw her mirror image flush to realise what she wanted the answer to be. He managed to bring out the most scandalous side of her, although she hurriedly reined herself in as she heard the fitting room door handle turn.

The door rattled on its hinges but didn't open. The handle turned again and Emily waited for Mrs Sedgwick to appear, mildly puzzled when the door still didn't move. There was some low muttering and another round of rattling, and then Lady Gouldsmith's voice came from the other side.

'My dear? Are you all right in there?'

'Yes,' Emily called back, puzzlement beginning to turn to slight alarm. 'Why?'

There was a brief pause and some more scuffling.

'Not to worry you, but we're just having a little trouble opening the door.'

A second voice followed the first. 'I'm so sorry, Miss Townsend. This door sticks sometimes, although my carpenter assured me it had been fixed.'

'No need to be concerned, however,' Eleanor finished reassuringly. 'We'll get you out…somehow…'

Emily's chest tightened.

They can't open the door.

Ever since she was a child she'd hated being confined in small spaces and, now she knew she was trapped, the fitting room suddenly seemed very small indeed. There were windows but they were too high to see out of, giving only thin slivers of bright blue sky and offering no hope of climbing through. Until the door opened there was no way out, and she felt her heart begin to flutter, the muffled voices in the corridor not filling her with much confidence as the walls seemed to draw in around her.

The muttering ceased abruptly, which didn't come as much comfort either. There was a shuffling noise, as if several long skirts were being swept out of the way, and then another sound made Emily's already cantering heart break into a full gallop.

'Can I be of assistance?'

Andrew's polite enquiry held a world of suppressed amusement. Probably from the outside there *was* something to laugh at—three elegant ladies scrabbling at a door that refused to open—although Emily's sense of humour had temporarily evaporated. She was stuck in a small room dressed only in her shift, with a handsome Earl waiting just outside, and she couldn't recall ever having been in such a mortifying situation in all her life.

There was some murmuring as the predicament was explained, and then:

'Stand back, please, ladies… Further than that. I don't know if the wood will splinter.'

Emily's eyes flew wide. Surely he wasn't going to—

'Move away from the door, Emily. I'm going to force it open.'

Alarm hurtling skyward she looked wildly about the fitting room. For all her scandalous daydreams she couldn't *really* allow him to see her in such a state of undress, and yet her gown seemed to have disappeared into thin air. The only place it could be was inside the armoire, and she lunged towards it with desperate haste, her fingers closing around a handle and tugging open the first drawer—

But she was too late.

With a crack of breaking wood Andrew stumbled into the room, the door sagging off its hinges beneath the force of his heavy boot. He swiftly regained his balance and looked around, visibly relieved when he saw her now leaning against the far wall.

'Are you all right?'

He moved as if to come towards her…but something stopped him in his tracks.

Perhaps he hadn't realised immediately what she was wearing—or *not* wearing, Emily thought vaguely as she watched him grow very still, the relief in his face changing to a different thing entirely that made her breath hitch in her throat. His eyes swept over her, seeming darker than ever in their intensity, and with boldness she hadn't known she possessed she made no attempt to hide from them. She couldn't seem to move. Covering herself had felt so important seconds earlier, when he had been on the other side of the door, but now he was before her the hairs of her nape stood on end at his inability to look away. He probably meant to, usually too polite to stare, but there was real hunger in the way he gazed at her, sudden tension in the small room stretching like a rope about to break, and Emily had no idea what might have happened if Mrs Sedgewick hadn't come hurrying in to dampen the embers that had begun to smoulder somewhere shamefully low down.

'Miss Townsend! Are you hurt?'

'No.' With difficulty Emily dragged her eyes away from Andrew's, slightly breathless beneath the weight of his stare. 'I'm quite well.'

'I'm so very, very sorry for such an unforgivable ordeal. I'll speak to the carpenter at once. He'll think twice about carrying out such shoddy work in the future…'

Mrs Sedgewick went on but Emily hardly heard her. Over the modiste's shoulder she saw Lady Gouldsmith had entered the fitting room alongside the hapless assistant and outnumbered by ladies, Andrew took his leave. Without a word he withdrew to the ruined doorway, slipping out unnoticed by the others—apart from Emily, whose stomach turned over at the glance he gave her before he disappeared.

At least I have an answer to my question.

Under cover of Mrs Sedgewick's threats towards every

carpenter in England, Emily laid a hand over her chest, feeling how it rose and fell as rapidly as if she'd just run a mile.

It certainly seemed as though he liked what he saw.

Chapter Seven

Lady Gouldsmith's birthday fell less than a week after their visit to Leamington.

She had loved the theatre for as long as Andrew could remember, and even during their meagre years had managed to take him to see something every Christmas that had delighted her as much as him. He could afford now to take a private box as a gift to her and was touched by her excitement, although the presence of Emily, currently sitting across from him in the carriage as they drove into town, made the excursion more…complicated.

He kept his eyes firmly on the window but even that didn't help. He could still see her reflection in the darkened glass, the nights drawing in now that autumn had begun, and he wished he could ask her to stop swaying in her seat. The movement reminded him of dancing— or something more intimate—and he gritted his teeth as he tried to focus on the moon instead of the ghostly outline of her face.

I shouldn't have broken that door down. I should have let the carpenter come instead of bursting in.

He hadn't known a moment's peace since he'd gone crashing into the fitting room, and he was still paying for his heroism even now. Nothing he tried seemed to work, the image of her in the thinnest of linen shifts appearing before him at the most inopportune times, and he was half afraid he might be losing his mind.

Eating breakfast?

Emily in her shift, the pallor of her skin clearly visible through the almost transparent fabric.

Gone for an early-morning ride?

Emily in her shift, her secret curves all but laid bare.

Enjoying a brisk walk out on the estate?

Emily. In. Her. Shift.

Belatedly he realised he was drumming his fingers against the leather seat, and he made himself stop before his mother noticed. She'd know at once something was bothering him and he had no intention of explaining what it was, Emily's constant unconscious movements in time with the carriage catching at the corner of his eye.

I have to keep a clear head.

Deliberately he checked his pocket watch, although he already knew the time. Turning it over in his fingers gave him something to do other than let them resume tapping, and he watched the second hand jerk its way around the dial as he attempted to curb his wayward thoughts.

Until he'd spoken to her about her father he couldn't let himself be carried astray. His attraction to her was becoming difficult to hide—if indeed he had hidden it at all—but he *couldn't* allow himself to do anything more. She tempted him so much it was hard to think straight, and that was just what he needed to do, the conversation he was putting off too important for him to attempt while distracted. The longer he took to gently help her see reality, the longer she would have to build up her expectations, and then her pain when she found her father had no interest in her would be even greater than before.

How she had managed to deceive herself was entirely understandable. Growing up in such a cold and loveless environment she must have been desperate to believe that someone cared about her, and her relentless desire to have her father as part of her life was one Andrew sympathised with wholeheartedly. The void his own had left could never be filled. Like an itch he couldn't quite scratch, it needled at him, more a dull ache now than the fresh agony it had been at first, but still one he carried with him every day, and it was easy for him to see why Emily was so keen to escape the same thing.

'Are you looking forward to the play?'

At the sound of her voice he instinctively looked up, although she was addressing his mother rather than him.

'Very much so. Are you?'

'Yes...'

'You don't sound sure.'

Even in the semi-darkness of the carriage Andrew saw Emily shuffle in her seat. 'Oh, I am. It's just my first true public outing among the *ton*. You said the theatre is one of the places people go to see and be seen, and I'm not sure I like the idea of the latter.'

She tucked a non-existent strand of hair behind her ear, the gesture betraying her nerves. It was a feeling he well understood. The desire to make his mother happy chafed against the knowledge that half of Warwickshire Society would be staring at him as soon as he entered the theatre and he didn't want to be gawped at either, even if having Emily at his side somehow managed to subdue the worst of his unease.

'Don't worry too much about that.' He leaned forwards, wishing he hadn't when he caught the faintest hint of the rose water on her hair. 'We'll be sitting in a private box. Once seated you'll be able to look at other people as much as you like without them being able to see you in turn.'

'That's a relief.' Emily's shoulders dropped and he realised she must have been holding them tense, whether knowingly or otherwise. 'I must confess some hypocrisy, however. While I don't relish the prospect of being studied myself, I'm intrigued to look around to see if any of the gentlemen there might be my father.'

She smiled, although she didn't hold his eye for long. Ever since that fateful moment at the modiste's shop she hadn't seemed to know how to behave in his presence any more than he did in hers, something unspoken now passing between them he didn't dare try to unpick. But for once the shy lift of her lips didn't make him entirely forget everything else.

'There are certainly likely to be more than a few lords in attendance,' he conceded cautiously. Apparently her apprehension wasn't enough to stop her from pressing ahead with her plans, and his own concerns returned sharply to the fore. 'We won't know all of them well enough for introductions. Even if there was someone you thought could be a possibility, it would be better to wait until you were sure.'

The carriage turned a corner, the squeak of the wheels and beat of the horses' hooves making her quiet reply almost imperceptible—but not quite—and Andrew felt his heart sink at what he only just caught.

'I've waited twenty-one years already. I'd rather not hold on for much longer.'

The theatre was packed to the rafters.

In every direction silk and satin gleamed in the light of countless candles—jewels and gold thread sparkled at necks and knuckles and everywhere in between. The moment Andrew steered his mother and Emily through the doors, the noise and heat hit them like a brick wall, the raised voices and press of cloying bodies not serving to take the edge off his disquiet. It seemed his prophecy had been correct. Most of Warwickshire's upper class thronged the room, affecting to take their seats but in truth hoping to show off their finery to the envy or ad-miration of everyone else, and he had never been more grateful that Uncle Ephraim's avarice now allowed his reluctant heir the luxury of a private box away from the crowds.

Looking down to check neither his mother nor Emily were being crushed as they fought their way towards the stairs, he saw her eyes were round. She was staring this way and that—at the velvet curtains around the stage, the candelabras hanging from the ceiling, the glittering splendour of the gowns and waistcoats on all sides—and he felt his stomach contract. Was she simply admiring her surroundings, or had she already begun the hunt he feared could only end in tears?

He leaned down so she might hear him above the buzz of conversation. 'Are you all right? Not too anxious among all these people?'

'I'm fine.' Her fingers tightened on his arm, only slightly, but the momentary pressure still shot straight to his chest. 'Are you?'

Her glance was swift but searching, and Andrew wondered whether she was remembering the card party he had hosted against his will.

'Of course. You never need worry about me.'

It was only half a lie. He couldn't pretend to be enjoying the curious glances in his direction, as ever drawing more interest than he liked, although now there was a difference. When he'd first come down from Derbyshire he'd had to weather those stares alone, but now he didn't have to. Emily walked at his side with elegance any Society lady would strive for, resplendent in a silvery new gown he had paid extra to have made in half the time, and an ember of pride kindled inside him. She looked every inch the Countess-to-be, and he couldn't imagine anyone better suited to the role, her outside lovely but the feeling her presence gave him more valuable than any pretty face.

'Up here. Our box is on the very top balcony.'

With girlish excitement Lady Gouldsmith let go of his arm to ascend the stairs, Emily close behind. Candles set in alcoves along the stairwell walls cast a glow over her every time she passed one, her curls shining gold beneath a crown of gilt flowers he privately thought made her look like a fairy queen. With every floor they climbed the number of people grew smaller, until they reached an ornate door, which at a nod from Andrew was thrown open by a waiting servant.

Lady Gouldsmith sailed in without hesitation, but Emily stopped dead on the threshold.

If Andrew had thought her eyes were wide downstairs then now they were like saucers. 'This is just for us?'

'Yes. Just the three of us.'

She stared at the extravagantly upholstered seats turned towards the front of the box, where an uninterrupted view of the stage stretched out before them. A rich carpet underfoot and gold tassels on the curtains were lavish touches he had to admit added to the general splendour, illuminated by candles in gilded sconces that wouldn't have been out of place in a palace. As if to underscore the air of luxury a bottle of champagne stood in a bucket of ice that Emily went immediately to dabble her fingers through, her face alight with amazement it was a pleasure to behold.

'It's *wonderful*.'

She crossed to stand beside his mother, leaning over the railing to look down at the crowds below. In such skyward seclusion nobody on the lower floors could see them unless they specifically craned their necks upward, but that didn't stop Emily from being able to peer down on *them*. If any man resembling her enough to pique her interest was there she was sure to spot him, although as he caught another glimpse of her delighted face Andrew considered whether his worries might have been premature.

Perhaps he wouldn't have to caution her. Perhaps her enjoyment would make her forget the task she had set herself, the one he feared would make her more unhappy than she'd been before. He could only hope so, as well as do his best to distract her. All without getting too distracted himself, of course, the memory of her beneath the negligible cover of her shift never far from his mind.

Emily sat very still, hardly blinking as she watched the actors move across the stage. Anyone looking at her could have been forgiven for thinking she was entranced by the tragic scene unfolding before her…but appearances could be deceiving.

In truth her focus was trained on Andrew, his seat very near to hers. Each time he scratched his chin or touched his mouth she knew he was going to move before he even raised his hand, so attuned to his presence that even the steady rhythm of his breath sounded loud in her ear. His leg was almost touching hers, her skirts *just* brushing his knee, and the tension of wondering whether his next stretch would bring them into contact made her feel as though she was balanced on the edge of a knife. Since their visit to Leamington she had half feared he'd been avoiding her, but there was no chance of him doing so while they were corralled in the same box, now so close together he could only have escaped her if he shut his eyes. He certainly seemed as though his attention was fixed on the stage rather than on her, although her heart slammed into the front of her bodice when he suddenly turned his head.

'Are you enjoying yourself?'

His voice was lowered and the deep pitch sent a delicious shiver down the back of her neck as she nodded, hoping he hadn't noticed she'd instinctively leaned closer.

'Yes. Even more than I imagined.'

Seated on her other side Lady Gouldsmith's gaze never left the actors. One of them was now lamenting the death of another and a tear glinted on Eleanor's cheek, clearly moved by the action Emily had been too distracted to absorb. She was indeed enjoying her first ever visit to the theatre, although not necessarily for the reason Andrew had in mind, and she sat up a little straighter in her seat.

This won't do. I'm supposed to be watching the play and looking out for my father, not trying to get as close to Andrew as I can without climbing into his lap.

Trying not to make her intent too obvious, she let her eye wander over the audience seated below. There had been no attempt to extinguish the candles even after the play had begun, and she could see the other patrons as clearly as if it had been daylight, their clothes and faces brilliantly lit by innumerable flames.

The distance between them was another matter, however. From her lofty seat she couldn't make out the details of their faces, illuminated but too far away to clearly distinguish one from another. Someone she knew well could have been among the patrons clustered below and she wouldn't have recognised them, her place up in the rafters an obstacle she hadn't foreseen.

Disappointment prickled through her.

First the card party and now this.

Once again her hopes had been built up for nothing. For the second time she had strayed into the *ton's* natural territory, summoning all her nerve to try to pretend she belonged, and for the second time there was nothing to show for it. Her father might have been in that very room and she'd never know. The disappointment wending through her took on a sharper edge as she considered an unwanted possibility.

What if she never found him?

If she never found her father she'd forfeit the love she'd hoped to gain—for where else could she obtain it? As much as Andrew seemed to like her, he was still marrying her for their mutual convenience above anything else. He had already committed to giving her a home and a lifestyle more comfortable than anything she'd ever dreamed of, and to delude herself into thinking he might offer his heart on top of that would be folly. He'd needed a wife and she'd needed shelter, and if she never reunited with the one person she was certain already loved her then she would have to go the rest of her life without.

Her throat tightened and she made a conscious effort to swallow the aching lump. Just because her own feelings for Andrew were shifting didn't mean his were doing the same. Friendship interspersed with some fleeting desire seemed to be the extent of it, and even for that she ought to be grateful… A difficult concept to hold onto when he leaned forward in his chair, the candlelight casting shadows over his face that made his jawline look like it was chiselled from stone.

The activity on the stage seemed to be reaching a crescendo. Too intent on her inner turmoil to understand what was happening, she followed the audience's lead when they stood up, the curtains pulling shut to the sound of thunderous applause.

'Wonderful. Wonderful!'

On her feet like everyone else, Lady Gouldsmith daintily blotted her eyes with a lace-edged handkerchief, giving Emily a watery smile. 'Look at me, moved to tears! I only hope the second act will compare.'

'The second act?'

'This is just an interval, for people to move around after sitting for so long.'

As if to illustrate her point Eleanor waved over the side of the balcony to where the audience were in a state of flux. But then her eyes narrowed. 'Andrew, is that Lady Sandwell? I *think* I see her—over there, in the box opposite. I don't know who else would wear such an unusual hat. I've been meaning to speak with her about her recommendation for a new gardener—if you'd excuse me.'

Before her son could either confirm or deny the presence of Lady Sandwell and her hat, Lady Gouldsmith disappeared, vanishing through the box's door in a swathe of lilac silk, and abruptly Emily and Andrew found themselves very much alone.

From the balcony Emily returned to her seat, aware of a new unsteadiness in her legs. She hadn't been on her own with him for the best part of a week. Not since she had been so brazen as to allow him to admire her in her shift, and she hardly knew what to do with herself as she pretended her insides weren't swooping like a bird in flight.

Andrew remained at the railing for a moment. Whether he was watching the crowds below or just affecting to she didn't know, although when he turned to her his face was carefully blank.

'Would you care for some champagne?'

He nodded to the bottle still lying in its bath of melting ice. It was already open—Lady Gouldsmith had required refreshment after a particularly gruelling scene—but Emily hesitated.

'I'm not sure. Like everything else the *ton* seems to enjoy, I've never tried it.'

'Do you want to?'

'Perhaps a drop. If I like the taste, I might have a real glass afterwards.'

Andrew inclined his head. Taking a glass from beside the bucket he poured out a thimbleful, seeming to pause before he moved towards her.

The theatre was noisy. Laughter and a hundred different conversations made a clamouring din, but somehow the only thing she could hear was the soft swish of his coat as he leaned down to place the glass in her hand. He was easily close enough for her to touch him, and she willed her fingers to stay still as she took the champagne, staring fixedly at the bubbles rather than his too-near face.

He stepped back—again his footsteps the only thing her ears saw fit to register—just as Emily took her first tentative sip.

'What do you think?'

The bubbles tickled her tongue but the taste wasn't unpleasant, and when she informed Andrew of the fact he gave a dry laugh.

'It improves on further acquaintance. Will you have more?'

'Please.'

She held out her empty glass, bracing herself when he came forward again and bent to fill it.

For all her efforts she realised her hand wasn't completely steady. The surface of the champagne rippled slightly, betraying the tremor inside she was trying so hard to disguise—and when his fingers brushed her knuckles she couldn't help the sharp breath that escaped her parted lips.

Andrew's eyes locked with hers.

If he had been within touching distance before, now he was closer still. He was so much taller that he had to bend almost double to reach down to her chair, still towering over her but his face now all she could see. He seemed to have forgotten the bottle in his hand. He'd ceased pouring the moment he heard her gasp, and she felt heat climb up from her neck when his gaze swept from her eyes to her mouth with the same dark intensity as a few days before.

Andrew didn't move, and neither did she; and yet somehow the champagne bottle was set down, and the glass vanished from her hand, and when Andrew fell into his seat Emily somehow fell with him to end up in his lap.

His lips were sweet with the taste of passion and champagne and she never wanted him to stop, his kiss deep and powerful and chasing out everything else. Her hands were in his hair, pulling him towards her, his grip on her so firm she almost couldn't breathe, half suffocated by her desire to be pressed against him even more. His tongue danced with hers, delving, exploring, twisting, only to break away as he trailed kisses down the length of her neck, burying himself beneath her chin to nip where her pulse bounded at the base of her throat.

It seemed Andrew's pent-up longing was just as great as her own. He cupped her cheek, tipping her head back so he could reach the sensitive jut of her collarbones above the neck of her gown and graze them with his teeth, scattering stars in front of Emily's glazed, half-open eyes. Whatever spell the burning tension of the modiste's fitting room had cast on them was unstoppable, and now the thread had been broken it couldn't be repaired, unable to hold back even in the knowledge that they were in public. All the aching, all the desire to touch him, the fight against doing so abandoned as Emily's fingers tightened in the short hairs on the back of his neck, and her heart sang to hear him swallow a guttural groan. It was impossible to tell where he ended and she began, a seamless melding together that set her alight…

'Wait. Wait.'

Andrew pulled back, his cheeks flushed and eyes as dark as coals. He was breathing like a hunted animal and Emily felt her throat clench as he released her from his grasp, shakily slipping from his lap to collapse back into her own seat.

She huddled into the chair, trying to slow the wild pounding of her heart. Her blood felt like fire in every vein, and she suspected Andrew's was the same as he pushed back his hair, looking as winded as she felt.

'The *ton* would think Christmas had come early if they'd seen that.'

He passed a hand over his face—but when he looked at her his smile sent a static shock crackling in its wake. 'I don't want to give them anything to use against us. Engaged or not, I don't think it would be a good idea to do that again…however much I might want to.'

Emily's already heated blood all but burst into flames. Her hair had come loose on one side and she twisted it back, aware her fingers were almost too nerveless to move. Her mouth was dry and her mind drawn a near perfect blank, too pleasure-drunk to work properly, although from somewhere a single sensible observation cautiously raised its head.

'Them? You talk about the *ton* as though you weren't one of their number.'

'That's because I still don't truly feel as though I am.'

He gave her another of those heart-stopping smiles, although this time she thought she caught something lurking underneath.

She took a deep breath. For the most part all she could think of was the scalding pressure of Andrew's mouth, her neck still tingling where he had branded it with kisses, but her curiosity managed to find a crack to slip through. His past was as much a mystery as ever, and she might never be gifted such an opportunity to ask as now, when his defences were down and his vulnerability was as exposed as his desires.

'Why is that? You've never really told me.'

He was straightening his cravat—his hands not looking entirely steady either—and at the question he paused. For a moment Emily wondered if he would pretend not to have heard her, but then he slid her a sideways look, as ever the meeting of their eyes making heat spark in her stomach.

'I will, but not right now. It grieves my mother to speak of it and she'll be back at any moment.'

With perfect timing—or perhaps imperfect, depending on who was asked—the door to the box opened. Lady Gouldsmith came inside, granting a vague smile to her son and soon-to-be daughter-in-law, although it was Andrew's low, gravelly murmur as his mother turned to close the door behind her that caught Emily's attention like a butterfly in a net.

'Besides…there are other things I'd *much* rather think about at present than sorrows of the past.'

Chapter Eight

There was a slight crack in the flagstone closest to Andrew's boot.

He looked down at it, trying to ignore the sensation of a belt being tightened around his chest. The church was uncomfortably warm but he knew it wasn't the heat that had caused the neck of his shirt to feel damp, his silk cravat tied perfectly but somehow feeling like it was slowly strangling him with every breath. Even above the drone of the organ he could hear the slight shuffling and murmuring of the few guests who had been invited to witness his marriage, and he wondered if they could tell his state of mind from the back of his head, certain even his hair must look slightly tense as he waited for his fate to be revealed.

'Any moment now. She won't be much longer, I'm sure.'

The Reverend Figsbury peered expectantly down the

aisle towards the open front doors, but Andrew continued to stare directly ahead. He wished he had the reverend's confidence. Until he actually *saw* Emily walking
towards him there was still a chance she might not show,
a possibility that pulled his innards into a hard knot.

She had nobody there to support her, after all. The
bride's side of the church was empty—she had no family
and the necessity of concealing her origins meant her few
friends from among Miss Laycock's boarders weren't
invited. The only people she'd know were his mother
and himself, and if she'd changed her mind there was
no one to stop her from bolting, perhaps running from
the Dower House before she had to make the change to
Huntingham Hall...

Still staring at the back wall of the church he unconsciously shook his head.

She wouldn't run. How could she? She had nowhere
else to go, which was the very reason she had agreed
to marry him to begin with, and he shouldn't forget it.
If he was looking forward to seeing her every day he
shouldn't tell her, nor should he admit how much he liked
the idea of her making Huntingham her own, introducing the feminine touches his uncle's tenure had deliberately wiped out. To walk into a room and find Emily
sitting beside the fire or perhaps catching sight of her
picking flowers in the garden was a prospect that made
him happier than he thought safe, worry nagging at him
even as far more appealing things tried to distract him
from what he knew he still had to do.

But there's no point in thinking about that now.

Andrew glanced down at his pocket watch. The conversation regarding her father was something he would

only have to fret about if she actually came to the church—and she was now fifteen minutes late.

His unease stirred harder. If he turned his head a fraction he could just see his mother alternating between watching him and the door, a constant twist that must have made the person sitting behind her dizzy. She didn't seem worried yet—surely it was every bride's prerogative to arrive a little late—but the reverend was peering over Andrew's shoulder with more and more concern, and he became aware a low muttering had broken out behind him, the guests becoming restless as the wait went on.

'Ah. There she is.'

Reverend Figsbury broke into a beaming smile—and Andrew felt as though his heart had been shot out of a cannon.

He didn't mean to turn around. The previous night he had determined not to watch her walk down the aisle, not wanting to add to the nerves that were sure to be making her weak at the knees, but now the moment had arrived his resolve deserted him. As the organist launched into the wedding march he realised he was moving, spurred on by some force he was powerless to fight, and without knowing quite how it had happened he found his eyes suddenly fixed on Emily's approach.

Time stood still.

She was coming towards him, the sunshine streaming in through the door, swathing her in a halo of light. It lit up the copper brilliance of her hair to shine as though it was on fire, a circlet of flowers somehow sitting atop the flames without catching alight, although beneath it her countenance was pale. The pearly sheen of her skin was offset by a gown of the lightest grey that moved like mist around her and was hardly more substantial, her skirts brushing the ground in a trail of silvery lace more like a spider's web than anything made by hand. If he hadn't been there to witness the sight for himself he never would have believed a woman could look so beautiful, like something from a fairytale come to life, and he could no more have dragged his eyes away from her than he could have found words to describe his awe.

It wasn't her beauty that struck him the hardest, however.

Her steps were every bit as unsteady as he thought they would be, each one clearly costing her great effort. She tottered slightly as if she was walking the deck of a pitching ship, and Andrew's breath seized as he watched her draw nearer, the dirge of the organ suddenly too loud. She looked so small and vulnerable all alone beneath the church's great domed ceiling, every face turned towards her while her own was cast down to the floor, and he knew what he was going to do even before his mind came to a conscious decision.

Without stopping to allow it to catch up, he strode towards her, the wedding guests taking a collective breath as he walked past them down the aisle. Emily looked up at him, apparently startled to find him so suddenly close, but she didn't step back when he held out his hand.

'Here. We'll walk the rest of the way together.'

The murmurs from the pews around him grew louder but he didn't spare them a glance. Emily was all he could see, her white face tight with strain, and he knew that if she took his hand now he would never want to let go.

She would need someone to rely on. If she found her

father she would need a friend to help her through the pain of rejection that must surely follow. She might only be marrying him for security, but that was something Andrew knew he was happy to provide.

His cravat felt tighter than ever as he waited to see if she would place her hand in his. He took a half-step closer, bending slightly so Emily was the only person to catch his murmured words. To his delight she swayed as his breath tickled her neck, but he hardened himself against the urge to follow it with a kiss, the memory of that heated moment in the theatre's rafters streaking through his mind.

'This is how it will be. From this day on, if you wish it, you'll never have to face anything alone.'

Her eyelashes flickered, fluttering over cheeks that now glowed the ready pink he so loved to behold. She seemed to be looking down at the floor, or perhaps at the toes of her dainty new slippers; but then those hydrangea-blue eyes locked on his and the church around him fell away as Andrew felt her fingers settle in his palm.

Afterwards, Emily had no idea where she'd found the nerve.

To enter the church all alone and stand at the top of the aisle, knowing everyone had swivelled to stare at her, was one of the most frightening things she'd ever done. Her heart had been slamming against her breastbone and her stomach had churned nauseatingly, and with every step she'd felt as though she was about to vomit or faint.

But then—Andrew.

She cut him a sidelong glance. The familiar shape of his profile was sharp against the Dower House's drawing room wall. He was talking to yet another person she didn't know, the receiving line at her own wedding breakfast made up of strangers, but for the moment at least she wasn't afraid. All her fear had fled at the first touch of his hand; strong and warm and steady enough for the both of them, and as he had led her to the altar she'd known that he wouldn't let her fall. She was his wife now and he was her husband, and despite a world of uncertainties and concerns for the future she'd never been so glad of anything in her life.

Someone was talking to her and, with immense difficulty, she dragged her attention away from Andrew. What she really wanted was to continue to stare at the man she had just married, still hardly able to believe what she'd done, but her guest was not to be deterred.

'My lady. May I offer my most sincere congratulations.'

Sir Montfort, whom she vaguely remembered from the card party Andrew had held all those weeks before, rose from an elaborate bow. 'A wonderful event. I'm sure I'm not the only one pleased to see a Countess Breamore at Huntingham Hall once again.'

'Thank you, sir. I hope in time to prove myself worthy of the honour.'

Such a thing was impossible, she knew even as she spoke the obvious lie, but what else could she have said? The fact she was now the mistress of a nine-hundred-acre estate, a truly enormous house and the bearer of a centuries-old title was still so bizarre she might have given a hysterical laugh if a fingertip hadn't suddenly traced down the back of her bare arm, sending a rush of blood directly to her head.

'I have no doubt my wife will make the perfect Countess.' Andrew's smile was charming, although Emily couldn't help but suspect he'd guessed exactly what she'd been thinking. 'I can't imagine anyone more deserving of a life of comfort and privilege than the woman I have been fortunate enough to wed.'

She managed a smile in return, hoping Sir Montfort was too short-sighted to see how she'd flushed.

'The woman I have been fortunate enough to wed.' Fortunate...

Probably he was merely being polite...but that didn't stop a secret thrill from tingling down her spine.

He had kept his word until the very last. He'd assured her he wouldn't change his mind about marrying her and he hadn't, their fates bound together now by the ring gleaming golden on her finger. It was the most costly thing she'd ever worn—more expensive even than her cloud-hued gown—but the price didn't dictate its true value. The ring on her third finger represented reliability and trust, the mark of a man she could place her faith in, and she could barely credit that somehow the quest to identify her father had resulted in something so unexpected instead.

Not instead. Resolutely she corrected her mistake. *As well as. I'll find my father as well as having gained a husband—of that I'm still sure.*

Andrew was immersed in conversation with Sir Montfort, and for a moment she watched him without being seen. He couldn't have been truly interested in what the old knight was saying—something about rebuilding a chimney, having moved on from compliments—but his polite pretence was convincing. He would never want to offend or hurt anybody's feelings, one of the things she liked best about him, although now his kindness left a bittersweet taste on her tongue.

Until she tracked Lord *Somebody* down she wouldn't have answers as to who she really was—and she wouldn't be loved, either. The consideration Andrew showed her was the same he showed everyone else, and yet she yearned for more, still missing the unequivocal acceptance and approval she'd wanted since she was a child. It was a gap only her father could fill and she knew she shouldn't lose sight of that fact, even if the temptation to hope Andrew might step into the breech grew stronger every day—and wasn't likely to diminish now they were joined together until death did them part.

The afternoon wore on in a whirl of eating, drinking and relentless good wishes. Lady Gouldsmith had outdone herself as hostess for the newly married couple, with cakes and ices and fruit of every description piled high and champagne flowing, and the guests took advantage with full glasses and faces that grew pinker and pinker as day turned into evening. Having barely slept the night before, Emily felt herself beginning to flag as the candles were lit, although when Andrew came to find her, sitting in a chair half hidden behind a curtain, she found herself suddenly wide awake.

'Well, Lady Breamore? As you appear to be falling asleep in your seat, shall we go home?'

The upward curve of Andrew's lips was distracting— half courteous, half amused, and so wholly absorbing that Emily could barely find a reply as he helped her to her feet, his strong grip once again lighting fires beneath her skin.

'It sounds so strange to hear you call me that.'

'I'm afraid you'll have to get used to it. From now on you are a Countess, the equal—or perhaps better—of everyone here.'

He glanced around the room, his eye lingering over their guests, and to her puzzlement the smile segued into abrupt seriousness.

'No matter what the future brings, nobody can ever take that from you.'

His solemnity was short-lived. Perhaps he remembered a wedding was supposed to be a joyful occasion, or he thought whatever had just flitted though his mind was a matter for another time. Whatever the cause he hitched the smile back into place, and only one looking very closely could have noticed it didn't seem entirely effortless.

'I imagine you've long been desiring to leave the party. What do you say to sneaking out unobserved?'

At her nod Andrew held out his hand—and Emily took it without hesitation.

It was easy enough to creep away without being seen. The amount of champagne the wedding guests had ploughed through was impressive, and Emily doubted whether some of them were now even capable of recognising the bride and groom as they crept towards the door, keeping to the shadows thrown by crystal chandeliers. They moved stealthily until Andrew took hold of the door handle and eased just enough of a gap for her to slip through, following close behind and shutting the door again with the softest, most inaudible of clicks.

Out in the corridor the sounds of laughter and voices were dimmed, but it seemed Andrew didn't intend to linger. Still hand in hand, Emily's heart scurried faster as he led her to the entrance hall and through the open front door, the evening air just beginning to hold a crisp note. Above them the moon hung among countless stars, but all she could focus on was the warmth of his palm pressed against hers, walking quickly to keep up with him as Huntingham Hall loomed tall and magnificent out of the darkness.

At the bottom of the steps, Andrew paused.

'Wait.'

He turned to her, at last releasing her hand. 'I only intend to marry once, so I need to do this properly.'

The question of *what* he needed to do balanced on the tip of her tongue—but it fled when he swiftly bent down and scooped her off her feet.

'Isn't it tradition for a man to carry his new bride over the threshold?'

All her breath exited in a squeak of surprise as he drew her against his chest, cradling her as easily as if she'd been a paper doll. With one arm around her back and the other behind her knees she could feel his strength, as solid and unshakeable as the trunk of a tree, and she was too shocked to do anything but lean closer as he climbed the steps and kicked open the Hall's front door.

The butler must have left it unlocked or else Andrew's boot sent the bolt flying. With another of those bone-melting smiles he carried her inside, the smooth linen of his shirt pressed against her ear as she huddled against him, not wanting him to let go. Somehow her arms had found their way around his neck, bringing their faces almost level, and she gave an involuntary shiver when she felt the trace of stubble on his jaw rasp against her temple. The entrance hall was dark. In all the excitement the maids must have forgotten to light the candles, and to find herself alone in the shadows, held tightly against her new husband's chest, was like something from her most scandalous dreams.

Andrew showed no sign of putting her down. Instead he carefully adjusted his grip, splaying his fingers wider at the small of her back, the accidental—or deliberate— caress sending a wave of sensation that drenched her from head to foot.

'You seemed tired earlier. Are you still?'

His voice was low, a deep rumble in her ear. There was something in it she couldn't quite identify, some- thing barely restrained; but she didn't have to know its name to know she felt it too.

Slowly she lifted her head. He was watching her, even in the darkness the gleam in his eye dangerously clear, and with all the brazenness she possessed she shook her head.

'No? That's a shame.' He raised an eyebrow—and Emily's breathing raised its pace. 'I was about to sug- gest we go to bed.'

Her throat contracted, immediately dry.

What happened on a wedding night wasn't a mystery. The thing she struggled to understand was how Andrew could make her so weak with just one word—*bed*—spo- ken with such intent that she could give no answer but to slide a hand up to the back of his neck and guide his face downwards.

He needed no other instruction. Even as his mouth

found hers Emily felt him moving, knowing without opening her desire-heavy eyes that he was heading for the stairs. Clearly he could walk and kiss at the same time, pressing her against himself as tightly as if trying to fit her beneath his clothes, chest to chest and both aching to get somehow closer still. With tongues dancing and breathing ragged they stumbled upwards, wrapped together in building heat, her first glimpse of his bedroom a single snatched glance as he kicked the door shut behind them and broke the kiss to lift her higher against his mouth.

She sucked in a gasp as his lips sought the neckline of her gown, ghosting over the lace edge to scald the skin below. His hands were gripping her so forcefully it almost hurt, but she didn't want him to loosen them, her palm at his nape pressing him to her with scarcely any room left to breathe. Any thought of restraint or modesty vanished as he gently nipped along her collarbone, still holding her high off the ground, and her fingers curled into his hair when the tip of his tongue delved down into her bodice.

They were moving again, towards the bed now, Andrew parting the curtains with one knee to lay her down on the coverlet. Above her head a canopy of red damask stretched out like a scarlet sky, gleaming in the light of a fire roaring in the grate, but she had no interest in *that*. Her husband was beside her on the mattress, leaning down to kiss her again, and she pulled him to her so the darkness of his smile was the last thing she saw before her eyes fluttered closed once more.

He bore down on her, pressing her into the bed, but the feel of his body flush against hers filled her with the most wanton delight. If her hands skimmed lower she could feel the muscles of his back, and she seized hold of his shirt, pulling it up so her fingertips could graze his skin. He felt as good as she'd imagined, or better— taut and toned and burning at her touch, something she wanted to savour as she dared to slide one hand beneath the waistband of his breeches...

'If you go much further, you'll unman me.'

Andrew's voice was a growl in her ear, hot and urgent as his lips fastened around her lobe and struck sparks of pleasure somewhere much lower down. Somehow he had managed to slide her gown off one shoulder and his mouth went there at once, kissing from her throat to the soft peaks now almost escaping from their bounds. He was everywhere at once, his mouth and his hands, the scent of him all around her and the blazing heat of his skin taking her closer to the brink. She wanted him to do and say and touch *everything*, leaving no part of her a stranger, and although she had no words to express her longing Andrew seemed to know exactly what she meant.

With deliberate slowness he trailed a hand down-wards, his fingers lingering on the inside of her leg to force a whine from deep in her throat. She thought she felt him smile against her neck and dug her fingernails lightly into his back in retaliation, triumphing when she heard him groan in reply—but her victory didn't last for long.

He'd reached the hem of her gown and she gritted her teeth to feel him stroke a long line from her ankle to her knee, lifting her skirts along with it until they pooled around the tops of her thighs.

His hand dawdled there, drawing lazy circles across

her skin, and only when she thought she might burst or run mad did he lean back on his elbow, positioning himself so he could look down at her as he lay close to her side…and then he dragged his hand the last most essential fraction higher, and began to show her exactly how delicious being married to an Earl would be.

Chapter Nine

⧜⧜⧜

A bird was singing somewhere, the only sound in the quiet of the morning, but Emily didn't open her eyes.

She huddled deeper into the bedclothes, drawing the covers around herself more tightly as she waited to awaken fully. She couldn't remember the last time she'd slept so well. There was a slight soreness in her muscles and the secret depths of her core, but she felt loose and limber and more *alive* somehow than she'd ever felt before, realising belatedly that she had awoken with a smile on her face.

The cause of her happiness was obvious; but when she finally cracked open one eyelid, finding an empty pillow beside her made the smile fade.

Pushing herself up she saw she wasn't wearing her nightgown. She wasn't wearing anything at all, in fact, a discovery that made her already warm cheeks flush, although that was the least of her concerns.

Where was Andrew?

On his side of the bed the covers had been thrown back and the hangings were partly open, allowing her a narrow view of the rest of the room. It had been dark when they'd stumbled into it and she hadn't noticed the pretty wallpaper or ornate fireplace that greeted her now, just visible in the dim light that crept in beneath the heavy curtains. Last night Andrew had taken up her entire focus, his hands and the insistent press of his body blocking out everything else, and it was slightly disconcerting to wake in a room she had no real memory of entering. Her husband's—*husband's!*—touch was all she could recall, how he had made her writhe and gasp and finally, breathlessly, fall apart beneath him, and as she combed her fingers through her disordered hair she felt a pang of disappointment.

After all that, had he simply got up, dressed and gone out?

The night before had been wonderful, but not *just* for the things he had done to make her call out his name. Falling asleep in his arms, listening to the steady beat of his heart against her ear, had filled her with such peace she'd wished she could stay awake to hear it for longer, although eventually exhaustion had won. The very last thing she remembered before sleep claimed her was how much she had always wanted to be held like that, safe and warm and content in the knowledge that the strong arms around her would never let her down. It was the feeling she'd longed for since she was a child, and to encounter it from the man she was now tied to for the rest of her life was not something she had foreseen…

There was a noise from the other side of the closed

bedroom door. It sounded very much like someone—a maid, probably—intending to come in, and she hastily pulled the bedclothes higher, clutching them to her as the door creaked open.

'Ah. You're awake.'

A loaded tea tray was borne into the room, but not by a servant, and Emily felt her heart turn over as she watched Andrew come towards her.

In the low light she could see his bare chest scattered with the dark tangle she'd run her nails through the night before, snaking down in a line over his taut stomach to disappear beneath the waistband of his unbuttoned breeches. They hung loose around his hips as if they might be persuaded to drop at any moment, and she found she couldn't look away from the matching pair of indents on either side of his navel, razor sharp diagonal lines that pointed the way to the fascinating part of his anatomy she had so recently discovered.

He set the tray down on a small table beside the bed, his smile bordering on wolfish. It seemed she wasn't the only one struggling not to stare. His eyes lingered on her bare shoulders peeping out above the coverlet, and she had to fight the sudden shameless temptation to let it slip lower.

Instead she wrapped the cover around herself more firmly, secretly delighted by the fleeting disappointment that flitted over Andrew's face.

'What's this? Do you usually bring up your own tea?'

She tried to appear offhand, although she wavered when he sat on the edge of the bed, his broad shoulders now directly in her eyeline. It was only a few hours ago that she had gripped them so tightly he had sucked in a harsh breath, and she flushed now to wonder if she'd left a mark, perhaps a series of tiny crescent moons where her nails had dug into the skin.

'Sorry. I should have told you. I gave the servants the day off.'

He leaned forwards, the muscles of his bare back moving distractingly as he passed her a cup. 'I thought that on your first day as mistress of Huntingham Hall you might like the place to yourself…apart from me, of course.'

The wicked curve of his mouth widened and Emily looked hurriedly down into her tea, not daring to meet his eye. If she did he was sure to read the unladylike thoughts currently swirling, and she felt she ought to at least *attempt* some pretence at decorum, even if the bedclothes were currently the only things preserving her precarious modesty.

Surreptitiously she watched him tending to his own cup, wielding the teapot with more skill than one might expect from an aristocrat with servants to attend to every whim. As could describe her too now, she supposed, the ring on her third finger gleaming as she lifted her hand to take a sip. It was her first day as a Countess and yet she didn't feel very different, her new title paling into insignificance beside the other things currently crowding her thoughts.

Andrew sat back again, his shifting weight pulling slightly at the bedclothes, and Emily had to move quickly to prevent herself from revealing more than she intended. It was awkward to hold a cup with one hand and the covers in the other, and she was left with nowhere to hide when he fixed her with those dark, inviting eyes.

'How did you find yesterday, in the end? Was the wedding as you'd imagined?'

He raised his cup to his lips but didn't look away, his direct gaze holding her captive until she answered. Thinking clearly was difficult when he was sitting so close, his warm, bare chest easily within arm's reach and she struggled to block out a sudden skin-tingling memory of it bearing down on her.

'It was less frightening than I'd anticipated...apart from when I first walked into the church, of course.'

She saw him nod, probably remembering her pale, terrified face. Until he had come striding down the aisle to rescue her she'd been almost too afraid to move, nobody sitting on her side of the church to support her and every set of staring eyes belonging to a stranger. There had been no familiar figure to give her the courage to go on, apart from that of Lady Gouldsmith and the groom himself, and despite her current happiness the sting of that knowledge still remained.

'I would have liked to have had some guests of my own. Most brides are given away by their father at the very least.'

She shrugged as though it was of little consequence, but Andrew didn't seem fooled.

'Their father.'

There was something in the way he repeated her words that she didn't quite understand. His eyebrows drew together and he studied the gilt rim of his cup, his scrutiny abruptly leaving her face.

'This desire to find him. I understand it. After I lost my own I would have done anything to get him back again. But...'

His words tailed off into uncertainty, the furrow of his brows deepening. It wasn't often that he seemed discomforted, but he was now, and even the enticing ridges of his chiselled abdomen couldn't distract Emily from wondering why.

After a moment he tipped his head back, addressing the canopy spreading above the bed instead of her. 'It wasn't easy, but I've learned how to live without him. I'm certain, given time, you could do the same regarding yours.'

Emily realised she was frowning likewise. 'What do you mean? I'm already without him. That's what I'm looking to change.'

She saw his fingers tighten on his saucer. There was something teetering on the tip of his tongue, she could tell, but then he shook his head.

'It doesn't matter. Forget I spoke.'

Still without looking at her he drained his cup, placing it back on the tray with a sharp rap of China against metal. It was a restless movement and didn't help to convince Emily that nothing was amiss, although his evasiveness nagged at the back of her mind.

There had been another time recently when he had said less than she knew he'd been thinking—and perhaps now, with the ghost of their perfect night together still hanging in the air, was the time to ask.

Carefully setting her own cup aside she leaned forward, aware the cover of the bedclothes became more and more perilous every time she moved.

'Speaking of things you've had to learn…'

Andrew half turned towards her. Unless the low light

was playing tricks on her, his expression was slightly guarded, although his tone was even as ever.

'Yes?'

'That night at the theatre. You said you'd tell me about what happened when you were younger, but not when your mother might overhear and be upset. Surely there's no danger of that now?'

To her surprise he laughed. 'No. She's far too tactful to think of visiting newlyweds the day after their wedding.'

For the briefest of moments he paused, then stood abruptly, pacing over to the window to twitch aside a curtain and look out.

'It's a beautiful day. I think I'd like to show you the maze.'

Caught off balance by the rapid change of direction, Emily blinked. 'The maze?'

'Some Lord Breamore of yesteryear designed it. It's on the other side of the ornamental gardens, somewhere I fancy you've yet to explore.'

Andrew tweaked the curtain a little wider, a slice of sunshine cutting across the floor. If she didn't know better she might think he was trying to avoid the subject she had just raised, although she had no intention of letting him off so easily.

They'd known each other for so long now, were *married*, for goodness' sake, and yet she still knew next to nothing about him before his earldom had brought him crashing into her life. He knew everything about her— every detail of her shameful origins, her unwantedness, her yearning to belong—but had offered little detail in return, and she needed to learn the truth about the man she had wed.

'That sounds lovely, but there are other things I'd like to explore more.'

'Other things?'

Andrew glanced back at her over his shoulder, one eyebrow raised provocatively, and Emily felt herself blush.

'Not *that*. You know what I mean.'

He laughed again, although more ruefully than before. 'I'm to have no secrets? Is that it?'

A magpie flew close to the window and they watched it wheel away, a black and white blur against the sky. It wasn't much of a distraction but it seemed to help Andrew make up his mind, perhaps giving him the shortest of reprieves in which to marshal his thoughts.

'Very well. How about this...'

He turned away from the window, the early-morning sunshine throwing his silhouette into sharp relief. Outlined against the light, the breadth of his shoulders was more impressive than ever, and Emily couldn't even pretend to not stare as he came towards her and sat beside her on the bed.

'If you can find your way to the centre of the maze without my help, I'll tell you everything you want to know. Is that a deal?'

A small smile tugged at the corner of his mouth, a mouth now *definitely* close enough to kiss. If she just leaned forward a little more her arm would brush his, far more solid and muscular than her own, and on the end of that arm was a hand whose skill she wouldn't mind experiencing again...

The hand in question moved, held out towards her.

'I said, is that a deal?'

Before he could change his mind she pressed her palm to his, sealing their bargain with a firm shake. His strong fingers gripped hers and she had to bite back a breath at the current that crackled through her even at that contact—perfectly innocent, and yet the sudden intensity of his eyes making it feel anything but.

He let go of her hand, watching attentively as she tucked the bedclothes around herself more securely. His smile had grown somewhat strained, and she was mildly bemused at how swiftly he levered himself off the bed.

'If you'll excuse me, I'll leave you to get up.'

'Oh. Of course.' Disappointed at the idea of him exiting the room—taking his shoulders with him—she tried nonetheless for a casual nod. 'You have something important to do?'

'Not especially. It's just that if I stay here with you much longer there's a danger I might not let you get out of bed at all.'

As the hem of Emily's skirts whisked around yet another corner—one he was confident led to a dead end—Andrew wondered how much time he had left. The maze was large, but not huge, and despite her false starts they were drawing nearer to the centre, the clock counting down to the conversation he had hoped to postpone for another day.

He *could* have pursued the subject of her father while they were in their bedroom, he admitted to himself, as he waited for his wife to re-emerge from behind the hedge. But he'd deliberately let the moment slip. Emily had given him the perfect opportunity to warn her against building her hopes too high and he should have taken it, although he knew very well why he had not.

Sitting up in his bed she had looked like an angel, all rosy cheeks and tumbled hair, the early-morning light gilding her pale skin, and he hadn't wanted to ruin it with something as ugly as the truth. For today at least he had hoped to spare her that unhappiness, but she'd continued asking questions. He knew she wouldn't rest until he answered them, and posing the challenge of the maze was a final attempt to give himself more time in which to think.

'Am I going the right way, at least? Can you tell me that?'

She peered back at him, smiling at the shake of his head. From his position a few paces behind he could make any number of long, leisurely examinations of the subtle curve of her hips, and it made deciding what he was going to say much more difficult, each step she took a distraction he could have done without.

The air had taken on an autumnal freshness, but the sun was still bright and Andrew clenched his hand into a fist against the sudden temptation to stare. When the sunshine was in front of her—as it was at that moment— he could see through the thin fabric of Emily's cream gown, and the sight took him straight back to the night before, the image of her lying beneath him making his breath claw at his throat. It had been intense—the heat, how she'd curled around him and refused to let him go— and it had confirmed the suspicion that had been growing inside him almost from the first day they'd met.

She might have wed him as a means to an end…but for him, things now went far deeper.

She looked back at him again and he forced a grin, hoping it didn't look as tight as it felt. His feelings for her were blossoming, unfurling like a vine scaling the walls of a fortress, and yet soon he would have to cause her pain. Speaking about his past wasn't something he relished, but it was what it might lead to that really made him reluctant, more talk of fathers something he had little reason to desire.

'I think we must be close now.'

Emily lengthened her stride, the sound of her new silk slippers pattering faster. A curl had come loose from her chignon and it dangled teasingly down her back, inviting him to catch up with her and wind it around his finger in an imitation of her wedding band. Every time she moved her hand he saw it shining there, a tiny golden crown on her slender finger, and as she rounded another corner he tried not to revisit how he had kissed that very same hand so passionately only a few hours before.

Focus. You have other things that need attending to.

She was right, after all. The centre of the maze was only a few turns away, and he braced himself for the moment she'd discover it. When he'd first found his way through as a boy he'd been so proud of himself, doubtless as Emily would be too, and he could still remember how he'd gone running to tell Uncle Ephraim about his triumph.

The old Earl hadn't cared. His nephew's news had been a pointless interruption, and Andrew realised he was frowning as he recalled the pang of childish disappointment. He'd resolved long ago that when he had his own children he would celebrate every single achievement and he still felt the same, the prospect of having a family so much closer now Emily had entered his life.

'Is that it?' She pulled up short, looking directly ahead. 'Have I found the end?'

The winding hedges had straightened out and a clearing lay before them, partly visible beyond a metal arch set into a tall bank of greenery. There could be no mistaking it—certainly not for Andrew, who had already seen it once that morning—and in spite of his circling unease he couldn't help a spark of pleasure at Emily's smile.

'Well done. You got there far more quickly than I did the first time I tried.'

She darted ahead, ducking beneath the arch to enter the clearing, and he followed the loose curl still beckoning from between her shoulder blades. Gravel scrunched beneath their feet but he wasn't surprised when her slippers fell still again almost at once, knowing she wouldn't have expected what was now in front of her.

She spun round to look at him, eyes wide.

'Andrew! When did you do this?'

It had been time-consuming to make repeated trips from the Hall to the centre of the maze, each time carrying something with him, but her delight made the effort more than worthwhile. A glance over the top of her head showed the scene was just as he'd left it—a small table taken from the drawing room flanked by two chairs, laid with cakes and sandwiches sheltering under net cloches to keep out the flies. He couldn't take the credit for the cakes—for that he'd have to thank Huntingham's cook—but the sandwiches were his own work and he felt an absurd twinge of pride as he tried for a nonchalant shrug.

'This morning, while you were getting dressed. It

takes an age for a lady to dress even with a maid helping her, so I hazarded a guess that without any servants
you'd take twice as long.'

'You guessed correctly. What a wonderful surprise.'

Moving towards the table, Emily touched the vase of
flowers set down in the middle of it, the petals stirring
beneath her fingers. Andrew had picked them himself,
and he was glad he'd bothered when he saw her face was
alight, that alone something for which he would happily
have gathered a whole field full of blooms.

There was quiet appreciation in it, her pleasure just
as genuine for a simple bunch of flowers as for the most
expensive gown, and it only confirmed his certainty that
he had made the right decision in his choice of bride.
When he'd had little money he'd had to grab any small
joys he could find, and Emily's smile as she picked up
one of the cloches to peep underneath told him she'd
been much the same.

'This was so kind of you. How do you know how to
do these things? First a tea tray, now this... How is it an
Earl is so well domesticated?'

It was a real question, asked with real interest, and
Andrew sighed internally as he readied himself.

'When I said I'd answer all your questions I hadn't
expected them to start the moment you found the middle
of the maze. Will you at least sit down first?'

He pulled out one of the chairs and Emily sat obligingly, although the interest in her eyes didn't dim for so
much as a second. They roamed over the array of deli-
cacies in front of her and, although Andrew's shoulders
seemed to have tensed, he still enjoyed the puzzlement
mixed with her curiosity.

Her reaction was understandable. Not many men would know how to make a luncheon, and still fewer Earls, and as he took his own seat he wondered where to begin.

'You wanted to know about my life before I came back to Warwickshire. In part that explains why I know one end of a kitchen from the other.'

She leaned forward eagerly. 'I do want to know. I'd like to hear as much as you're willing to tell me.'

To buy himself a few extra seconds Andrew passed her a plate. On his own he arranged a few sandwiches and a generous slice of honey cake, although he seemed to have left his appetite back at the Hall. Emily took a carraway bun but he could tell her full attention was fixed on him, waiting with polite impatience for him to start.

'You remember my Uncle Ephraim.'

'I certainly do.'

'Of course. I suppose there's little chance you'd forget him.' Andrew raised a sardonic brow, wishing he hadn't started so clumsily. 'He was my father's older brother.'

At Emily's encouraging nod he went on, more hesitantly than he liked, but her unspoken reassurance drew him out almost against his will. 'My father was intended as his heir and so, beginning when they were just children, my uncle determined to wield as much control over him as possible. For the most part it worked. A younger son has little money of his own, and by withholding it Uncle Ephraim was able to keep my father in line…or, at least, until he met my mother.'

He paused to make himself take a bite of honey cake. Emily nibbled at the carraway bun, but he could tell she

174 *A Marriage to Shock Society*

barely tasted it, too focused on him to be distracted by anything else.

'What happened when he met her?'

'My uncle tried to forbid the match. My mother was respectable, you see, but had no fortune, and that wasn't good enough for my uncle. My father, however, was determined, and no matter the objections he was set on making her his wife. Ephraim was furious. But, in the absence of anyone else to proclaim as his heir, there was nothing he could do, aside from being as unkind to her as possible, in the hope of driving her away. As my existence suggests, his attempts didn't work.'

He laughed shortly, but there was no real humour in it. What came next was his least favourite part. It was only Emily's intent gaze that made him inclined to tell it—not a secret, but still something he would rather not have voiced.

'When I was five years old my father died,' he pushed on, trying not to be swayed by her immediate murmur of sympathy. 'Of course, there was no chance of Uncle Ephraim stepping in to help my mother in her grief. He was content to leave us almost penniless and alone, my mother not having any family left after the death of her parents before I was even born. My uncle named me his heir, but that was as far as his interest in me went until I was a little older, when he began to think of trying to mould me in his image just as he had my father many years before.'

Emily shook her head, her eyes holding a world of compassion. There was still vivid interest, but pity outstripped anything else, the kind that from anyone else would have made his hackles raise; but his wife's was somehow much more appreciated.

'What happened after your uncle cut you and your mother off? Where did you go?'

'Up to Derbyshire. Houses were cheaper there and the little bit of money my mother could scrape together would stretch further.'

He sat back in his chair, briefly studying the clouds overhead. Aside from a couple of wisps the sky was clear, reaching out into the distance in a blue so bright it hurt his eyes, and he thought back to the times he'd gazed up at it as a child and wished things were different.

'My upbringing wasn't exactly what you'd expect for a boy in line for an earldom. My mother was able to somehow find the money to fund my education, but not for much else. We had no servants or any of the luxuries of the *ton*, even though by rights she was still Lady Gouldsmith…which is how I came to learn proper use of a kitchen.'

There was a pinch between Emily's sandy eyebrows. 'But… I don't understand. Without your uncle's assistance, how did you survive?'

'The same way as everyone else.'

A lone butterfly alighted on the vase and Andrew watched it daintily sip from one of the flowers, its tiny tongue like a straw. 'As soon as I was old enough, I found work. Tutoring, mostly, for local families that liked the idea of their sons being educated by a gentleman. It brought in enough money for us to live, although by that time I was a lost cause as regards to behaving like a proper Earl-to-be—much to the aggravation of my uncle, who you could argue bore the blame for it.'

He managed a smile. Not a particularly convincing one but the best he could do, although Emily didn't see it. She too was looking at the butterfly, but he had the impression she wasn't really taking it in, no doubt too busy unravelling his story.

'So that's what you meant. When we first met you said we had more in common than I might have assumed.'

'Just so. I believed—still believe—we're of a similar kind. We both know what it's like to struggle, to feel we don't fit in, and that was far more important in my choice of wife than money. There are some things it can't buy.'

For a moment she was quiet. Birds called among the hedges and a gentle breeze played with the hedges' leaves, but Emily didn't speak, whatever she was thinking hidden behind veiled eyes until at last she turned them on him.

'Thank you for telling me that. I understand it probably wasn't enjoyable.'

She looked at him with such tender understanding that anything else he might have intended to say was instantly forgotten, wiped away by the sweet empathy he hadn't known he'd craved. For years he'd balked at dwelling too long in the past, but she had a way of making him feel seen, perhaps briefly even glad he'd finally laid himself bare—but then she went on.

'We're alike in another way you're too kind to mention, however. We both had to grow up without our fathers, albeit for very different reasons, and I believe that too makes us more similar than an outsider looking in might first imagine.'

Andrew felt his stomach contract.

Careful, now. This is what you knew was coming.

It was the turn he'd predicted the conversation would take even as he'd hoped it wouldn't. Sympathy still radiated from Emily so strongly it was almost tangible, and he knew her remark was based in concern for him that did her credit. She imagined they shared another mutual pain, and in some ways she was right; although unbeknownst to her, *her* pain was only just beginning, whereas time had dulled the worst of his own.

'I meant what I said before.' He began carefully, feeling his way like someone walking on cracked ice. 'It's possible to overcome that loss. The ache will never quite go away, but you can soothe it in other ways and with other things.'

The faint crease reappeared between her brows. 'I understand that, although… Forgive me. I would never want to compare our situations or be insensitive to your very real loss, but I still have hope that I'll find him. Until I've exhausted every avenue I won't give up.'

She picked up the bun that had lain almost untouched on her plate and Andrew watched with growing unease as she brought it to her mouth.

He was going to have to be more obvious if he intended to make his point. Clearly she hadn't taken his veiled meaning, and he would have given anything not to press harder, only the desire to make her see sense insisting he go on.

'Even if there's a chance it won't bring you the happiness you expect?'

Emily hesitated, a carraway seed held daintily between finger and thumb. 'What do you mean?'

'Just as I say. The very last thing I want is for you to

be hurt, either by your father or by building your expectations of him too high.'

The sapphire brightness of her eyes dimmed into confusion, but he couldn't let himself halt the charge. It was a conversation he'd been dreading, but now it was upon him he had to see it through whether he wanted to or not.

'Have you considered there might be a possibility, however small, that he wouldn't want to see you?'

The delight when she'd realised she'd solved the maze, her appreciation of his efforts to lay the table, her powerful compassion when he'd told her of his past unhappiness—every trace of those emotions vanished as she sat in front of him, hurt clouding where once she'd worn a smile he'd never wanted to forget. His aim had been to spare her upset, but looking at her now he knew he had only caused more and internally he cursed himself for his blunder, his attempts to help somehow managing to make things worse.

'He cares for me. I know he does.' Emily spoke quietly, although nobody could have missed her conviction. 'He wouldn't have paid for my schooling if he didn't. For some reason he was unable to keep me with him, and so he tried to do the next best thing, even if placing me with the Laycocks turned out to have been a mistake.'

'Emily—'

She cut him off with a single shake of her head and Andrew found he didn't have the heart to overrule her. She had such strength in her beliefs that it would have seemed cruel if he'd carried on trying to squash them, and yet he became aware of a growing ache in his chest as she sat stiffly in her chair, all her prior openness snapping shut like the jaws of a hunter's trap.

'I understand what you're saying, and I appreciate your concerns, but I'm certain I'm right. If I can find him I will, and I truly believe he'll be glad I did.'

The urgent desire to reach out for her gripped him, to take hold of her hand and press a kiss on the soft palm, but he knew it was too late. She was standing up and good manners dragged him to his feet likewise, although he wanted to catch her in his arms rather than bow with unhappy civility as she began to move away.

'Thank you for this morning, and all the effort you went to arranging luncheon. If you'll excuse me, however, I think I'll return to the house.'

'Of course.' He took a step towards her, one hand outstretched. 'Shall I escort you?'

The hurt in her eyes cut through him as she shook her head, subtly moving back out of his reach. She was trying to hide it, as always so attuned to the feelings of others, but he knew her too well to be blind to her pain, and the knowledge that he had caused it was a punishment like no other, only able to watch as she began walking away.

'No, no. Please, do finish eating. I'm sure I can find the way back by myself.'

Chapter Ten

The music and laughter were far too loud but Andrew forced himself to keep up a polite smile as he moved through Admiral Strentham's ballroom, nodding whenever an acquaintance caught his eye, although it was Emily he was looking for among the glittering hordes. She'd disappeared soon after they had arrived and he knew she was avoiding him, an air of awkwardness hanging over them since his ham-fisted efforts to talk to her three days before.

He hadn't particularly wanted to come out this evening, much preferring to have stayed at home, attempting to cajole his wife into speaking to him without keeping her eyes trained on the ground. But the Admiral's invitation had been of many months' standing, and in the end he'd been left with little choice but to staple on a smile and hope Emily would spare him a friendly glance.

Not that he felt he deserved one, he acknowledged

gloomily, bowing as Lady Fortescue and her daughter glided by. His attempt to talk sense to her had failed miserably and he could tell he'd cut close to the bone. It was little wonder she didn't seem to want to be in the same room as him. There had been no repeat of the heady passion of their wedding night and it was a torture to lie beside her at night, unable to touch her while memories of doing just that ran riot through his sleepless mind. He needed to apologise and he needed to do it soon... although the fact he still believed in what he'd said made an apology somewhat more complicated.

It was *how* he'd said it that he ought to beg pardon for, he thought, vaguely aware of being approached by a couple of gentlemen he recognised from his club. He'd hurt her feelings, and for that he reproached himself, but surely the message itself had been sound? His intention had been to save her from future pain, if he could, and if that meant upsetting her *now* perhaps that was the price that must be paid, although it was not an idea he liked and he realised he was frowning as the gentlemen now in front of him each offered an unsteady bow.

The two men straightened up and Andrew made sure to keep his face carefully blank. Neither was someone he would have sought out given the choice. He'd first met them years ago, on one of his ill-fated visits to Ephraim, and the condescending manner in which they had addressed him when he'd had little money still rankled now he had more than both of them put together. Standing with them was a waste of time he could have been using to look for Emily, but he had to exchange at least a few words, even if only to prove the impoverished upbringing that had once amused them hadn't left him with equally poor manners.

'Good evening, Sir Reginald, Mr Lewis.'

He managed to sound civil, or at least enough for Mr Lewis to clap him—with a touch too much familiarity—on the shoulder.

'Breamore. We've come to congratulate you, sir. On your very recent, very swift marriage.'

Sir Reginald nodded in agreement, his colour just as high as his associate's. The ruddy cheeks were those of a man who had already drunk a fair amount and probably intended more, no doubt accounting for the unexpected friendliness.

'Swift indeed,' the slightly swaying knight hiccupped. 'Not to say I'd have waited either. The new Countess is a very beautiful woman.'

'Yes. Easily the handsomest in the room, or perhaps even the neighbourhood. Small wonder you were in such a rush.'

The two men chuckled and Andrew felt himself bristle. Emily wouldn't enjoy being spoken of with such libidinous undertones, and he didn't appreciate it either, his protective instincts coming immediately to the fore.

'She is without question handsome, yes.' He tried to keep the dislike from his voice, although probably his unwanted companions were too deep in drink to notice either way. 'But she is also clever and kind. Fond of music, skilled in the pianoforte and well educated. There are many aspects to Lady Breamore than just a comely face, and I consider myself extremely fortunate to have found her.'

Mr Lewis peered up at him dully. 'Well...quite.'

He didn't sound entirely certain. Clearly in his view such virtues in a wife were less important than having a pretty face, and he seemed to forget all about them as soon as Andrew finished speaking, leaning forward again with intoxicated sincerity.

'But her hair, Breamore. That striking coppery gold. I was saying to Reginald that it reminds me of someone.'

Sir Reginald nodded so hard his watch danced on its chain. 'Yes, although we just can't place it. Has the Countess family hereabouts that we would be acquainted with? Nobody seems to know anything about her. It's as if she appeared out of thin air.'

Hidden by the high collar of his shirt, the muscles of Andrew's jaw tautened.

It had only been a matter of time before someone asked outright about her background. He owed the two overly intimate men nothing—nothing about Emily was any of their business, he thought coolly—but he knew the *ton* too well to think Lewis and Reginald were the only ones who had been wondering, drunk enough now to raise the subject that must have been on countless lips. Whatever he replied would spread like wildfire, passing from one ballroom gossip to another until every Society family had heard whatever answer he gave, and it occurred to him that his mother had been right.

She said ages ago I'd need to guard Emily against the ton if they came sniffing for answers. At least this way I can try to influence what they believe.

Affecting to consider for a moment, Andrew beckoned them closer.

'I'd only tell you gentlemen this on account of your

attentions to me when I was a child. You remember, I think, when I used to come to visit my uncle?'

'Oh, yes. We always thought you such a promising young man.'

Either Sir Reginald had forgotten how scathing he had been about a shy boy's ill-fitting coat, or he imagined he was being cunning, but his falseness didn't make Andrew hesitate. The two men could be of use to Emily if he could just strike the right note, and he even went so far as to lay a friendly hand on Mr Lewis's back, drawing him closer against the ballroom's noise.

'I'll tell you this in confidence, then,' he murmured, glancing around as if worried about being overheard. 'My wife has no family to speak of. She lost her parents when she was very young and was instead raised in a genteel establishment by respectable guardians, the best, naturally, but of course not quite the same as family. She doesn't speak of it, for fear of seeming proud, but you can tell her quality just by looking—as I'm sure you've noticed.'

He was almost amused by Sir Reginald's immediate nod, accepting the fudged version of events without question. It wasn't a lie; she *had* been raised by respectable people in a school with the potential to be called genteel, although 'the best' might be stating the case a little too strongly. She had indeed lost her parents, however, one in death and the other through his choice to abandon his illegitimate child, and there was some satisfaction in hearing Emily praised now by the very same people who would have scorned her if they had known that truth.

Attempting earnest concern, Andrew looked from one inebriated gentleman to the other. 'That will remain strictly between us, I trust? My wife is a very private person. She wouldn't want to think she was being spoken of.'

Mr Lewis held a finger up to his lips. 'On our honour. We won't tell a soul.'

That was precisely what Andrew had wanted to hear. There was no way they would hold their tongues, and such an outrageous lie only proved it. By the time the Admiral's ball was over everyone would know the amended account of Emily's background but would be loath to mention it to her, and her acceptance by the *ton* would have become assured with no real effort at all.

'Thank you, gentlemen. I knew I could rely on you to keep your counsel.'

He bowed, moving away before they could rise from their own unsteady stoops. Talking of Emily made him want to find her all the more, and he redoubled his search, scanning the crowds but still catching no glimpse of her crown of autumnal curls. She should have been easy to spot and yet there was no sign of her, and his unease was just beginning to build when a voice from behind sent something skittering down his spine.

'Are you looking for someone?'

He turned, knowing there was only one person who could make the hair on his nape stand up with just five words.

'Not any longer.'

Emily stood at his elbow, a vision in ivory crape that fell around her like an angel's folded wings. Her hair was threaded with pearls and they gleamed when she moved, which was almost constantly, her head turning this way and that as if she'd rather look anywhere than directly at him. Part of him was simply glad to see her, relieved she hadn't slipped away while his back was turned, but a larger part cursed himself for having made her now so clearly ill at ease.

'I thought I hadn't seen you in some time. Where have you been hiding?'

'I wasn't hiding.' She looked down at her hands, carefully adjusting the silk fingers of her gloves. 'Your mother wanted to introduce me to some old acquaintances of hers. I've been speaking to them this past hour, until it was suggested I might want to return to you.'

She seemed on the brink of shooting him a glance, perhaps a swift flash of blue from beneath lowered lashes, but then she switched her attention to the dancers taking the floor and Andrew's stomach clenched.

He had to act. On their wedding day he could have sworn she'd felt something for him, some emotion mirrored by his own heart, and when she'd lain beside him in the midnight heat of his bed he had known for sure. There was a connection there worth saving, worth tending like a sapling that might one day become a solid oak, and unless he found a way to make things right he might have ruined his marriage before it had truly begun.

The band had struck up again, accompanying a rousing quadrille, and under the pretence of making sure she could hear him he moved a cautious pace closer.

'Perhaps you weren't hiding, then—but you *have* been avoiding me.'

Emily kept her gaze trained on the dancers, but the edge of her cheek flushed a dangerously pretty pink. 'That's not the word I would use.'

'Is it not? When every time I've entered a room you've

left it, and we've barely exchanged ten words since you
left the maze?'

He saw the line of her jaw tighten and knew instinctively what she was thinking. Her mind had scrolled
back to the same moment as his, that of three days before, when she had excused herself with unhappy courtesy, disappearing among the hedges before he could say
anything more to sour the dream she'd cherished since
she was a girl. Watching her hurry away had brought an
anchor down over his heart and he could see she wanted
to do the same again now, only his hand on her arm stopping her from fleeing all over again.

'If you were avoiding me, it's my fault.'

His chest tightened as she looked down at his hand
but she didn't shake him off. She allowed him to keep it
there, the first real contact they'd had in days, even that
chaste touch coming as a relief.

'I realised as soon as I opened my mouth that I'd hurt
you,' he continued, revelling in the warmth of her bare
arm through the palm of his glove, 'and I wanted so much
to tell you I'm sorry. Please believe that was never my
intention. I'd meant to express concern, but—'

'Not here.'

At last she turned, and his pulse leapt to finally feel
her eyes on him. 'I would like to listen to you, but not
now. Not while we could be so easily overheard.'

She studied him for a moment, her cheekbones lit
by that ready blush, and he was powerless but to agree.

'Of course. Whenever you'd prefer.'

The ballroom was still hot and noisy, but that didn't
seem to matter as much as it had only a few minutes before. He had apologised, or at least begun to, and Emily

had stayed to hear him out, and although she had resumed watching the dancers she seemed to have drawn a fraction closer to his side, making no attempt to move away even when he released her from his gentle grasp.

For a few steps they observed the couples without speaking. Emily seemed absorbed in the music and Andrew was content to bask in the pleasure of having her close to him, until she raised her voice above the scrape of violins.

'Do you dance? I've never asked.'

'I've been known to. Do you?'

'Whenever I can. I love music, as you know, although Miss Laycock would frown if we ever used it for something so trifling as enjoyment.'

Andrew nodded, a picture of her dancing springing forth immediately. It was something he'd like to experience for real rather than just imagining. She'd be graceful, her shoulders back and chin perfectly parallel with the ground, the skipping and twirling showing the supple lines of her figure to their very best advantage. It would be a sight to make every man in the room stare, himself among them, and he was only sorry it seemed unlikely he'd get the chance to see it.

'Did you intend to dance this evening?'

Emily hesitated. 'I would have liked to, but I think not. The only man I'd care to stand up with is you, but I understand that among the *ton* partnering with one's own husband is not the done thing.'

She didn't look up at him, which was probably for the best. His lips itched to curve upwards at being dubbed *the only man* and he thought it unwise to let her see, his position in her good graces still too precarious for comfort.

Perhaps I haven't chased her away after all.

The first glimmerings of an idea sparked at the back of his mind.

If Emily wanted to dance, but was too shy to partner with anyone else…

He glanced around. Nobody seemed to be watching them, and still concealing the beginnings of a smile he dipped his head closer to his wife's alluringly delicate ear.

'It's true the *ton* has their way of doing things. It's fortunate for us, then, that neither of us truly considers ourselves of their number.'

He felt her shiver, perhaps from the soft warmth of his breath on her neck, and he had to pause briefly to bring himself back under control. When she stirred with instinctive pleasure like that it reminded him of their wedding night, his hands and mouth roaming wherever they had wanted to, and he had to remind himself that he still had some way to go before she was likely to grant such an honour again.

'Come with me. I think you'll like what I have in mind.'

Emily could feel her heart beating all the way down to her silk dancing shoes as she followed Andrew through the crowds, still with no idea of where he was taking her. All she knew was that he had said to go with him, and she'd been quick to agree, being near him again a relief after the days of distant unhappiness since she'd hurried away from him in the maze.

At first it had seemed things were coming together, falling into place with an ease she'd realised afterwards she shouldn't have accepted so readily. He had finally opened up to her, telling her about his childhood and filling in the gaps she had wondered at since the first day they'd met, and the trouble he'd gone to with the table and flowers had touched her already receptive heart.

Armed with the knowledge he had been raised in genteel poverty—even forced into employment akin to that she had so narrowly escaped herself—she had made the mistake of thinking he had been right. Perhaps there were more similarities between them than she'd believed, the chasm between his world and hers maybe not so insurmountable after all…but then it had all fallen apart.

Clusters of well-dressed ladies and equally well-oiled gentlemen filled the room, curious stares tracking her progress among them, but Andrew didn't falter in his purposeful stride. He seemed to be heading towards the back of the ballroom. A set of tall double doors were propped open, leading out into the night beyond, and Emily made sure not to lag behind as he led her to them, her already thudding heart making an extra hard thump when he glanced over his shoulder to make sure she was still close by.

'Out here. The terrace.'

With the smallest trace of a smile he plunged into the darkness, his smart navy coat disappearing into the gloom. None of the revellers cluttering the doorway seemed sober enough to have noticed him leave, and so Emily followed suit, slipping between the curtains and taking a deep breath of cool air as she stepped onto the patio beyond.

Andrew was waiting for her a few paces from the door, a tall figure bleached by the moonlight. The terrace was empty apart from the two of them, and it was something of a surprise to find herself suddenly alone with him after the jostling clamour inside—although not an unpleasant one.

'This is better. It was suffocating in there.'

'Yes. Too loud to think clearly as well.'

The relentless babble of voices was indeed quieter, but the ability to think clearly was still slightly out of reach. Andrew's dark gaze was to blame for that. Fixed on her face, his eyes were two obsidian pools, almost the same midnight black as the sky stretching out overhead, and she wasn't sure whether it was his unwavering attention or the autumnal breeze that raised goosebumps on her skin. It was the same involuntary reaction to his presence she'd felt on their wedding night, and she tried not to let herself stray back to it, some last vestiges of what had occurred the day after still lingering.

He hadn't *meant* to hurt her, of that she was sure. There was some truth to his accusation she'd been avoiding him, but it hadn't been from pettiness or injured pride that she'd kept herself apart. Deep in the very darkest depths of her soul she held a fear, a secret worry that had haunted her since she was a little girl, and without knowing it Andrew had reached inside her and dragged it out into the light.

There's a chance my father might not want to know me. Something I never dared admit to anyone, not least myself.

It had been too painful to spend much time with him after he'd unwittingly voiced her worst nightmare, she thought now, watching the moonlight play across his sculpted face. Shame had overcome her: the mortification that he too imagined she might be rejected, unable to inspire any affection in her erstwhile papa—and perhaps, by extension, himself?

If Andrew doubted she could capture her father's heart, then wasn't there a chance he thought her incapable of securing *anyone's*, the growing feelings he inspired in her therefore unlikely to be returned? Because her feelings *were* growing and she couldn't deny it, widening and lengthening until soon they would encompass her entirely, and if it transpired that he thought her somehow unfit to be loved then her misery would be complete.

But she couldn't tell him that. To reveal the inner workings of her heart when she couldn't be sure how such a thing would be received was out of the question, and she rubbed her arms as she tried instead to turn her mind to more practical things.

'Why are we out here? If the ballroom was too warm, I fear this terrace isn't warm enough.'

In a puzzling reply, Andrew cupped a hand to his ear. 'Do you hear that?'

Emily stood very still. What was she supposed to be listening for? The night-time breeze whispered around her and a hum of voices came from the other side of the open terrace doors, but aside from that she could make out nothing but the merry din of the band.

'All I can hear is the music from inside.'

'Exactly.'

With an impressive flourish Andrew bowed, holding out his hand as he rose. 'You said you wanted to dance. Here on the terrace there's nobody to frown at us—if you'll do me the honour?'

Surprised, Emily looked from the outstretched hand

to his face, a slow warmth spreading through her at what she saw there. His countenance was in shadow now, whatever expression was on it hidden by the moon dipping behind a cloud, but even in the darkness there could be no disguising the intensity of his eyes. They watched her without wavering, and she was certain she saw relief when she placed her fingers into his palm.

At once he drew her to him, his arms around her as she'd longed for even during the self-imposed exile she'd thought so necessary. The band were playing a waltz, a new dance considered somewhat risqué given how closely the partners were required to twine together, and she had never been gladder to hear the soar of a cello that allowed her to sway in Andrew's hold.

One of his hands was on her back, pressing them almost chest to chest as they began to move in a smooth rise and fall. He stepped in perfect time with the music, surprisingly light-footed despite his height, but Emily barely had any attention to spare for something so irrelevant. Her hand was on his shoulder and she could feel the muscle beneath his coat, a constant undulation that lit sparks in her blood, and when his thumb moved in the tiniest caress, scant inches from her waist, she thought she might see stars.

They travelled and turned, the terrace their own private dance floor away from prying eyes. Andrew kept watch over her head in case they should be disturbed, but that didn't stop him from looking down at her every other step, the heat building low in her gut flaming higher when he pierced her with the smile she saw even in her dreams.

'Will this do?'

Her own lips had lifted without her even realising. 'It will indeed. I had no idea you were so graceful.'

'I can take little credit. A man can only move well if he has a good partner.'

He revolved them skilfully, Emily's heart slamming into her ribs when his leg brushed lightly against her skirts. She should have kept her chin elegantly raised, but somehow it insisted on dropping closer to his chest, her head almost resting against it as his hand on her back encouraged her ever nearer. In truth she would have been happy to stay like that for ever, cradled in his strong embrace with no one to whisper or stare, the unfortunate conversation that day in the maze fading into the background as Andrew's palm burned through her gown. He had tried to make amends and she knew it was genuine— but it seemed he had more to say, her nerves tingling as he spoke into her ear.

'Now that we won't be overheard… I truly am sorry for the misunderstanding between us. Causing you pain was never my intention.'

She lifted her head to peer up at him, the tingling growing more intense as she realised just how close she was to his mouth.

'I know that. I know you would never purposefully hurt me or anybody else.'

Almost imperceptibly she felt him relax, his shoulders dropping the smallest degree. She hadn't realised quite how tense he had been, and she wondered that her acceptance of his apology had been the key to his release, touched that he should care so deeply. Perhaps her good opinion was more important to him than she had assumed, a thought that made her glow warm, although something still stood in the way of the harmony she so earnestly wanted.

He didn't altogether agree with her quest to find her father. That much had been made clear, and it seemed unlikely they would come to terms that suited them both. While she understood his perspective, he didn't appear to comprehend hers, but if they were to move on he would have to meet her halfway.

Still looking up at him she tried to think how to explain, the knowledge that she was easily within reach of kissing him making it much more difficult.

'I know you meant to warn me, but still believe he'll be glad I found him. I *have to* believe that. Do you see?'

She could tell by his face that he didn't. His jaw had tightened again, his brows on the verge of drawing together, and she went on quickly before he could reply.

'You grew up knowing that you were loved. I did not. The only thing that kept me going through my loneliness was the idea of one day meeting my father, the one person in all the world I was convinced might care for me, and I clung to that hope throughout everything. At one time that belief was all I had and I can't abandon it now I'm so close to the end. Do you understand?'

Her words came in a rush, half to get them out without being interrupted and half because Andrew's hand was drifting lower. He cupped the small of her back and she realised she was tilting her body against his, the space between them now far narrower than was strictly polite, but apparently neither of them inclined to mind.

'I'm trying to.' Andrew's voice was delightfully low against her earlobe, more vibration than sound. 'If it's important to you then it's important to me, even if I don't fully follow your reasoning.'

He gazed down at her with such frank honesty she felt her cheeks kindle, only realising when he settled both hands on her waist that they had stopped moving. The music had finished and she hadn't even noticed, too bound up in his sweet words and even sweeter grip to care about anything else, and when he lightly brushed his thumbs over her lower ribs she almost crumpled to the paved ground.

In the moonlight he was handsomer than ever. His eyes held hers and it wasn't in her power to look away, black locked onto blue in a connection that awakened every nerve. 'But he isn't the only one who could care for you. Just so you know. There's someone else who thinks very highly of you indeed, and he isn't very far away.'

With heart-stopping gentleness he brought her towards him, encouraging her closer until the thin crape of her bodice was pressed to his shirt. Without thinking her hands went to his shoulders, sliding together so she could lace her fingers together behind his neck, and the touch of his lips was worth every moment of the unhappiness she'd felt for the past three days.

It wasn't a kiss to set fire to the air around them, as on their wedding night. This was slower, softer, holding a different kind of passion from before, but no less powerful for its quietness. When they first wed there had been urgency, finally able to act on the desire that had overwhelmed them both, but now there was something more in the unhurried meeting of their lips, and in the tiny part of her not yet given over to bliss, Emily knew Andrew felt it too.

There was a deeper meaning to the way he kissed her now, the terrace and the noise of the ball beyond it paling into insignificance with the movement of his mouth. He had admitted he cared for her and, with every ragged breath, Emily told him the same thing in reply—and if a shadow from the doorway hadn't fallen over them, she thought she might just have uttered three words that would surely have changed their marriage for ever.

'Breamore? Is that you?'

Leaning away from her Andrew uttered a curse, although he didn't surrender her completely as a man weaved his way towards them, evidently a little worse for wear. For her part Emily could hardly see, her head swimming with pleasure and the honey-sweetness of Andrew's confession, and she knew her curtsey was somewhat unsteady when Mr Lewis offered her an equally untidy bow.

'Good evening, my lady. The Admiral sent me to find you. He wants to toast you as our neighbourhood's new first lady. Shall I tell him you'll come in?'

Even in the darkness she could see his smirk. She had a horrible suspicion he had just seen more than he ought to, although the sensation of Andrew's hand sitting unseen on the base of her spine gave her the courage to lift her chin.

'You may. I shall be along directly.'

Her determined dignity seemed to do the trick. Mr Lewis's grin faded and he bowed more respectfully, staggering back to the doors and vanishing with only a faint scent of port left behind.

Immediately she turned to her husband. 'Do you think he saw us?'

Andrew shrugged. His hand traced circles against her now, tempting her to shudder with feral enjoyment that had no place at a respectable ball. His eyes were on the door Mr Lewis had just disappeared through, but when he bent to murmur into her ear Emily knew all his attention—and more—was fixed on her.

'To be honest, I don't much care if he did. Shall we go in? The sooner they toast you, the sooner we can leave—and I think we have more making up to do.'

Chapter Eleven

The days turned into weeks, the changing colour of the leaves on the Huntingham estate keeping track of how much time had passed since Emily had taken up residence. As autumn wore on she found herself feeling more and more at home in her new role as Countess, much to her surprise, although her growing contentment brought problems of its own.

Every day her feelings for her husband grew a little deeper while, with aggravating irony, her reluctance to tell him so developed at much the same rate.

Quite when she had fallen in love with him she wasn't sure, she thought as she examined the milliner's window display, noting the pallor of her reflection in the glass. It had happened so gradually that she'd mistaken it first for mere attraction until finally realising—once it was far too late—that there was no way back. With every kind word and thoughtful gesture Andrew had won her heart, now so firmly his it seemed impossible she would ever be free, and the knowledge frightened her right through to her core.

There was a particularly interesting bonnet in the window and she pretended to study it as she tried to quiet the tumultuous voices of various trains of thought all vying for her attention. Andrew had business with his lawyer in Leamington and she'd gone with him, thinking a stroll around the various boutiques would help distract her from the constant push and pull of her mind, but so far nothing had succeeded.

All she'd managed to do was wonder if he would prefer her in a pink gown she'd seen or the matching blue, whether he'd choose a white parasol or a cream to accompany her walking dress—and what he'd say if she confessed that she loved him, a conversation she'd rehearsed in her head so many times she could imagine it word for word.

Andrew, I have something to tell you...

Andrew, I have something to say...

Belatedly she realised the milliner's assistant was watching her from the other side of the window. From the girl's expression it seemed she was worried Lady Breamore had lost her wits, and it dawned on Emily that staring vacantly into space without appearing to see what was before her was *not* proper conduct for a Countess. Hurriedly she moved away. Andrew took up so much of her consciousness now it seemed she couldn't escape even in window-shopping, although she knew that no matter how much she thought about it her situation remained the same.

She couldn't tell him. There was now too much at

stake. In a cruel paradox, the more she came to care for him the less she could admit it, her heart ripe to be broken if Andrew's response wasn't the one she longed for. He had affection for her and certainly desire, and since the Admiral's ball she had begun to suspect he might feel the same—but the risk was too great, baring her soul to him a step she couldn't undo. If it turned out she was wrong it would plunge them into awkwardness they might never overcome, the fact they had wed out of convenience seeming less crucial now but still not one she'd forgotten. It would be far safer to wait, biding her time until he spoke first, and until then she would just have to try harder to keep herself in check.

'Not, of course, that he makes it easy,' she muttered as she walked, reflecting that talking to oneself probably wasn't any more acceptable than slack-jawed gawking, but carrying on all the same. 'If there was ever someone more capable of making a woman fall in love I'm sure I don't want to meet him.'

Out of the corner of her eye she saw a man touch his hat to her and she responded with an automatic smile, followed just as automatically by the same thought as always. Precious few of the *ton* who now treated her with such civility would have behaved the same when she was plain Miss Townsend, unwanted semi-orphan with a made-up name, and for what felt like the thousandth time she scanned the street for any oddly familiar stranger, more from habit than any real hope.

She'd moved among Society for months, admired and respected wherever she went now that she bore Andrew's name, but the one person she wanted to meet still hadn't crossed her path. Either her father had fallen off the face of the earth or she'd been mistaken, perhaps blundering down the wrong path for almost the entirety of her life, and her disappointment weighed heavily on her spirits when combined with her uncertainty as to the secret workings of Andrew's heart.

Feeling somewhat under a dark cloud she checked her dainty gold watch, one of the gifts with which Andrew had filled her trousseau weeks before. He would be at least another hour at his lawyer's office and she hesitated, trying to decide what to do. There was a coffee house at the end of the street that smelled extremely enticing but she wasn't sure whether an Earl's wife was supposed to frequent such places, making a mental note to ask Eleanor next time she came to tea. In a way there were more restrictions on an upper-class lady than her lower counterpart, she mused, not for the first time, and she was just about to turn to wander slowly back the way she'd come when a loud noise from behind made her start.

A carriage had come bowling down the high street, moving far too quickly for a road with so many pedestrians, and the bellow of the coachman for people to stand aside sent Emily reeling back. The horses clattered past her at a tremendous pace, so close to the pavement that she could smell their sweat as they rushed by, and indignantly she looked up to see which gentleman thought himself so important that his haste was worth risking others' lives.

She only caught the most fleeting of glimpses as the carriage hurtled around the corner, a figure at the window little more than a pale blur—but even that fraction of a second, less than a single blink, was enough to steal every last ounce of her strength.

She stood rooted to the spot, staring after the carriage even after it disappeared from view. All around her other shoppers frowned and grumbled, irritated or startled by the coach's dangerous approach, but Emily barely heard them. Her heart was too loud and her breathing too fast, and when an urgent order came from her brain to her legs it took her a moment to force them into action.

The first step felt like she was wading through treacle, but when she hit her stride she found she was running, her skirts flying out behind her as she dashed for the corner. Heads turned to follow her, some mildly disapproving and others curious as to why a Countess might be moving so inelegantly fast, although she couldn't possibly slow down. There wasn't a second to waste—if she let the carriage get too far ahead she might lose it and the man inside, that single snatched peek at him sending a skewer through the very centre of her chest.

A coat of arms was painted below the window he had peered out of, the crest she *knew* she had seen a smudged version of before, although it was the man himself that had helped her make the connection. His hair was a striking copper-gold, still vibrant despite approaching middle age, and the sidelong shape of his nose was one she knew very well indeed. It reminded her of one she'd seen countless times before, able to look at it whenever she chose…

As long as she stood in front of a mirror.

Her lungs ached with each gasping breath of cool autumn air but she kept throwing herself forward, her slippered feet hardly touching the pavement. A respectable young lady didn't run, and the unfamiliar effort of it hurt her throat, a stitch burning into her side as she flung herself round the streetcorner, almost colliding with a couple walking the other way. A wheezed apology was all she could manage and she knew they'd turned to stare after her as she hurried away, the curls coming down beneath her bonnet the same colour as those of her quarry.

The street ahead was just as busy as the one she'd left and her stomach turned over when she saw the carriage caught behind another, brought almost to a standstill on the narrow road. The driver was straining up from his seat in an attempt to see what was causing the problem, and Emily fell back into the doorway of a butcher's shop as the coachman cast an aggravated eye behind him, his impatience at being forced to a crawl obvious indeed. What his passenger thought of the delay she had no way of knowing, although she was glad their predicament gave her the chance to catch her breath.

She closed her eyes, leaning against the closed door as she tried to wrest back control. Her heart was racing and, despite the cold wind, her forehead was damp beneath the lace edge of her cap. She'd acted on instinct, dragged along by a voice that wasn't her own, but now the first urgency had passed reality came trickling back like water on the brink of causing a flood.

Who is he? And why do I feel I know him, despite never having seen him before?

The answer was obvious; and yet she didn't dare acknowledge it, pressing her back against the door so hard she felt the handle bruise her spine. The possibility wouldn't be deterred, however, circling round again so there was no hope of ignoring it, and when she opened her eyes the gleaming black hulk of the carriage suddenly seemed one of the most spellbinding things she'd ever seen.

Tentatively she slipped from the doorway, cautiously following as the coach trundled slowly along. No matter how the fine pair of matched horses tossed their heads they couldn't move any quicker, and Emily had more than enough time to gain ground, twitching the brim of her bonnet lower as she tailed behind.

All her attention was on the window, or, more precisely, the scant gap between two almost fully drawn curtains where she had seen the occupant's face. There was no sign of him now and a sense of unease began to filter up through the layers of her excitement and shock, a vague apprehension that she had somehow made a mistake.

I need to see him again. I need to be sure.

The carriage in front had begun to speed up and Emily realised her stride was lengthening to keep pace. In desperation she looked around, hoping some serendipitous event might present itself, and at the very same moment her fervent prayers were met with a decided answer.

The impatient coachman shouted for a young lad selling fruit to mind out for the wheels—at which the curtains were pushed aside and a man appeared briefly behind the narrow slice of glass.

Emily's legs failed her.

She'd meant to keep after her prey no matter what, but the face at the window made following any further impossible. It was another fleeting thing, lasting no longer than the first, but the second blow to her windpipe convinced her beyond all doubt.

The coach was drawing away from her, gaining speed as it careened down the road, and she watched it go with eyes suddenly clouded by tears. The final detail she caught before she was blinded completely was the coat of arms painted proudly on the door, a distinctive image that imprinted itself into her mind as firmly and indelibly as a blacksmith's brand.

I wonder what Andrew will say when I tell him.

In a daze she turned to totter back to the high street, hardly aware of where she was placing her feet. Probably she made an interesting spectacle, with her hair half tumbled down and mud spattered on the back of her skirts, although that didn't seem to matter much now. There was only one thing on her mind and it brought a smile to her face, tears still beading her lashes but happiness bubbling up all the same, and at that moment seeing her husband was all she wanted.

I wonder what he will say when I tell him I've found my father at last.

Descending the steps of Lambeth & Sons Solicitors, Andrew looked around for Emily. She'd agreed to meet him at half past the hour but evidently some shop or other had delayed her, and he found himself pleased rather than annoyed that she was nowhere to be seen. It had taken all his powers of persuasion to convince her that his money was now hers to spend as she wished and it was a joy to see her quiet pleasure at a new pair of stockings or penny bouquet, inexpensive trifles that brought her as much delight as a new barouche would to many of the other ladies of his acquaintance.

In most other ways she was a natural Countess, elegant and dignified as if she'd been born into the title, but the disinterestedness he'd liked so much before they wed was still very much in evidence, and he supposed there was little chance it would change now.

Reaching the bustling street, he peered left and right, wondering from which direction she would appear. There was a fashionable dressmaker across the road that seemed a likely candidate for a distraction, as did a confectionary shop a little further down, and he was just weighing up whether he had time to slip inside for a twist of barley sugar—one of the only indulgences he'd been able to afford as a boy, and still secretly enjoyed even as a grown man—when a flicker of red cloak caught at the corner of his eye.

With the same leap of his heart that always accompanied any glimpse of his wife he turned towards her, ready to tease her for being late, but then his stomach dropped down to his boots.

His first thought, hot and raging, was that she'd been attacked. Her usually beautiful, piled-up hair streamed from beneath her bonnet as she stumbled towards him, somehow pulled loose from its pins, and her wide eyes glistened with unshed tears. One or two had already escaped to leave tracks down her flushed cheeks, and he blazed with the sudden need to know who had caused them, hardly aware that he was moving as he strode to meet her.

'Emily? What's happened? What's wrong?'

He took her hands, feeling at once that they were shaking as though she was gripped by a fever. She was pale aside from a crimson blotch over each cheekbone, and it crossed his mind that she might be about to faint, quickly drawing her to him to thread a steadying arm around her waist. Even the thrill of holding her against him couldn't replace his urgency to know who he needed to hunt down and thrash, his blood beginning to burn that someone had dared cause her distress, but his anger segued into confusion when she shook her head.

'Nothing's wrong. I think, finally, everything might be right.'

She peeped up at him from beneath the brim of her bonnet, her head resting against his shoulder, and his bewilderment climbed up another ten notches. The tears she'd been holding back were falling freely now, but she was smiling unrestrainedly, and the combination of opposing emotions were more than he could immediately understand.

'I see…'

Carefully, not unlike how a doctor might treat someone having recently sustained a blow to the head, he guided her away from the middle of the pavement, depositing her against Lambeth & Sons' railing. It was a busy afternoon and plenty of passers-by cast inquisitive glances at a crying woman and her brooding companion, although it seemed Andrew's expression was enough to prevent any of them from thinking to interfere.

'You need to sit down. Let me call for the carriage, then you can explain exactly what's going on.'

Giving her no time to argue he crossed to the roadside. His carriage waited a few shops away and he signalled the driver to come closer, returning to Emily's side when the horses began to move.

'Here. Let me help you.'

The carriage pulled up alongside and Andrew half lifted her into it, the perplexing fight between happiness and tears still waging its war on her face. She all but collapsed into her seat and he felt obliged to sit close beside her, always glad of an excuse to be near, but still at a loss as to her current state of mind.

When the carriage jerked forward, carrying them the first few yards towards home, he gently took her hand.

'So? What's happened to make you so…troubled?'

It wasn't quite the right word, but it was the best he could do. In truth he had no idea how else to describe her and it wasn't a surprise when she shook her head again, the loose splendour of her hair shifting over her shoulder as she moved.

'I'm not troubled. In fact, I don't think I'll ever feel troubled again.'

At his frown her smile widened. How she managed to look so beautiful with her eyes raw and skin mottled he didn't know, although the sight transported him abruptly back to the day he'd found her in the forest, on the first occasion he'd been privileged enough to see her unvarnished feelings. *Then* there had been no half-concealed joy in her face, only resignation and despair, and the memory of it would have driven him to take her in his arms if it hadn't been so obvious she had more to say.

'I couldn't wait to tell you but now I'm not sure I know how. I suppose the best way is to just come out with it, but…'

She looked down at her hands. One of them still lay in his keeping and, in spite of every other distraction, he felt a spark when she tightened her fingers around his, even the slightest touch enough to bring him under her control.

'I found him,' she murmured, her voice wavering with

suppressed emotion. 'As much as I've ever been of anything in my life, I'm certain I've found my father.'

There was a flash of hydrangea-blue as she glanced at
him, eager to see his reaction, but Andrew felt as though
he had been turned to stone.

'Your father?'

Emily's nod was so enthusiastic he might have feared
for her neck if he'd had any attention to spare. Instead
every fibre was consumed by sudden dread, and it was
all he could do not let his instant dismay come flood-
ing into his face.

She'd found him at last? Could it be true?

And if it was…how long would it be before she wished
she hadn't?

The carriage rattled over a bridge, the horses snort-
ing loudly as wood rang hollow beneath their hooves,
but nothing could divert his focus.

'When? Where?'

'In a carriage, speeding down the high street.' She
spoke more strongly now, allowing her elation to shine
through. 'I caught only the swiftest glimpse but I'm willing to wager everything I own that it was him.'

Emily leaned towards him, alight with hope that
plunged a knife into his heart. 'His hair was identical to
mine, both in colour and curl, and his nose might have
been my very own. He was exactly the right age and the
coat of arms painted on the door of his carriage was the
same I saw on my papers, the imprint left when his signet ring got covered in ink.'

With every word the gleam in her eye had grown
brighter, although it dimmed a fraction as she looked

up at him and he realised his countenance was at risk of betraying his concern.

'I can see you doubt me. If you had seen him yourself, however, I'm confident you would not.'

The faintest touch of disappointment blunted the edge of her joy, and inwardly Andrew cursed himself for causing it. He was caught on a tightrope, trapped between dampening her excitement or encouraging it, knowing that she would end up unhappy either way.

He had to do something, however. He couldn't sit idly by while she careened so close to the edge, and cautiously he squeezed her hand, hoping he could find the words that had been so elusive in the maze.

'It isn't that I doubt you. I just think one glance seems a fragile foundation to base your hopes on. The last thing I would want for you, above anything else, is to have the pain of finding them dashed.'

Her head came up, her faded smile coming once again to the fore.

'They won't be. I have every intention of seeing him again to make doubly sure.'

'How do you intend to do that?'

'The coat of arms wasn't smudged this time. I saw it clearly. Two lions, two swans and a set of crossed swords, quartered on a background of yellow and red. Do you know it?'

Eagerly she watched him, not noticing when the carriage hit a bump that made the whole thing bounce on its axis. Nothing was of interest to her except following the thread of discovery, and he saw there was no hope of escape, drawn into her quest whether he liked it or not.

'Yes. I know it. As a boy I was very interested in heraldry. Every crest I ever saw I committed to memory, although I never dreamed such useless knowledge would one day have value.'

He tried to smile, attempting to muster something that might mirror the glow on her face, but his mouth didn't want to oblige.

Of its own volition his mind spun back over twenty years, clicking to a halt on some rainy day he could only half recall. The thing he remembered clearly was gazing up at a coat of arms affixed to the tack of an enormous horse, which blew and stamped as Papa spoke to the rider seated high up on its back. The man's face was lost to the mists of time, but the shield-shaped plate was as clear as ever, swimming in front of him now as if he'd seen it mere hours before.

'That particular coat of arms belongs to an old and noble family. The current bearer left to live abroad many years ago but it seems he must have returned.'

Emily nodded jerkily, appearing to be holding her breath. 'And his name...? What is his name?'

A creeping coldness spread through him as if he'd swallowed a bellyful of ice. Once he gave her that final piece of the puzzle there would be nothing standing between her and having her dreams ground into dust. It was the key that would allow her to unlock the truth and he had no choice but to give it to her, knowing with crystal certainty that she wouldn't rest until he did. Everything in him recoiled from it, wanting to turn away—but her eyes were too wide and full of anticipation, and they made it impossible for him to disobey.

'Lord Wagstaff. Lord Cedric Raleigh Wagstaff.'

Her slender hand, which he had no intention of letting

go of, trembled against his palm. Her shoulders slumped and for one alarming moment he feared she would slide off her seat, all strength seeming to leave her as her lips parted in a breathless gasp.

'Lord Wagstaff? That's his name?'

Andrew nodded, the tendons in his neck hard as iron bars. 'Yes. He has a small estate just outside Warwick. I'd heard his father died just before Uncle Ephraim did. He must have returned to take whatever inheritance was left to him if you saw him in town.'

Falteringly Emily loosened the fastening of her cloak, giving him a glimpse of opaline throat. In the dip between her collarbones he could see her pulse fluttering in much the same way it did when he kissed her by candlelight, although now wasn't the moment to revisit such infinitely more agreeable times.

Her hair was still half loose around her shoulders and carefully she gathered it to one side of her neck, her hand quaking all the while. She appeared to be trying to compose herself and Andrew waited, the deep thud of a warning drum loud in his ears.

At last she took a shuddering breath, exhaling slowly. 'I've learned at least *some* caution. I won't appear on his doorstep uninvited as I did with yours. But how can I bring about a meeting? There must be some way for us to be introduced…'

Her fair brows twitched together. In the sunlight streaming through the carriage windows they were almost translucent, but he still saw how they shot up when she was struck by an idea.

'Lady Merton's garden party! It's Saturday next. Do you think Lord Wagstaff will have been invited?'

'Perhaps. I couldn't say.'

'I think he must. Such an important figure in Society is sure to be included.'

She gripped his hand harder, so sweetly delighted he was tempted to lift her fingers to his lips, despite his mouth feeling too stiff to deliver anything close to a kiss.

'I can scarce believe it. After all this time...'

Her free hand was pressed to her bodice, doubtless to steady the wild leaping of her heart. It must have been flinging itself about like a bird in a cage, although when she turned in her seat to properly study his face she seemed to have seized back at least some control.

'You *are* pleased...? You don't seem it.'

'I am. Of course I am.'

The lie lay heavy on his tongue. It was bitter, more like a mouthful of bile than words, and he had to force himself not to grimace as it fell from his lips. 'If you're delighted, I'm sure I am too. Your happiness means more to me than anything else.'

That at least was true, he thought as he watched Emily's smile regain all its previous strength. Her happiness *was* the most important thing to him, growing in significance over the weeks and months until he could think of nothing that concerned him more. From his first sight of her in Huntingham Hall's parlour in her shabby dress and downcast face she had intrigued him, a fellow adventurer looking for a place to belong, and somewhere along the way from would-be governess to Countess he had fallen in love with her.

She leaned against him, gazing out of the window with that lovely curve still shaping her lips, and he slid his arm around her, a lump rising in his throat as she nestled closer. She trusted him now, he was certain of it, and perhaps her feelings matched his own, something unspoken between them that would carry on growing with each passing year. Surely there was no need to put into words what she inspired in him, so obvious even a simpleton would have realised the truth? Because Emily was no fool, in spite of her wildly misplaced naivety, and as the coach carried them homeward Andrew wondered if it was *he* who might be wrong.

Was there a chance—slim, but maybe not completely non-existent—that Wagstaff would indeed be pleased to meet his daughter again after so many years…?

Chapter Twelve

Emily's hands were shaking so much she could hardly tie the ribbons on her mask, the curling feather attached to the topmost edge waving with every tremble of her fingers. For the entirety of the past week she'd ached for the moment she'd get to wear it, but now the time had come she felt like she was struggling to breathe.

She glanced again into the mirror, seeing herself lingering in Huntingham's grand entrance hall. Night had fallen beyond the front door. If she didn't hurry they would be late, a snub sure to be noticed by their hostess, and yet...

'Do you need some help?'

Eleanor appeared from the drawing room, resplendent in a gown of midnight blue with her own mask pushed up into her hair. She would pull it down once they arrived at Lady Merton's house, but for now Emily could see her mother-in-law's expression clearly and her heart sank as she recognised the same unease that had been on Andrew's face for the past week.

With some effort she forced the realisation aside. 'Yes please. I can't seem to remember how knots work.'

Lady Gouldsmith came up behind her in a rustle of expensive skirts, and Emily watched as her reflection's mask was tied into place, hiding the determined set of her mouth.

Andrew might have been harbouring some reservations, just as his mother was, but she wouldn't be changing her mind. Her whole life had been leading up to this evening and she had to see it through, every unanswered question she'd ever had now ringing like a deafening cacophony of bells. The one person who could throw some light into the darkness would be there tonight, and nothing would stop her from speaking to him, even if she had to walk to Lady Merton's party in her bare feet.

There was no danger of that, however. The carriage stood waiting at the bottom of Huntingham's steps and the time to set out came closer as Eleanor gave the ribbons at the back of Emily's head a final tweak.

'You look wonderful. It seems a shame to cover such a pretty gown with a cloak. Quite what she's thinking, having a garden party at night…in autumn…'

Lady Gouldsmith shook her head at their hostess's irrationality. It was a fair observation. The cold night air made cloaks not just necessary but essential, and Emily readjusted the one that hung around her in soft folds. It had a cowl she could draw over her head and she raised it now, the hood hiding her distinctive hair beneath a swathe of shimmering ivory. Combined with the mask she was unrecognisable, an anonymous stranger gazing back at her in the mirror, and she wasn't quite sure why she felt a sudden chill skitter down her spine.

Trying to ignore it she smiled. 'I'm glad you're coming too. Andrew has been so quiet of late. Even when we're in the same room it's as if he isn't really there.'

Eleanor possessed excellent manners, but she also wasn't afraid to speak her mind. 'He's worried about you,' she replied shortly, firmly brushing a speck of lint from Emily's shoulder. 'As am I. If I thought you'd listen I'd try to persuade you not to do what you intend this evening—but as I know you won't, I'll save my breath.'

Somewhat stung, Emily opened her mouth to respond—or to defend herself? She wasn't quite sure—but the sound of boots made her close it again as Andrew stepped into the hall.

He looked from his mother to his wife and she found herself momentarily distracted from the whirl of excitement and apprehension swooping through her innards.

In the evening shadows his eyes seemed darker than ever, or perhaps it was the deep navy of his coat that made them so richly obsidian, his hair likewise almost black in the candlelit hall. Every trace of stubble was gone from his jaw, the subtle cleft in his chin more prominent in the best possible way, and despite having seen him every day now for months she still felt herself stir when he raised one quizzical eyebrow.

'Is everything all right?'

'Of course.' Eleanor stepped in before Emily could stumble onto an answer. 'I was just helping Emily with her mask.'

She drew back as her son came forwards, although Emily thought she caught one last concerned glance before Lady Gouldsmith turned away. If Andrew saw it likewise he didn't remark on it, instead stopping so close she could smell the warm scent of his cologne.

'You look beautiful. From what I can see of you, that is.'

He smiled, slightly more tautly than she would have preferred, and she saw his mother was correct. One glimpse of those stiff lips told her he was ill at ease and she was glad of her mask to hide how her forehead gathered into a frown.

Was he really *that* perturbed? He'd had a full week to voice his misgivings and hadn't uttered a word, either against or in favour of what she had planned, and she had assumed he had accepted it at last. She knew he hadn't always grasped the importance of what she was doing, but surely now he understood, perhaps uncertain but at least not planning to stand in her way—although even if he'd wanted to, the time for an intervention had passed.

'Shall we go?' With resolute cheerfulness she turned around, looking directly at him rather than his mirror image. 'I imagine it would be considered extremely rude if we were late.'

'It certainly would.'

He stood aside so she could see past him to the front door where Eleanor stood waiting. She had pulled her mask down and Emily felt another of those unwelcome shivers at the smooth, blank face that gazed back at her, a strange thrill of the uncanny that made her apprehension suddenly surge upwards.

'Ladies first. After you.'

Even with so many other things demanding her attention, Emily couldn't help but stare at the wonders before her.

As Eleanor had hinted, most of the *ton* had thought Lady Merton half mad to hold a party outside at night, but in truth it was a triumph of hostessing, and more than one lady was heard to wish she had thought of it first.

The guests bypassed the house completely, welcomed in through a side entrance that led directly into the sprawling back garden where strings of paper lanterns were festooned from every available tree. Torches guttered in elaborate holders staked into the ground, so many that the night-time chill was eliminated almost entirely, although great piles of shawls and blankets were available to anyone who might be even the slightest bit cold. In the middle of the vast lawn a bandstand had been erected, bedecked with flowers picked from her famous hothouse, with an area nearby as a makeshift dance floor on the carefully levelled turf. At every turn there were candles and vines twined around statues, gazebos made from metal wrought as fine as filigree, and a rumour was fast spreading that there were to be fireworks after the main event of a real pineapple had been cut and served to the crowds of astounded guests.

'This is… Have you ever seen anything like this?'

'No.' Andrew was peering incredulously up at a man on stilts, whose job seemed to be distributing glasses of champagne to anyone who came near him. 'Even by *ton* standards this is something else.'

The band had struck up and a few couples were already forming up to dance as Emily took Andrew's arm, his mother drifting away to speak to some acquaintance she had recognised despite her disguise. The sea of blank faces was mildly discomfiting and, as they moved further into the crowd, Emily was again glad of her own mask. When she'd first stepped into the garden amazement fleetingly managed to overshadow everything else, but now her breathless anticipation resurfaced and she had to will her fingers not to cling too tightly onto her husband's sleeve.

Together they made slow progress through the chattering throng, stopping occasionally to return a nod or curtsey to some faceless acquaintance. The masks made it difficult to tell one person from another, although her mind raced too fast to wonder if she had sailed past anyone she knew, her gold-ringed eyes darting this way and that in search of the only person whose identity she was truly interested in uncovering.

'I can't tell who's who. With their faces covered everyone looks the same.'

Anxiety began to trickle in. Rising up onto her tiptoes, she scanned the crowds around her for some flash of the tell-tale copper-blonde hair she'd glimpsed at the window of Lord Wagstaff's carriage. Wherever she looked porcelain facades gazed back at her, unnerving with their dark eye holes that lent them a faintly sinister aspect, while bright snatches of coloured gowns peeping from beneath cloaks were like slices of daylight in the gloom.

The smell of woodsmoke and roasting meat hung in the air, interspersed by the occasional scent of roses so at odds with the time of year, and from every direction came a din of music and laughter and voices that rose and fell without end. If she had wanted to feel as though she was at a carnival she would have enjoyed herself immensely. But in her current state the tumult of sounds and smells and strange visuals was dizzying, pulling her in too many directions at once, and she felt her chest begin to grow tight.

How am I to recognise him? Someone I caught only a glimpse of and is now hidden in plain sight?

Andrew's arm shifted slightly beneath her fingers and hurriedly she loosened what she realised was a biting grip, although a glance up at him gave no indication as to whether her accidental pinching had hurt. Just like everyone else his face was covered. His mask was painted navy, perfectly matched to his coat, and it did a frustratingly good job of hiding his expression. The only clue she could glean as to how he was feeling was in the stiffness of his shoulders, as ever able to draw her attention despite everything else clamouring for it, although for once even their charms couldn't distract her for long.

Pressing a hand she wished was more calming to her chest, she took another sweeping survey of the revellers spread out across the darkened lawn. Expensive coats gleamed in the torchlight but no one man stood out among them, the hair peeping from beneath every hat either brown or blonde or grey. For a few of them it was impossible to tell the colour, and with the feeling she was clutching at straws she turned back to Andrew.

'Do you know how tall Lord Wagstaff is? Even that small hint might be of some use.'

'I'm afraid not. I haven't seen him since I was a very young boy.'

His voice was noncommittal, its vagueness fanning the embers of her frustration.

Couldn't he at least *try* to be of more help? He couldn't have failed to see she was on tenterhooks, turning left and right like a weathervane as she searched through the darkness, and yet he stood unmoving beside her as if his boots were nailed to the grass. It was on the tip of her tongue to ask him to be more proactive, perhaps using his impressive height to see over the tops of people's heads—but then Lady Merton glided past them, her hands held out towards a guest standing half hidden beneath a nearby tree, and all at once Emily wondered how she hadn't seen him before.

The world around her grew dim as she watched Lady Merton take the man's hand and pull him out from the shadows, the moonlight glancing off the carved ivory of his mask. It concealed his face, of course, and his hat hid almost the rest of his head; but his sideburns were exposed, grown long in the latest fashion, and the colour of them made it impossible for Emily to see anything else.

A bright, unmistakable copper-gold.

'Emily? Are you unwell? You're trembling.'

She heard Andrew speaking to her but it was as if he was on the other side of a closed door. He seemed far away, or perhaps it was her that had been transported, time and distance meaning nothing as she stood and stared.

If he said she was trembling then she believed him, although she wasn't aware of any unsteadiness in her hands. In truth she felt the exact opposite, suddenly certain instead of unsure, any doubts falling away like a tree shedding its leaves. Lady Merton and her friend were too far away for Emily to hear them but sight alone was enough, a quiet amazement stealing over her as Andrew bent down to catch her reply.

'It's him. Over there.'

She barely managed a croak, her throat immediately

dry. Under her numb fingertips she thought she felt Andrew's forearm tense but it barely registered, her attention fastened on the man she was now so convinced she
had seen somewhere before.

'That's Lord Wagstaff. I'm positive that's who I saw
in Leamington, looking out of his carriage window.'

The tremor that had so alarmed Andrew grew in intensity, Emily at last registering the weakness in her
limbs. It would soon be a struggle to walk and a frantic
fear washed over her that she might be about to collapse,
allowing the moment to slip through her fingers as she
lay insensible on the ground. She had to approach him
before her nerves could stop her in her tracks, and without truly realising it she found she'd taken the first step.

But there wasn't a second.

At once she spun back to Andrew, wildly impatient
when he didn't move. Her hand still lay in the crook of
his arm and he held on to it firmly, forcing her to wait
or risk straining her wrist.

'What's the matter?' She stared up at him, trying to
contain the temptation to get behind him and push. 'This
is what we've been waiting for! Please come with me, I
need you to introduce us.'

Again she stepped away from him, certain that this
time he would oblige, but again his immovable arm held
her back.

'I can't. Forgive me, but I can't have any part in this.'

She wheeled to face him, unable to grasp what she
had heard. The music was loud and the voices all around
them were raised, and it would have been easy for her to
have mistaken him if the eyes behind his mask hadn't

been filled with such anguish that any response died on her lips.

He looked down at her, the terrible sadness in his eyes sending a fist of ice into her chest. 'Please reconsider. I've held my tongue out of respect for your feelings, but now I *must* speak. If you do this you *will* be hurt, and you *will* regret it, and I would much rather you spared yourself the pain.'

'But…' Confused, Emily faltered, suddenly wishing she could see his face rather than expressionless porcelain. The unhappiness in his eyes and voice cut into her, and her first instinct was to draw closer against him, only the bewilderment of his abrupt change of heart holding her back. 'I thought you understood now. I thought you knew what this meant to me. Why are you saying this again, when everything is just about to fall into place?'

Incomprehension held her almost unmoving, but the swiftest glance over her shoulder showed Lord Wagstaff still near the tree. Caught between the burning need to run to him and the desire for Andrew to explain himself she swayed, the unsteadiness in her legs ramping up its efforts to bring her to the ground.

Frustration clawed at her, hot and almost angry as she waited for Andrew to speak. Hadn't they talked about this already? Hadn't she told him in no uncertain terms why she had to carry on? She hated that he was so clearly worried, the knowledge cutting deep, but couldn't he try harder to understand? She was on the brink of gaining the love she'd always wanted, and the ache inside her that had first taken root when she was a child came again to make her feel as though she was being eaten alive.

Andrew tried to bring her closer, gently increasing the

pressure on her hand, but she didn't move. If she took a step towards him her nerveless legs might not let her come back again, although the longing to lay her head against the front of his shirt was strong when she saw the unfeigned tenderness in his eyes.

'I can't support you doing something to hurt yourself. Don't you see? You think you need to find your father so you finally have someone who loves you, but I—I want to tell you—'

There was a crashing of broken glass.

Instinctively Lady Merton's guests turned as one to see the stilt-walker sprawled on the ground, surrounded by the shattered remains of a great many champagne glasses. It seemed something had caused him to lose his balance and there was a whirl of activity as their hostess sprang into action, calling for servants to clear up the mess and a doctor to see to the injured man. Her guests gathered to get a better view, even the band ceasing to play as attention shifted to the scene of the accident, and in the commotion Emily saw her chance.

Even Andrew was momentarily distracted, and a moment was all she needed to extract her hand, slipping away from him before he could say a word to stop her. A flicker of guilt accompanied her as she wove through the crowd, alongside a powerful curiosity as to how he would have finished the sentence he left hanging in mid-air, but her heart was pounding so hard she could barely hear herself think. Lord Wagstaff was still by the tree and with Lady Merton gone to take command he was now alone, and there was nothing to stop her as she bore down on him, every step an effort but sheer force of will driving her on.

He was attempting to see the face of his pocket watch when she reached him, tilting it so it might catch the light of a nearby torch, although when he heard her approach he snapped it shut.

'Good evening.'

His bow was slightly hesitant, as Emily might have noticed if she hadn't been wrestling to control her breath. It came fast and shallow and she knew she sounded strangled when she replied, her curtsey more of an untidy bob than a Countess's regal sweep.

'Good evening, sir.'

She rose unsteadily, her heart trying to punch a hole through her ribs. Lord Wagstaff peered at her—his eyes green in place of her blue, but perhaps a similar shape beneath his mask?—but didn't say anything more, doubtless wondering why a strange woman had come charging over to him without a word of introduction. He shifted uneasily, clasping his hands behind his back and Emily thought she might have to do the same. The urge to fling herself into his arms was overpowering, and she was only just able to hold it back, squeezing her hands into fists so tightly her nails bit into her palms.

My father. I'm talking to my father.

A surge of dizziness swelled and to her horror she felt herself sway, her vision filled with sudden lights. Under other circumstances she would have leaned on Andrew for support, but he was on the other side of the crowd, his attempt to follow her blocked by the army of servants who had descended to surround the stilt-walker, and so there was no one except Lord Wagstaff to lurch forward to steady her when the garden around her began to spin.

He wasn't as tall as Andrew, but his hands were almost

as strong, and a streak of lightning lanced through her as she felt him take hold of her arm. Up close the giveaway shade of his sideburns was more vivid than ever, and she nearly choked to spy a reddish curl peeping from beneath his hat, containing a thread of grey but still identical to her own. She couldn't see his face and yet she had all the proof she needed, the shock when he touched her surely an instinctive reaction to having found the truth at last, and as he propped her against the tree she was glad to have something to hold her up.

There could be no denying it. Nobody could look at him and disagree he was the man who had signed her over to the Laycocks, the mysterious lord whose name she had longed to discover for almost twenty years. By some miracle she had found him, at last on the cusp of finding the love she had craved for so long, and she had to bite her tongue to stop happy tears from prickling at her eyes.

'Thank you, sir. I'm not sure what came over me.'

She tried to smile, remembering too late that he wouldn't be able to see it behind her golden mask, but she realised he wouldn't have noticed it even if her countenance had been exposed. He was looking at the top of her head rather than her face, and for a split second she wondered why before a cold breeze around her ears answered the question.

Somehow when she'd stumbled her hood must have been knocked back. Her hair was no longer covered by her cowl and the soft pile of curls had seized Lord Wagstaff's unwavering attention, his gaze fixed on them as if he was powerless to drag it away.

He made an odd movement, checking some reflex, but

then he turned his head away, muttering to himself as he fumbled with the ties at the back of his mask.

'This wretched thing… Perhaps I can't see properly…'

Emily froze, watching mutely as he pulled the mask away from his face. At first she couldn't see it clearly, his head still turned away—but then he looked directly at her and she had to cling to the tree or risk sliding to the ground.

'Have we met before, ma'am?'

Lord Wagstaff's expression was guarded—wary, even, but Emily couldn't see it. The shape of his nose was of far more interest, so similar to her own, and she was certain there was a likeness in the sandy arch of his eyebrows. It wasn't quite like looking into a mirror, but there were too many shades of familiarity to be a coincidence, and her voice shook with emotion too strong to be contained.

'I think so. It was many years ago, but I believe we have.'

Her arm felt as though it was made of paper, but she just about managed to raise it. Lord Wagstaff followed the movement without blinking, seeming to have turned into a statue as she reached for the ribbons on the back of her own mask and carefully, tremblingly, untied it from her face.

She lifted it free…and Lord Wagstaff's reaction was immediate.

He stared at her, his mouth falling open, and even in the moonlight she saw he'd blanched bone white. His eyes darted from her hair to her face to her shaking hands, taking in every inch of her with wordless shock, but then he reeled back, stumbling away as if she was a snake about to strike.

'No. Forgive me—no.'

He held up both hands to fend her off and Emily faltered in the act of reaching for him, her arms dropping loosely to her sides. Confusion and dismay roared up all around her, snatching away the exhilarated wonder of mere seconds before, and she could only watch as he moved further and further away, his face as white as the ivory of the mask he had let fall onto the grass.

'Wait. I think there's been some mistake—'

She tried to follow but he shook his head. It wasn't an angry gesture, more imploring, desperate, and she staggered to a halt as he turned away, almost running from her now in his haste to escape.

'Wait! Please!'

Lord Wagstaff didn't look back. He reached the edge of the crowd and began to push his way through, willing to risk such rudeness to put distance between them, and in her mounting bewilderment she heard her voice crack as she called out far more loudly than she should have.

'But—you're my father!'

He didn't stop. But the conversations of those around her most certainly did.

Every head turned in her direction, every face still hidden behind a mask lighting up with the scent of scandal now drifting in the air. At first there was silence...but then the muttering began, a low buzz that Emily barely heard above the blood rushing in her ears.

She stood staring at the gap in the crowd through which he had disappeared, feeling the eyes trained on her as if each was a needle digging into her skin. A tiny kernel of pain had started to unfurl inside her, somewhere dark and so deep down she hadn't realised it was there, and it grew larger and more agonising as her sluggish mind caught up with the reality of what she had just done.

She had found her father, who'd had no desire to be discovered, and with the very same act she had revealed the truth to the *ton*.

Falteringly she looked around the sea of empty faces, seeking the only one that could bring her comfort—but the next moment she was hit with another flare of pain that almost made her double over. She wanted Andrew, the husband in whose arms she had come to feel so safe, but the agony in her gut flashed again to remind her she shouldn't wish for him any longer.

If her own father didn't love her, as she had managed to delude herself that he would, instead fleeing from her while all Society watched, what hope was there that Andrew could ever return the feelings that had grown in the once barren ground of her lonely heart?

It was a fact that hit her squarely in the chest, knocking the wind from her as she huddled into her cloak, wishing it could shield her from the empty-eyed stares. The cruel irony was that she had never wanted him more and yet she had no right to look for him, the proof she was unlovable laid out for all to see. She should have listened to his warnings instead of clinging stubbornly onto her futile hopes, she saw now with perfect clarity; but there was no way of turning back the clock, and with one last blind glance at the whispering crowd she put her head down and began to stumble towards the gate that led out of the garden, wishing she still wore her mask to hide the tears pouring down her cheeks.

* * *

The crowd was too thick for Andrew to reach her but over the tops of too many heads he saw how Emily's face crumpled before she hurried away, his heart shattering as the first tear glinted in the moonlight. All around him word of what had just happened was spreading, details already being embellished until by morning the truth would no doubt be barely recognisable and the ice in his belly turned to fire as he ripped the mask from his face.

'I hear Lady Breamore's name on many lips, but is there anyone who has anything to say to me directly?'

He managed—barely—to keep his voice steady, although his expression must have given him away. Nobody met his eye, the mutters petering out to leave behind a taut silence, and he felt the grimmest of contempt for the hypocrisy surrounding him on all sides.

While they thought her a highborn lady they couldn't bow and curtsey low enough, but now...

She might be a Lord's daughter, but her illegitimacy cast her in a very different light, as the murmurs showed. Rumours and counter-rumours would abound now as to her mother and other mysteries, and there was no hope of stopping them, although everything in him wanted to try. Unhappiness rose in his gullet, bitter at the back of his throat, and with every blink he saw the image of Emily's grief as she'd tried to run from her shame.

'Perhaps it could be remembered that my wife has treated every one of you with nothing but respect since she came to Huntingham.' He raised his voice so it carried on the still night air, giving every gossip the opportunity to hear him. 'The true value of a person lies in their actions and nature, not the accident of their birth—

a fact that cuts both ways, from the poorest orphan all the way up to the Regent himself.'

The hushed muttering started up again at such an inflammatory declaration, but he had no desire to listen. Somewhere out in the darkness Emily was all alone, her soul in tatters and her dreams torn apart before her very eyes, and without a further word he turned on his heel and began to stride away, pausing only to offer an apologetic bow to Lady Merton as he passed.

'Please forgive me for making a scene at your party. I hope you understand.'

She gave him an appraising look, but then she smiled, the movement clear even behind her mask.

'A man must defend his wife, my lord. You'll hear no censure from me.'

With another civil nod Andrew moved away, heading towards the gate Emily had fled through. Out of the corner of his eye he saw his mother approaching it likewise, her mask now pushed up off her face, and he recognised the same pained determination in her countenance as he imagined was on his own. His chest felt as though it was in a vice, every breath a battle, although he had no thought to spare for his own feelings when Emily's had been so completely destroyed.

I knew that this would happen... But I would have given anything in the world to have been wrong.

Chapter Thirteen

The breakfast tray on top of the dresser lay untouched. By now the tea must have been stone cold and the toast hard and dry, but Emily didn't stray from beside the window, staring out as a new day slowly came to life around her.

The sun was up now, casting a deceptively temperate light over everything it touched, although no such warmth bloomed in the icy hollow of her chest.

From somewhere in the hall she heard a clock strike. She'd been standing there without moving for over an hour, she realised dimly, only just able to recall how the servant who had crept in to make up the fire had been startled to find her already out of bed. Sleeping had been out of the question—the look on her father's face as he'd backed away from her had seen to that, his horror so vivid even a child would have understood it, and it thrust a knife between her ribs every time she closed her eyes.

What felt like a lifetime's worth of pain and misery had kept her company all night, from the moment she'd run from Lady Merton's garden until faint birdsong signalled the approach of dawn, but it wasn't only Lord Wagstaff's reaction that had laced her blood with frost.

Andrew had been kind to her afterwards, when he'd handed her into the carriage and whisked her back to Huntingham without a word—but she knew the damage was done.

The place beneath her bodice where her heart should have been felt curiously empty. For the past twenty years it had held hope, a stubborn little flame that had refused to be extinguished, but now there was nothing but sorrow as deep as the ocean. In one night she had snuffed out that spark, not only regarding her father but her husband as well, and the knowledge that Andrew must be lamenting the day he'd met her was the worst feeling of all.

She raised a hand to her cheek, surprised to find it was dry at last. Perhaps she had no more tears left, finally knowing for certain that her husband would never return her love having made her cry more than she'd realised a woman possibly could. She had brought shame on him, every member of the *ton* now aware how far beneath himself he had wed, and he'd seen with his own eyes the rejection that illustrated she was unable to be cherished. If she had any sense she'd hide herself away before she could drag his name even further through the mud and she meant to start her penance that very day, keeping her distance from him so that even the sight of her wouldn't cause him further regret.

I should have listened. If I had, perhaps...

Slowly she sat down on the window ledge, barely registering the cold glass against her shoulder. There was no point in 'ifs'. 'If' she hadn't confronted her father, 'if' she had chosen to do things differently—these were all paths she hadn't taken and now she never would, her only choice to lie in the bed that she had made. Lord Wagstaff didn't want to know her and she had to accept it, just as she had to accept the fact she would spend the rest of her life without knowing the joy of being loved, and if the prospect made her want to weep then she would make sure to do so only in the silent seclusion of her room.

Because of her pride and foolishness, in believing a lie of her own making, she deserved nothing else.

Her stomach gave a groan but the idea of filling it brought nausea rushing to the fore. Even the thought of eating was more than she could stand, and she closed her eyes until the sickening plunge of her innards settled. She hadn't touched a morsel since luncheon the day before, too excited to manage even a mouthful at dinner, and now she might never have an appetite again. Not even Lady Merton's fabled pineapple could have tempted her, the thought of it bringing forth yet more pictures from the night before, and she wrapped her arms around herself as she tipped back her head and prayed for the strength to withstand the pain.

There was a knock at the door.

'My lady?'

The voice of her maid came as a relief as well as a crushing disappointment. For an instant she'd imagined it might be Andrew, and a longing to see him seized hold of her before she could stop it, the desire to feel his arms around her so intense she almost gasped aloud. He had spent the night in one of the guestrooms and the bed had felt far too big without him, although that was no longer any of her concern. If she was to withdraw from him—as he no doubt now wanted—she shouldn't let herself think of the former passion they had found together or the way he had held her as she slept, and with shame blazing a trail from her throat down into her belly she made herself stand up.

'Yes, Mary. Come in.'

The door opened and the maid appeared, hesitating on the threshold when she saw her mistress already dressed.

'You're up, my lady. But are you unwell? You look pale.'

Summoning a smile was impossible, but Emily tried at least to hide the strain in her face as she shook her head. 'I had trouble sleeping, that's all. I'm a little tired.'

The maid gave her a doubtful glance but didn't press any further, too well-trained to pry, and turned her attention instead to tidying the bottles and brushes on the dressing table. Evidently she hadn't yet heard the lurid tale of what had happened in Lady Merton's garden. But she would, along with the rest of Huntingham's servants, and Emily's innards twisted again to think she soon wouldn't be able to escape the whispers even in her own home.

'You haven't even looked at your breakfast, ma'am.' Mary picked up the tray, eyebrows raised in restrained curiosity. 'Are you sure you're not unwell?'

'Quite sure. I just don't find myself very hungry this morning. If you wouldn't mind, it can go back to the kitchen.'

'Of course, ma'am.'

With a neat bob the maid crossed back to the door,

the sound of it closing behind her feeling more like the clanging of a prison gate, and once again Emily found herself alone.

Moving back to the window she leaned forward until her forehead touched the glass, the chill of it matching the ice in her veins as she stared blindly out at the grounds below.

Was Andrew somewhere in the house, perhaps doing something similar? Or had he gone out, unable to stand being within the same four walls as the wife who had rewarded his gamble in wedding her with a mountain of shame?

She screwed her eyes shut but it didn't help ward off the hiss in her ear, the sharp little voice set on compounding her misery. There was no hope of ignoring it and she realised she was pressing her knuckles against the windowsill, the wood hard and cold against her skin.

I can't do this to him. I can't let this go too far.

If it was just herself that had been damaged by her actions the previous night she could have borne it, but she could not bear pulling others down with her. Her father would be subjected to mutters now, the same as Lady Gouldsmith, whose only crime was always having shown kindness to one in dire need of it. Was it fair to repay her now with notoriety, to be known among the *ton* as the woman whose daughter-in-law was nothing but an unclaimed indiscretion? It was a poor return for everything Eleanor had done…and as for Andrew…

It was just as well she had no tears left. The thought of him dragged so low would have made her cry if she'd been able to, the image of his kind, handsome face a torture Emily could barely endure.

Wonderful, sweet, thoughtful Andrew—who she should never have thought, even for so much as a moment, could ever truly be hers.

He deserved the world, not the ridicule she knew was certain to follow. People would stare now, for reasons other than his status and pleasing countenance, and to avoid exposing him to those intrusive gazes she would have done anything.

She stood up slowly, bracing herself against the windowsill. The room around her swam slightly, either from her not having eaten for so long or the sudden rush of grim determination that swept over her, and she breathed deeply as she waited for her head to stop spinning.

She couldn't erase the past. Nothing could undo all the mistakes she'd made, in her haste and desperation taking one wrong step after another until she had tripped and taken those she cared about down with her, but she could at least try to prevent any further damage. Shame and rejection followed her like a plague, and only by removing the source could those she'd come to love ever, in time, regain the respect she had caused them to lose.

The mirror on top of her dressing table gleamed in the morning sunshine and she made herself look into it, meeting her reflection's cool blue eyes.

Mary was right—she *was* pale, her face taut as if stretched too tightly over the bone beneath, purple shadows betraying her sleepless night. Her ghostly twin gazed steadily back at her and she watched its lips part, hearing the crack in her own voice when she spoke her decision out loud.

'There's only one thing to do, and I should do it now.'

With bleak resolve she crossed the room, stopping

before the armoire in which her beautiful gowns hung in a silken parade. Somewhere beneath them was the small trunk she'd brought with her from Miss Laycock's school, pushed to the very back so only the battered leather handle showed, and with her mouth set in a tight line she bent down to pull it out.

Despite the chill wind Andrew had almost broken a sweat by the time he strode back up the Hall's front drive, his head down as he threw himself forward. Going for a walk had been supposed to help him make sense of the situation, but it had been an utter failure, his thoughts in just as much of a whirl now as before he'd set out.

He'd yet to see Emily that morning. She'd fled into their bedroom the moment they had returned from the party and he hadn't thought it prudent to follow, giving her space even if everything in him had instead yearned to take her in his arms. Her white, anguished face was imprinted upon his heart and it made him grimace to recall how she'd looked in the moonlight, all hope and happiness drained from her as she'd watched her father turn his back and run.

'What do I say to her? How am I to proceed?'

The greyhound trotting at his side had no answer. It seemed he would have to decide on his own, and his frown was ferocious as he took the steps two at a time and pushed open Huntingham's heavy front door.

With the uncanny intuition of all good servants the butler materialised immediately, his hand already out to take his master's hat. 'Good morning my lord. Did you have a pleasant walk?'

'Not especially, but thank you for asking.'

Shrugging off his coat Andrew shot the butler a glance, seeing the other man's face was impassive as ever. Either he wasn't yet acquainted with the gossip currently spreading through Warwickshire or he was too professional to hint at it, and Andrew tried to smooth out the worse of his scowl.

'Is her ladyship down yet?'

There was the briefest of hesitations that reflected well on the butler's grasp of a sensitive subject. 'No, sir. The Countess is still upstairs. Mary enquired after her health and gathered Lady Breamore is tired after a poor night's sleep.'

'I see.'

Andrew's stomach contracted. Past eleven o'clock, and Emily still kept to their room? It confirmed his fears that a new morning had not brought better spirits. His spine felt rigid as he gave the butler a nod and made for the stairs, cursing Lord *damnation* Wagstaff with every upward step.

What kind of man could look his own daughter in the face, he thought savagely as he climbed, and just turn away, cutting her off as if she was a stranger rather than his child? It was the outcome he'd always predicted, but to have seen it play out in front of him was cruel beyond imagining. Emily had tended to the little ray of hope inside herself for years, feeding it and keeping it alive throughout the entirety of her sad childhood, then as a lonely young woman, and at the very moment she had dreamed of her father had pinched it out to leave her in the dark. It was harsh and callous and the memory of it made Andrew curl his hands into fists, sorrow and anger curdling together in a mixture more bitter than anything he'd felt before.

On the upper landing he paused to try to regain his composure. Getting so agitated would be of no help and he still had no idea how to begin. His ire with her father clouded his mind, causing any soft words he might have grasped at to evade him, and he wondered if he ought to seek his mother's advice, before dismissing the idea just as quickly as it had appeared.

No. This is between me and my wife.

Her happiness was his responsibility, and besides, bringing someone else in would only add to her distress. She had already been humiliated in front of half the *ton* and he couldn't allow her to feel any more exposed, even if it was just his mother and not one of the gossips that had so delighted in the unhappy scene. How he and Emily went about working through the new strain on their marriage was nobody's business but their own and he had to remind himself to drop his shoulders as he approached their bedroom door, knocking gently on the polished wood and listening hard for any movement on the other side.

'Emily. Are you there?'

There was silence.

He knocked again. 'I believe you can hear me. Will you come out? I'd like to talk to you.'

This time he caught a faint sound from within, the slight creaking of a floorboard, and then the iron bar over his chest pressed down harder when he heard her speak.

'Please. It's best for both of us if you just leave me be.'

The quiet pain in her voice sliced through him, going

right to the space she occupied in his heart. 'I disagree. If you come out—'

'No.' She cut across him far more abruptly than she ever had before. By the sound of it she was standing very close to the door, perhaps even leaning against it, and he would have given almost anything to magic it away so she might fall into his arms.

'You've already been so kind to me and I threw it back in your face. You saw what happened last night. I don't deserve your consideration and that was the proof.'

Andrew felt his face harden into a mask as stiff as the one he'd worn the night before. 'You don't deserve...?'

He couldn't finish the sentence, too dismayed to find the words. Was that really what she thought? Why she wouldn't leave the room? He'd imagined she was hurt, wounded by rejection but not that Lord Wagstaff's rebuff had made her question her very value, and he leaned urgently closer to the door.

'Because of your father? You'd take the actions of one stupid man as proof you're unworthy of being treated well, of compassion, of being—'

He clamped his mouth shut, leaving the last word unsaid. It wasn't the time to unleash it, not when she was so grief-stricken and confused, but it echoed through his head nevertheless and he had to bite his tongue to stop it from spilling out.

Loved. You were going to say loved.

He'd almost said it in Lady Merton's garden, a split second before the stilt-walker's accident had interrupted him, and it was just as true now as it had been then. To him Emily was worthy of being loved and he was the one who loved her, a truth he had no desire to deny. It hadn't been his initial reason for marrying her, and there was a chance she didn't feel the same, but as he stood with his hand flat against the door, pressing his palm to the wood as if he could push through it, he swore he would confess all the first moment he could.

There was another silence. Now there was no sound at all from the bedroom. No squeak of floorboards or faint rustling of skirts, and it took all of his willpower not to seize the door handle. She was clearly determined to be alone and he had no wish to force his presence on her, although he couldn't stop himself from trying one more time.

'This isn't right. You can't stay in there for ever.'

'I know. I know that very well.'

Something in her voice stirred the hairs on the backs of his arms. It wasn't quite resignation—more like the bleakest resolve, and any reply he might have made died in his mouth.

There seemed little hope of her changing her mind and to stand guard outside her door wouldn't help. When she came out—as she'd have to, eventually—he'd speak with her properly, but until then there was frustratingly little he could do. The crux of the matter was Lord Wagstaff, damn his eyes, and the damage he had done to his daughter's sense of self, and Andrew was just about to lean wearily against the wall when an idea took him by the throat.

Perhaps her father would be more open to knowing her if he actually *knew* her?

He straightened up cautiously, allowing the notion time to unfold.

There was never a second chance at making a first impression. Lord Wagstaff had fled before Emily had been able to show him all the qualities that had made Andrew fall in love with her, but what if those qualities were set before him now? Surely he couldn't spurn his daughter once he knew of her kindness, her sweet nature and the pleasure she took in music, all attributes that would make any father proud?

What frightened him off was being confronted so publicly. Andrew followed the thread of his thought, careful not to let it slip away. *But what if I could reach him in a more subtle manner?*

He glanced at the door. It was still tight shut, giving no clue whether Emily was close behind it or on the other side of the room. Part of him hoped she would hear it when he softly laid his fingertips on the wood, as gently as he would have stroked her hair in happier times, and then he turned away, making for his study with new hope just beginning to rise.

Some hours later, however, his dogged optimism had begun to flag.

With a grunt he swept the latest attempt at a letter off his desk. It floated to the floor to join the other drafts abandoned there, some screwed into balls and a couple even torn in half, and Andrew watched it go with narrowed eyes.

'Why is this so cursedly difficult?'

His voice was loud in the empty room. The only other sound was the crackle of the fire and he pushed back his chair to walk over to it, throwing his quill down as if it was to blame for his inability to express himself as he wished. Above the mantle the portrait of Uncle Ephraim glared down at him—the same one that had been in the parlour until he'd had it moved—and Andrew glowered back, meeting the cold, painted eyes without flinching.

'You needn't look at me like that. Do you think you'd be better at writing to him? You, who never cared about anyone this much in your entire life?'

His uncle's sneer didn't soften; but then, it never had while he was alive, either. It was men like him that made people like Emily feel so worthless, Andrew thought fiercely, with their rules as to who was acceptable and who wasn't, and he realised he was pacing as angrily as a lion in a cage as he tracked back and forth across the hearth rug.

How was he supposed to sum up all her good qualities in a letter, when a lifetime wasn't long enough to list them? That was the question he was struggling to answer, demonstrated by the mountain of half-finished drafts scattered across the study carpet.

With a sigh he raked a hand through his hair, the cogs in his head working relentlessly. Was she still in their room? Had she decided to come out now he was no longer outside the door? For his part he was determined not to leave the study until he had committed enough to paper to change Lord Wagstaff's mind, although that now seemed more of an undertaking than he'd thought. Her agony was as real as if from a physical wound, and he couldn't let her go on suffering, his pacing increasing as he tried to force his brain to work harder.

He stopped in mid-stride.

It was no use. It wouldn't matter how long he spent with a quill in his hand. His feelings for Emily were too deep now to be contained by any piece of paper and it would be a waste of time to keep trying, especially when there was a far more direct way of telling Lord Wagstaff exactly what he would be missing.

It was what he should have done from the very beginning, and Andrew shook his head at his foolishness as he went to the study door, throwing it open and hurrying down the landing towards the stairs. Her father might have run away in public, with the eyes of the *ton* fixed on him as he'd fled, but a private visit would be different. In his own territory Lord Wagstaff would be less evasive, perhaps more inclined to listen—and at the very least he couldn't escape, even if Andrew had to follow him from room to room to make himself heard.

Outside the air was crisp but the speed with which he walked to the stable yard kept him from feeling any kind of chill. Constance whinnied from over the top of her stall door at his approach, and he remembered how he had lifted Emily up onto her back all those months ago, a wry smile twisting his mouth as he opened the stall and led the horse out.

If I'm successful perhaps we'll go riding again, only this time without the sprained ankle.

He saddled her as quickly as he could, only glancing up when one of his grooms appeared, looking unnecessarily apologetic as he took off his cap.

'I'm sorry, my lord. I didn't know you wanted your horse made ready. If you step back I can do that for you.'

'I know you can.' Giving the girth a final check Andrew turned to the groom, the dry half-smile still in place. 'And I don't doubt that you'd do it very well. But sometimes a man has to do things for himself—whether he's an Earl or not.'

Without another word he swung himself up into the saddle and shook the reins, urging Constance into a smart trot that flowed smoothly into a canter, and he felt his determination rise as he left Huntingham Hall behind.

Standing at her window, half concealed behind a curtain for fear Andrew might look up, Emily's aching heart tore in two as she watched him ride away, knowing that it was the very last time she ever would.

Chapter Fourteen

It felt like the longest wait of her life but evening finally came, bringing with it the moment she had both longed for and dreaded.

Emily looked around the flame-lit bedroom, the curtains now tightly drawn against the darkness outside. Everything was ready. Her small trunk was packed and her old cloak folded on top of it, alongside the tattered bonnet she hadn't worn in months, everything she'd owned before she came to Huntingham in that neat little pile and not a petticoat more. All the splendour Andrew had heaped upon her since they'd wed was to be left behind, every gown and necklace and even the silver hairbrushes on her dressing table, and only knowing without question that she was doing the right thing gave her the strength to cross to the door.

Slowly, taking care not to make any noise, she eased it open. There was nobody out on the landing, just as she'd hoped. All the servants would be in bed at this hour, and Andrew...

Pain lurched in the pit of her stomach and she grasped the edge of the doorframe until the first onslaught passed.

Don't think of him.

She straightened up, teeth pressed together so hard it made the muscles ache in her jaw. The stern voice in the back of her mind was right. If she allowed herself to picture his smile or the way his eyes creased when he laughed she might weaken, and she couldn't afford to lose her resolve, no matter how much everything in her yearned to unpack her trunk and pretend she had never intended to flee unseen into the night. The time was almost upon her, only one thing left to do before she slipped away, although the letter in her hand felt curiously heavy as she crept down the shadowy landing towards the half-open door of his study.

For one heartbeat she stopped to listen. Was there any danger he might still be inside? He'd spent hours in there earlier, or so her maid had told her when she'd come with another tray that had gone untouched, but then apparently he had gone out in something of a hurry and Emily had no way of knowing if he had returned. His comings and goings would very soon be none of her business, after all, and she gritted her teeth harder still on another wave of pain that tried to bring her to her knees.

Instead of crumpling, however, she willed herself forward. There would be plenty of time for grief once she'd left, when she would struggle to drag her trunk the five miles to Brigwell. If she stumbled on her way back to the school at least there would be no one around to see it, the long walk giving her time to think how best to persuade Miss Laycock to let her stay until she found a placement far enough away that she wouldn't expose her husband to whispers he didn't deserve.

Only a few months ago the prospect of exile had seemed so bleak she'd tried to seek out her father to avoid it. The irony that in doing so she had brought herself full circle was almost too cruel, now back where she'd started but leaving a trail of destruction in her wake.

The study was cold when she warily stepped inside. If there had been a fire in the grate it had long since burned out and the only light came from the full moon shining through the window, the curtains still open to the night beyond. The smell of tobacco smoke and leather from the books crammed onto every shelf laced the cool air, and she allowed herself to take one deep breath, trying to commit the scent of Andrew to memory. She would keep it locked inside her, hidden deep where nobody could take it away, and it would be the only thing that consoled her when missing him made her feel as though she would never be happy again.

He will be, though, and that's what matters.

She clung to that scant comfort as she slowly approached his desk, hardly noticing how her skirts rustled over various sheets of paper lying discarded on the floor.

Once she'd gone the *ton* would eventually move on to some other scandal, find some other poor soul to scrutinise beyond all endurance, and the humiliation she'd brought down on him would eventually be swept under the carpet. A man as rich and powerful as Andrew could obtain a divorce, the process difficult but not impossible for someone of his standing, and then he could marry again, the second time to a woman far more suited to being a Countess—who would never bring disgrace upon his name.

With a throat full of broken glass she walked around to the back of the desk. The chair was thrown aside as if Andrew had stood up abruptly, and she couldn't stop herself from tracing her fingers over the arm where his hand must have lain only hours before. With every second that passed her time at Huntingham Hall grew shorter, and the sorrow nesting inside her grew more intense, emotion almost choking her as she reached down to place her parting note on the pile of papers strewn across the green leather top.

A word scrawled on one of the crumpled sheets caught her eye.

She stilled, frozen in the act of retracting her hand. The myriad pieces of paper scattered on the desk were covered in Andrew's handwriting, some almost full while others contained just a few lines, but the one beneath her note was the shortest of all. The writing had been heavily crossed out but the text was still just about legible, and all the breath left her body as her wide eyes skittered over it in full.

Sir,

    Please allow me to begin by telling you how much I love and respect your daughter, Emily Elizabeth Townsend. While I understand...

It went no further, ending in an ink blot that looked as though it had been made by an impatient dash of the writer's quill, although all her attention was fixed immovably on the twelfth word of the second line.

She stared at it, four little letters hardly visible in the moonlight. The paper they were scratched on shone silvery and the words a deep black, and she had the strangest feeling they were staring right back at her as she picked the letter up, only realising she'd dropped into Andrew's chair when she felt the wood pressing hard against her back.

'What...?'

Again and again she skimmed the three lines, not trusting the evidence of her own eyes. Repetition couldn't help her take in what she was reading, and it was only when the words began to blur that she saw her hand was shaking.

Her breathing had become faster, her heart working at wild speed. Surely he hadn't *meant* for his sentiments towards her to be interpreted romantically? Wasn't that why the words had been crossed out and the draft left unfinished? There was no sense to be made of Andrew writing such a letter to Lord Wagstaff, confessing feelings he hadn't even admitted to the person who had supposedly inspired them.

In her unhappiness she must have misunderstood, for one wonderful moment thinking that perhaps her love was returned rather than the mere civility he no doubt intended, and her bewildered, tentative hopes came crashing down around her once more.

She let the paper drop from nerveless fingers, suddenly too wearied by her idiocy to hold it a second longer.

'Why do you insist on torturing yourself? Why be so stupid when you know that couldn't possibly be right?'

The silent study had no answer. In the quiet of the night she might have been all alone in the world, and she braced herself to stand up, suddenly desperate to be gone from the place she no longer belonged—if she ever had.

By the time Andrew woke she intended to be back in Brigwell, saving him from a scene his impeccable good manners were sure to find unpleasant. Out of a misguided sense of duty he would try to persuade her to stay, and in her weakness she might agree, the prospect of never being in his arms again making it hard to get to her feet. Everywhere she looked the ghost of him lingered, in every corner of the study as well as on every inch of her skin, and she was about to run away from the spectres of lost joy when her skirts brushed something lying by her feet.

Instinctively she looked down. Another piece of paper was on the floor, this time tightly folded and without knowing exactly why she bent to pick it up. Perhaps it was just to hold something Andrew had held, for one last time bringing him a fraction closer, but as her hand closed around it she felt the hairs stir on the back of her neck.

With immense caution she glanced at the other half-formed letters spread over the desk. *One* badly worded draft could be misinterpreted…but could half a dozen? Or more, if she were to pick up all the ones lying in screwed-up balls on the floor? Probably to do so would just cause her even more disappointment, and yet she found herself unfolding the paper in her hand, holding it up to the window behind her so the moon could illuminate the scribble within.

Sir,

Please excuse my writing to you. Such an imposition is rendered essential, however, by the love I

bear for my wife, Miss Emily Elizabeth Townsend,
as was...

Lightning lanced through her entire body.

There it was again. The single most beautiful word she'd ever read—*love*—spelled out in Andrew's handwriting so clearly it might have been daylight outside rather than the middle of the lonely night. Once might be a mistake, but to write it twice was surely intentional, and gripped by sudden fervour she cast about for another discarded page, snatching it up as though she feared it might escape.

Sir,
I hope you will not be distressed by this letter.
I write only to recommend to you someone I love
dearly, whom I believe would inspire similar sen-
timents in yourself if...

Again the writing ended abruptly, but it was enough to send her folding back down into the chair.

The room seemed to reel around her as she sat, gazing mutely at the papers spread out in front of her. With each halted attempt at writing the picture became clearer, but she didn't dare look at it, afraid that doing so might make it disappear.

Like wildflowers in a meadow her hopes had begun to bloom, and yet it seemed impossible they wouldn't be cut down, the blade of cold reality surely waiting to slice through the tender stems. Her head knew it was dangerous to dream, but her heart refused to listen, pounding inside her as if challenging the rest of her to keep up, and she was too distracted to hear footsteps growing closer until the study door flew open so violently it banged against the wall behind.

'Don't go. For pity's sake, don't leave.'

Andrew was halfway across the room before she could blink, although her subconscious recognised him at once, a thrill spilling through her as she took in his sliver of bare chest and disordered hair. It looked as though he had just leaped out of bed, perhaps pausing only to pull on a pair of breeches beneath his half-open nightshirt, and judging by the rapid shortness of his breath he had run all the way. She wanted to jump up likewise, meeting him with the same passionate urgency that clearly held him in its grip, but her legs had turned to water and her head was spinning and it was all she could do not to fall off her chair.

He came directly towards her, not stopping his charge until the desk would let him go no further. 'I had to speak to you. I was going to wait until morning but I couldn't let you suffer even a minute longer, and when I saw our bedroom door open and all your belongings packed—'

He broke off, running both hands through his chaotic hair. He looked like a man on the brink, and in that moment Emily had never loved him more, all his calm and suavity fallen away to show the naked emotion within. He wasn't an Earl as he stood in front of her, clearly desperate for her to stay. He was just her husband and she was just his wife, and suddenly all the muttering *ton* in the world couldn't have convinced her that he didn't know his own mind.

With unsteady fingers she picked up the first letter,

neither noticing nor caring that in her trembling it shook like a leaf. 'Did you mean this? Or should I say, these?'

She watched him glance down. In his haste it seemed he hadn't noticed what she was holding, and she saw his face change almost imperceptibly, the tight mask of dismay taking on an exasperated edge.

'Yes. Every word. The difficult part was finding the right ones, as I'm sure you've noticed.'

He tried to take the paper from her but she snatched it away, pressing it to where her heart leapt beneath the bodice of her old gown. 'The right words for what?'

'I thought that would be obvious.'

The darkness should have made it difficult to see what passed through his obsidian eyes, but somehow the fire in them burned bright enough to cut through the night. He looked down at her, slumped back in his chair hardly able to move, and the hopeless wonder of his smile was something she knew she'd never forget.

'To tell Lord Wagstaff that if he chose not to know my wife he would be missing out, of course—on the kindest, sweetest, most beautiful woman I ever met, who would take my heart with her if she left.'

Emily's lips parted but nothing came out. Everything she'd ever longed to hear hung in the air between them, and she couldn't seem to speak as he came around the desk and took her hand to raise her gently—but insistently—to her feet.

'I went to see him. I was certain that if I could just tell him about you, about the real person rather than whatever faded memory he might have had of you as a baby, he would change his mind. And it turns out, I was right.'

Andrew spoke quickly, earnestly, perhaps trying to

explain before she pulled away, but she had no intention of the sort. His free hand had found its way to her waist, and the relief of his touch almost felled her, the only medicine that could have made the pain inside her vanish without trace. His grip was light but so safe she never wanted to move, and she felt herself sway at the warmth of it, cutting through the ice of her misery to leave only sunlight behind.

If Andrew had read the growing shift in her expression he didn't show it. He went on, determined that she hear what he had to say, and she was happy to listen so long as he didn't let go of her hand or relax the heated pressure of his palm.

'He wanted to come to see you anyway, and my visit assured him he would be welcome. Apparently he immediately regretted his conduct at Lady Merton's party but was too ashamed of himself to call to apologise, fearing that he had pushed you away for ever. If you'll allow it he'll come to call on us tomorrow…or should I say, today.'

Emily's breath stalled in her throat. The pure elation of being close to Andrew again when she'd thought she would never get another chance had caused her mind to spin with joy, but now she tried to focus on more than just the movement of his lips. If her pleasure-addled brain had understood him correctly he had been to see Lord Wagstaff, and even more astoundingly had discovered that her father might not have abandoned her after all—something she struggled to comprehend, a delicious flicker licking over her when she felt Andrew's hand tighten to keep her firmly upright.

'He wants to see me? Truly?'

'Yes. I believe that deep down he always did.'

Carefully, evidently aware that her legs were hardly working, he brought her nearer, his other hand releasing hers so he could tilt her head up to look directly into her eyes. 'It was shame that kept him from you all these years. He was persuaded not to marry your mother by the threat of disinheritance, and he bitterly regrets his weakness in choosing his fortune over her. Apparently you look so much like her he knew who you were the moment you removed your mask, and he was so overcome with grief and remorse that he lost his head and ran.'

'That's why he never came for me when I was a child? Because he thought…?'

His nod made ending her sentence unnecessary. 'He felt he was a sorry excuse for a man and that you were better off not knowing him. In a misguided attempt to have you brought up well he paid the Laycocks to take you in, leaving a considerable sum set by for your schooling and other expenses on the condition they never revealed his identity. He was very upset when he learned Miss Laycock told you the money had run out on your twenty-first birthday, by the way—apparently you should have been given a substantial sum he left for you when you came of age, but it seems the dear headmistress had other plans than to let you have what was legally yours.'

He gave another of those bewitching smiles, although behind it she sensed a mountain of concern that almost made her smile in reply. Everything she thought she knew about her father, her childhood and even her old guardians had been thrown into disarray, and it was hardly surprising he seemed uneasy about the effect of his words, his fingers soft against her cheek as if to comfort her was his only thought.

'So it wasn't me he was ashamed of. It was himself.'

She let her gaze wander over his downturned face, fresh heat kindling inside her as she ventured from his eyes to his mouth and lingered there, his lips so close now the smallest stretch would bring her up to meet them. She knew she ought to be elated by what she had learned about her father, as well as angry at Miss Laycock's greed, but somehow all she could truly concentrate on was the man in front of her and the question that had risen unbidden to the tip of her tongue.

'And what of you? Are you ashamed? Doesn't it bother you what the *ton* will think of me now, and what they're likely to say about you for marrying me?'

This time there was nothing uneasy about the upward tick of his mouth, and it sent an involuntary shiver through her from head to toe. 'Even if I knew every word in every language on earth it still wouldn't be enough to express how much I don't care. As I said before, we're not really part of that world. Now everyone knows the truth we have nothing to hide—and their whispers be damned.'

It was the only answer Emily needed to hear.

She leaned forward, her heart singing as she felt Andrew's arms wrap around her, holding her to the broad expanse of his chest. He lowered his head and she raised hers and they met in the middle, each seeking the other and a glittering cascade of happiness washed over her as his lips found hers and stole every last sigh of sorrow she'd expected to make.

Twining her arms around his neck she pulled him

closer, revelling in the solid strength of his body pressed to hers. Through the open front of his shirt she thought she could feel his heart beating in time with her own, an intimate rhythm she never wanted a day to go by without hearing, and when he swept her off her feet it felt like the most natural thing in the world to lean against his shoulder and feel as though she'd come home at last.

'Did you know it's two o'clock in the morning?'

His voice against her ear made even her bones feel weak, deep and warm and full of promise, and she shrugged as she felt him begin to carry her towards the door.

'I thought it was late. Perhaps, as I'm no longer going anywhere else tonight, I ought to go back to bed.'

'May I escort you?'

'You may do much more than that.'

Epilogue

Two years later

The bundle of blankets his mother placed in his arms was warm and soft, and Andrew's heart felt full to overflowing as he looked down at the crumpled face nestling among the folds. The baby's nose was like his but the sparse hair was a distinctive copper-gold and he didn't know when he'd last seen something so beautiful until he looked up, meeting Emily's eye as she lay exhausted but radiantly happy in the middle of their bed.

With her usual brisk tact Lady Gouldsmith left the room—although not before thoroughly plumping Emily's pillows and pouring her a fresh cup of tea—and with extreme care he shifted the precious load into the crook of one arm, freeing a hand to seek out Emily's, lying on the hurriedly changed sheets.

'He's got your hair.'

'And your nose.'

She smiled, squeezing his fingers far more gently now than she had at the peak of her pains. She looked shattered after her long ordeal, during which he had stubbornly refused to leave her side, but already some of the colour was returning to her cheeks, and her face as she gazed at her brand-new son was so astoundingly lovely that, for a moment, Andrew struggled to breathe.

Sitting in a chair beside the bed, cradling his child while he held his wife's hand, he had everything he'd ever wanted. Nothing could replace the loss of his father, but his mother had taken such joy in her daughter-in-law and Emily loved her now in turn, the relationship with her own papa likewise deepening as they grew to know each other.

People still muttered about her occasionally, throwing the odd lanced barb when she and Lord Wagstaff were seen out in public arm in arm, but the opinions of such narrow-minded individuals didn't matter. Since their unconventional marriage Andrew had gained a wife he loved and now a family, too, and so long as Emily was happy he couldn't care less about the mumbling of the *ton* or anyone else who might venture criticism where it didn't belong.

'What shall we name him?'

At the question Emily eased herself up a little higher against the pillows, wincing slightly as she moved. 'I thought you might like Matthew. For your father.'

He stroked her knuckles with his thumb, touched by her consideration. 'I would. Thank you. And for a middle name?'

She was busy adjusting the coverlet with her free hand

but he could have sworn he caught a glimpse of a furtive smile. 'How about Ephraim?'

'Ephraim?' Surprised by such an unexpected suggestion he sat forward, quickly leaning back again when the movement caused the baby to stir. 'For my uncle? Why?'

Emily shrugged, the smile growing wider. 'If you think about it, it's because of him that we first met. If I hadn't come here looking for him, our paths would never have crossed and we wouldn't have found the happiness we have now.'

Andrew laughed, although he couldn't argue with her logic. 'He would hate that. The sentimentality of being credited with a love story? That would have put him in the foulest temper the world had ever seen.'

He laughed again and this time Emily joined in with the spiritedness he had adored watching grow over the past two years, no longer the shy young woman who had first appeared in the parlour of Huntingham Hall. She was confident now and he was glad of it, knowing herself to be worthy of love and to give it in return, and as he gazed down on the child they had made together he thought nothing could ever dampen their joy.

'Very well. Matthew Ephraim Gouldsmith it is. And here's hoping he grows to be more like his first namesake than his second.'

* * * * *